NO BOUNDARIES

By the Author

Healing Hearts

No Boundaries

NO BOUNDARIES

by
Donna K. Ford

2014

ISBN 13: 978-1-62639-060-7

This Trade Paperback Original Is Published By
Bold Strokes Books, Inc.
P.O. Box 249
Valley Falls, NY 12185

First Edition: May 2014

CREDITS

Editor: Ruth Sternglantz
Production Design: Susan Ramundo
Cover Design By Sheri (graphicartist2020@hotmail.com)

Acknowledgments

There is one person in my life who has always believed in anything and everything I wanted to do without question or hesitation. My partner, Keah, is my love, my best friend, and my strength. I am forever grateful for her support and patience as she helps guide me along my sometimes meandering and stubborn path. Her words of encouragement lift me beyond my doubts and fears to keep me moving in the right direction when otherwise I would be lost.

Thank you to all the wonderful readers who have reached out to me over this past year to share your kind words and push me to get the next book out. I had the pleasure of meeting many of you this year, and each one of you made this an amazing journey, and I can't wait to see what you have to say next.

Words can't describe my gratitude for my editor, Ruth Sternglantz. She has a way of getting into my head, and she pushes me deeper into my own story until it becomes something more. She is my teacher and my guide. Thank you.

I have to thank all the wonderful staff at Bold Strokes Books for the amazing work they do. You make all the difference.

Last, I want to thank my parents, Virgie and Don Ford, for showing me unconditional love and always standing up for who I am. That is my armor. As long as I have that love and acceptance, no one can shake me with their cruel words. I hope to always make you proud.

Dedication

For Keah, for her helping me believe in forever.

CHAPTER ONE

Andi Massey cut off the garden tiller and sifted through the soil with her gloved hand. The smell of the rich earth tickled her senses and roused memories Andi wished she could erase from her mind. Her mouth went dry when her fist closed around a small rock unearthed by the tiller. In a flash Andi could see the craggy, unshaven face looming before her. The smell of him mingled with the dirt beneath her. She tightened her grip on the rock and could hear the crack of the stone hitting his skull. Andi flinched and felt her stomach roll, threatening to be sick. She drew in deep calming breaths and tried to quiet her demons. She tossed the stone aside, an evil detested thing. She blew out a deep breath and cursed herself for her lapse into the past. She was always amazed at the simple things that still triggered the old memories.

Andi sat back on her heels and studied her work. She felt the dampness seep through her jeans where her knees pressed into the soil. Sweat trickled down her nose, and she brushed it away with the back of her gloved hand. With temperatures hovering around eighty degrees for a week, she wondered why she tortured herself with a garden. But she loved her garden. Her plants and her cat were the things that made her happy. They were the only things she dared love.

She shivered at the memories and tried to shake off the reminder of the life she had lost. These silent musings were becoming a common thing, and Andi had felt a disquiet seep into her life. She was lonely. When she wasn't working at her pet-supply store or delivering pet food to the elderly clients in town, she spent her time alone among her plants, and for the most part she liked it that way. She wasn't much of a people person...at least not anymore. She took a deep breath and told herself to stop this self-torture, as she tried to change her line of thinking. The ache of loneliness closed around her chest like a fist slowly squeezing the air from her lungs. That wasn't her life anymore. She'd moved to the sleepy little town of Norris, Tennessee, to escape all that and for the most part had done a good job. But the memories were something she knew she would never escape.

Andi was suddenly pulled from her thoughts by the sound of someone clearing their throat. She jumped, startled by the sound and the fact that she hadn't heard anyone approach. An instant later realization dawned, and she turned to greet the familiar voice. An old woman stood on the walk grinning at Andi. Her faded jeans were just a tad too short, her shirt was tucked half in and half out of her waistband, and her unruly hair stuck out from beneath a tattered straw hat.

"You know that's work, don't ya?"

"Yeah, some days I do. How are you, Mrs. Peterson?" Andi grinned at the sight of her neighbor. It never failed—if she was outside doing something, Mrs. Peterson was sure to turn up to inspect her work. Nothing got past this woman. She was the neighborhood watch program all in one person.

"It's too damn hot," Mrs. Peterson barked.

Andi laughed. "I'm surprised you're out then."

Mrs. Peterson harrumphed. "Didn't think you were going to sneak anything past me did you? I might be old, but I can still look after you, girl."

"Yes, ma'am. Would you like to come in for some tea?"

"Hell no. I'm going home and having me a beer." Mrs. Peterson cocked her head, peering at Andi over her glasses with a slight grin.

"All right then, have one for me while you're at it. Oh, and just so there are no surprises, I'll be mowing the lawn tomorrow. Just didn't want you to think I was trying to get one over on you."

Mrs. Peterson swatted her hand in Andi's direction. "Crazy girl."

Andi watched with hands on her hips as the old woman made her way back home. She loved these moments with Mrs. Peterson. She had been one of the first people Andi met when she moved in almost three years earlier. She had kept a close eye on the changes Andi made to the place, and at some point during the long inquisition, Andi had grown fond of their playful bantering.

She sometimes worried that Mrs. Peterson was lonely, living in her big house alone. But despite all Andi's efforts, Mrs. Peterson would never accept her invitations for dinner, or just a cool drink. She just showed up from time to time, shared a few words, and would leave again.

The more Andi thought of the solitary life Mrs. Peterson lived, the more she realized she had isolated herself in much the same way. She rarely felt lonely, but sometimes the emptiness in her life was like a deafening silence. During those moments she would go to the park or the hardware store just to watch people talk to each other, hear their laughter, and even watch them argue, and that seemed all the interaction she needed.

Now as she watched Mrs. Peterson go, the loneliness settled in again, and she wished she could put the past behind her and have a normal life. Andi shook herself and looked around at her work. Deciding she had done enough, she dusted off her knees, pulled off her gloves, and headed for a shower.

Gwen Palmer placed the last box into the U-Haul and closed the door. She had one month to get to her new home, set up some livable habitation, and learn her way around town before starting her new job with the Tennessee Department of Agriculture. At forty-five she had decided to start over. When she lost her job in Chicago, she had sold her house, found a new house online, found a new job online, and now she was finally making the move. She needed a change of scenery and a chance to start over.

Her friends thought she was crazy and her family was angry with her for leaving, but she just knew it was the right thing to do. Now that the day had finally arrived, she was filled with anticipation. This would be an adventure. Besides, she needed to get away. She didn't really have any solid ties anyway—sure, her family was here, and she had good friends, but it just wasn't enough. The women she dated were not the stick-around type, and she was tired of the transient relationships that were really nothing more than brief interludes or one-night stands. After the debacle with her last affair, she didn't think she could stay in this town for another moment. She felt humiliated. Miranda had used her and thrown her and her career away without a blink of an eye. She had to make a change, and she might as well take this opportunity while she had it.

Gwen sighed and took another look around the old bungalow one last time, as she remembered family dinners and movie nights and parties with friends. This had been the first place she had felt at home after leaving her parents' and going to college. But it was time to move on, time to grow up. She wanted a place she could grow into, share with someone, and perhaps have a family. She pulled a worn leash from the peg by the door. "Ready, Zeek?" Gwen asked the large black Neapolitan mastiff, who sat staring at her.

"What? Did you think you weren't getting to go?" Gwen smiled down at the dog who had been her constant companion for the past five years.

Zeek tilted her giant head to the side as if she wasn't sure what was happening. But recognizing the word *go,* she jumped up and placed her large paws on Gwen's shoulders. Tongue lolling, she happily nudged Gwen's chin with her nose.

Gwen laughed. "Okay, okay, I take it you're ready."

Taking one last look around, Gwen gave a quick salute to the house and closed the door, leaving her past behind her.

Ten hours later, she pulled into the drive and took in the view of her new home. She was surprised to find it looked in better shape than she had anticipated, based on the photos. But then again, it was dark outside. Who knew what surprises she would find, moving into an eighty-year-old house?

Zeek picked her head up from her makeshift bed on the bench seat to peer out over the dashboard. She sniffed feverishly.

"What do you think, Zeek?" Gwen ran her hand over Zeek's floppy ears as she studied the house with some trepidation. When she realized she was still sitting in the truck five minutes later, she laughed at herself. "What do you say we go check it out? Feel up to exploring after that long drive?"

In answer Zeek tried to shake herself, which didn't work out so well, since at 140 pounds, she took up most of the truck's cabin space. She stood and nuzzled Gwen's ear, breathing hot dog breath into her face.

Gwen laughed. "Okay, get off, you big oaf." She opened the door and climbed out of the truck, holding the door open for Zeek. "There you go, girl. Let's see what our new home is like."

The keys were in the lockbox attached to the door. Her realtor had given her the code at the finalization of the purchase. She punched in the code to retrieve the key. When the box opened, she let out a breath she hadn't realized she had been holding. Relief washed over her—she was definitely in the right place. She slid the key in the lock and heard the faint snick as the tumblers fell into place and the doorknob turned. Swinging the heavy wood door wide, Gwen stepped inside. Her fingers fumbled for a moment, searching for the light switch on the wall by the door. The sudden glow made her blink before her eyes adjusted to the light, and she settled on the view of the room.

The door opened to an average-size living room. The room was barren of course, and Gwen took in the beautiful hand-scraped wood floors and the dentil molding wrapping the ceiling. She guessed at least five layers of paint coated the delicate details of the woodwork and silently cataloged the many hours of labor ahead of her. Although the work would be tedious, she looked forward to making the house her own and bringing it back to its former glory.

"At least there's no wallpaper," she said, patting Zeek on the head.

Gwen made her way through the house and noted various repairs and updates to be made, the most substantial being to the kitchen. Besides the absence of appliances, this would be the best time to do the renovations to the floor, cabinets, and well, everything. She raked a hand through her hair as she scanned the room. She estimated the space to be about 200 square feet. The rectangular layout would be great for setting up a more user-friendly cooking space and separate dining area. The floors were covered in brittle vinyl flooring with large chunks missing in several places. Gwen leaned down until her knees popped in protest, tugged on a loose edge of vinyl, and pulled up a small section. The subfloor looked okay but would likely need some repairs as well.

Overall, Gwen was pleased. The house was cozy, with enough room to grow. She walked through the kitchen to the french doors and pulled them open. A large wooden deck wrapped the length of the house and around one corner. In front of the doors, the deck stepped down onto a smaller platform before turning to the right and stepping down onto a paved stone patio. At the bottom of the decking was a complete outdoor kitchen. The space was amazing, and she had to forgive the former owners their neglect of the interior renovations when she saw the amount of work that had gone into creating this outdoor oasis. The light from the house cast furtive shadows across the lawn, and Gwen could make out the tall custom privacy fence surrounding the backyard. This was one of the selling points as it provided the perfect place for Zeek to roam without Gwen having to worry about her getting into too much trouble with the neighbors. On cue, Zeek lumbered by, her nose to the ground as she took up patrol, thoroughly assessing every inch of the open space.

Gwen took a deep breath of the cool night air and felt some of the tension leave her shoulders. She listened to the still night and reveled in the silence, grateful to be far away from the push and demands of the city and memories of Miranda. She didn't know how she had managed to convince herself that Miranda loved her, that they were working toward a future together. The signs had been there all along, but she had chosen not to see them until it was all too late. She had paid the price for her indiscretion, far beyond the loss of her job. Gwen shivered as the memories and the pain still shimmered through her, filling her with disappointment and regret.

She hadn't doubted her decision to move. Not really. When Miranda had seen to it that she lost her job, Gwen decided she wanted to be somewhere where no one knew her. Maybe if she started over, there could be more to her life than work and one-night stands. Her best friend Holly was convinced she was having a midlife crisis and had lost her mind. Peter, her friend and colleague, had been the only one to support her move. He had seen the games Miranda had played with her life, and he knew what they had cost Gwen. Peter had come over with boxes, a bottle of red wine, and pizza from her favorite pizza dive.

Go, he had said. *It's a big world out there and it's calling to you. Your family will forgive you once they see that you're still close enough for them to invade if they need to. What've you got to lose? Go somewhere that bitch can't touch you.*

She had hugged him and kissed his cheek. He had been her voice of reason. She knew he wouldn't say anything he didn't mean, and she loved him for it.

Zeek bounded up the steps back onto the porch, her tongue lolling and eyes bright, luring Gwen out of the past and back to where she belonged. She smiled down at the dog, pleased to see she was happy with her new surroundings. "Come on, Zeek, let's get started." Gwen swatted the dog's behind and turned to go back inside to begin the task of assembling a place to sleep.

Chapter Two

The light pouring in through the bare window was a harsh assault as Gwen blinked the sleep from her eyes. Zeek lay on the floor beside her, the deep resonant snores rumbling through her chest, a clear sign she was sleeping well.

Gwen had been up most of the night moving as many of her things in from the truck as she could manage alone in the dark. Boxes sat piled in the living room and kitchen, and she wondered if she would ever get moved in completely.

She needed coffee. Gwen stretched and stumbled from her makeshift bed. She sifted through boxes marked *bath* until she located enough supplies for a shower. She gave up on finding her coffeepot.

The hot water beat against her skin, releasing some of the stiffness in her back and neck. She hoped that would be her only night sleeping on the floor. She stretched and messaged her aching muscles and remembered why she hadn't been camping the past few years. Either the ground was getting harder, or she was getting too old for this.

Once dressed in her faded jeans, a worn and tattered HRC T-shirt, and running shoes, Gwen pulled her white Range Rover Sport off the towing trailer and headed for the nearest place to find a hot cup of coffee. Her smartphone told her there was a diner only half a mile from her house. She chuckled at this. She seemed to be in the middle of nowhere. A coffee shop in this rural community seemed unlikely.

Meticulously following the directions, Gwen found the diner within walking distance of her home. She also found the town had a small bank branch, a grocery store, a post office, a service station for auto repairs, and a small pet-supply store. She took in the number of older residents coming and going around town and began to wonder if she had moved into a retirement community. Well, she did want relaxed. At least it would be quiet.

Gwen walked into the diner to find a small room with quaint booths lining the long window front. Tables were scattered throughout the room, covered with red-and-white checkered vinyl tablecloths that looked like they were as old as the building itself. The counter was white Formica with a strip of aluminum trim that was a throwback from the fifties, complete with red vinyl stools. Gwen smiled to herself as she took in the decor and noted that the patrons seated at the counter looked about as old and worn as the furniture. Gwen took a seat and leaned her elbows on the counter. She took a deep breath, drawing in the smell of fresh coffee, and her stomach growled in anticipation of sustenance. Something smelled delicious and she couldn't wait to have her hands wrapped around a steaming mug.

Gwen looked around at the occupants. Three old men sat at the counter next to her, sipping their coffee and engaged in a debate regarding some local politics. She caught something about a rock quarry they wanted to remain closed and a lawsuit to stop further excavation. As Gwen settled in, the only waitress in the room appeared in front of her.

"Hello there. What can I get you, sweetie?" the woman asked as she looked Gwen over.

"Coffee, please."

"How would you like it? Cream? Sugar?"

"Black is fine, thank you."

Gwen watched the waitress glide along the narrow work space. She efficiently filled coffee cups, cleared the counter, and managed to monitor the status of an order of bacon and toast she was preparing with movements so well-timed and smooth they could have been choreographed.

Gwen estimated her to be in her early- to mid-sixties. She wore her hair at shoulder length with loose curls that danced about her face when she moved. Intense brown eyes scrutinized Gwen as the woman placed the coffee on the counter along with a large muffin.

"On the house," she said smiling. "Are you new in town?" she asked, reaching beneath the counter and producing silverware.

"Yes," Gwen said before taking a sip. "I just arrived last night. I purchased the blue house on Pine."

"Oh yeah? That's the old Harman place. It's good to see someone take it on. Welcome to Norris."

"Thanks." Gwen extended her hand. "I'm Gwen Palmer."

"Glenda Ross," the woman answered, taking Gwen's hand with a smile.

Gwen noticed the three men had dropped their conversation and were appraising her openly, their expressions distrustful. She bristled under the scrutiny but attempted a smile.

Glenda swatted the counter with a towel in front of the men. "Stop that, you old busybodies. You're being rude."

The man closest to Gwen jumped at the scolding. "Sorry, miss. We didn't mean to intrude. We just can't help but notice newcomers. Most everyone in Norris knows everyone else. New faces always cause a bit of a stir."

Gwen laughed at the man's honesty. "Well, I hope you'll consider letting me stay."

The man peered at her for a moment as if trying to make a decision. "Maybe. You say you're in the old Harman house?"

"Sounds like it."

"Well then, I guess it'll depend on what you do with the place."

Gwen studied the old man thoughtfully, still not sure if he was being friendly. His expression gave nothing away about his mood.

Glenda interrupted the discussion. "Don't worry, Sam. I'm sure you and the boys will have plenty to keep you entertained with the upcoming festivities. Besides, I think that old place of yours has needed a little update for several years now. I imagine whatever Gwen here does to her own place will do just fine."

Sam harrumphed. "My place is just fine. I'm not as young as I used to be, you know." He turned to Gwen. "Anyway, good to meet you, Gwen." The old man shook Gwen's hand and gave her a wink.

Gwen felt relieved by the gesture. She made small talk with the other customers while finishing her coffee, then got a cup to go and thanked Glenda for the muffin. As she drove home, she was convinced she was in for a culture shock. Everyone who had come into the diner had been retired, and most had lived in Norris for twenty years or more. But she had learned that a good number of the patrons seemed to be transplants from other parts of the country and had landed in the area for various reasons, much like her own. That had to be a good sign. She hoped.

Despite the feeling that her life had suddenly been placed under a microscope, Gwen felt happy about her new surroundings. She got the impression that nothing went without notice in the small town and vowed not to give them reason to single her out. She wasn't looking to cause any ripples in the pond, but she hoped there would be a little more opportunity for her to meet someone closer to her own age. She was all about peace and quiet, but she wasn't ready to become the old maid in town.

At ten o'clock, two men arrived from a local moving company as scheduled. Gwen was relieved they were on time and eager to get the rest of her furniture moved into the house so she could return the rental truck. She had planned out each room and instructed the men where to put the heavier items. She didn't want to have to worry about moving them herself later.

The larger of the two men was broad shouldered, muscular, and eager to fill Gwen in on the history of the town. "My name's Mike, and this here's Joey." Mike gestured toward his partner, who stood a few feet away.

Gwen noticed Joey didn't make eye contact and stood with his hands in his pockets while Mike talked. The quiet one, she guessed. Joey was smaller than Mike, but the muscles in his arms and chest suggested he was not lacking in strength. Gwen had no doubt the two could get the job done. As they worked Mike gave Gwen information about nearby places to eat, where the nightlife was most entertaining, and where to have a beer and shoot a game of pool.

"Nice place you've got here," Mike said as he surveyed the house. "You know, most of these homes were built in the nineteen thirties, when the TVA built the dam for the hydropower. I'm guessing the original part of this house is one of those. You might want to see about the history of the house. They have lots of old photographs of the original town down at the local library. It's pretty cool stuff."

"Thanks. I'll do that." Gwen was enjoying the friendly chatter and realized she was feeling more at home as more of her belongings found their place in her new house.

With the last of the boxes and furniture unloaded, Gwen waved good-bye to Mike and Joey. She pulled the Rover back onto the towing rack of the rental truck and went inside to get Zeek.

Andi smiled to herself as she took in the blue skies and sunshine that marked the beginning of another beautiful day and listened to the chorus of birds singing in her backyard. She tightened the laces on her running shoes before setting out on her three-mile run. It was her usual Sunday morning routine and she looked forward to the scenery that awaited her.

Norris was a small community, nestled on the boundaries of the Norris State Park, which meant an abundance of wildlife coexisted with the people who called the area home. Andi didn't really like to run, but she made herself endure the three miles every Sunday. She thought it was a good change from her routine of riding her bike to work all week and the mornings of kayaking or paddleboarding she enjoyed. The pattern seemed to work. She felt healthy and her body kept the nice lean tone she preferred, without too much additional effort.

She had promised herself when she moved to Norris to take advantage of the beautiful landscape every day, her way of reminding herself there was still good in the world. It was part of the bargain she'd made with herself to shed the guilt of leaving her profession as a therapist to open a small pet-supply store and live a simple life after the brutal attack had changed her perception of life and her ability to trust. She no longer trusted herself with people and their emotions, no longer had faith in her ability to see beyond the surface and find the good buried within. She couldn't see beyond her own fear. She never regretted her decision to walk away from that life. Every morning when she stepped outside her small cottage home, she was greeted with flowers, trees, birds, green grass, and sunshine. At least, she liked to think so. Even the rain and snow were beautiful, and as long as she could hold on to that beauty, she had hope that someday she would find that trust again, maybe even find love.

As she ran, she worked through her mental checklist: things she needed to do at the store, errands she needed to run, she still hadn't finished the lawn. She took a left onto Orchard Road and cut across the street to the sidewalk. Sweat streamed down her neck, leaving wet trails that tickled her skin. She wiped her face with the back of her hand to ward off the inevitable sting as sweat dripped into her eyes.

At the corner of Pine and Crescent Road, Andi noticed a moving truck parked at the old blue house. She was surprised to see anyone there. The house had been empty for a couple of years, except for an occasional brief rental. She hoped this would be a more permanent tenant as the place was in need of some work. The windows and door at the front of the house reminded Andi of a face, and the lack of light and overgrown grass in the yard gave the place a forlorn appearance, like a lonely widow who looked out at the world passing her by.

Andi slowed as she neared the house. Despite her usual distance from neighbors, she was curious to see the newcomer in town. Just as she was passing behind the moving truck, a flash of movement startled her as a squirrel ran straight at her, leaping to the side at the last moment and scampering up a large oak tree. Before Andi could react, a large black form ran out from behind the van, apparently in pursuit of the squirrel. The sheer size of the animal made it impossible for either to avoid the inevitable collision. The animal slammed into Andi, knocking her over.

Out of breath and gasping from the sudden shock, Andi stifled a scream that consequently came out as a croak and sounded like she had swallowed a frog. She peered up at the massive animal that now stood with its paws straddling her shoulders and legs, its wildly drooping jowls hanging in her face. Before she could react, the dog dipped its massive head and licked the full length of her face. "Ick," she grumbled, but the rush of fear that had gripped her slid away. Obviously her attacker was harmless.

Looking up now at the friendly brown eyes and lolling tongue, Andi laughed. "Okay, okay. I guess you're forgiven."

A shadow fell over her suddenly as a figure came running up to them, and a stern voice called out to the dog, "Zeek, come!"

Zeek lumbered to the side and Andi leaned up on her elbows. She saw a tall woman with messy blond hair move to kneel beside her. The woman's piercing blue eyes were round with fear, and Andi stared into them, momentarily stunned by the woman's beauty.

"Oh my God, are you all right?" the woman asked, her voice strained with concern as her eyes roamed Andi's body, assessing her for injury.

"No. I mean, yes. I mean, I'm fine," Andi stammered as the woman pawed at her arms and clothes. She didn't know what to think of the sudden assault as she felt hands rake across her arms and legs. Andi was stunned by the pleasant warmth seeping into her skin from the stranger's touch. She was mesmerized by the gentleness in her fingers, the softness of her skin—and for a moment, Andi didn't want the feeling to stop.

"I'm terribly sorry about this. Zeek isn't used to the squirrels yet, and she gets a bit carried away. Are you sure you're all right?"

"I'm okay. Really." Andi caught the woman's wrist to stop the play of hands across her body, her face now hot with embarrassment. The woman was captivating, and as uncomfortable as the situation was, Andi was stunned by her body's response to the touch as every stroke of soft fingers made her skin tingle. She was sure this betrayal by her body was because it had been so long since she had been touched in any way. Now the simplest connection with another person was sensory overload. The woman froze, her eyes locked onto Andi's, and a faint smile began at the corners of her mouth. "Sorry. I guess I got a little carried away." She took a deep breath and shifted to stand. She put out her hand to help Andi up. "I'm Gwen Palmer and that lug is my dog, Zeek."

"Nice to meet you both." Andi took the offered hand, allowing herself to be pulled to her feet. A sudden stinging in her right hip told her she had a nasty scrape from hitting the asphalt when she fell. She hissed a little as the pain registered, distracting her from the warmth of Gwen's fingers gripping her hand. Andi pulled away reluctantly and dusted herself off. In the process she noticed a nasty abrasion on her left palm as well. Turning up her hand to inspect the injury, she saw tiny bits of dirt and rocks embedded in her skin, the wound angry and red. The sight of the injury made her wince again.

Gwen stepped close and took Andi's hand in her own, then turned the palm up to assess the damage.

At the intimate touch, Andi's heart began to race. She was stunned by the proximity of their bodies and the soothing, gentle caress of Gwen's hand. Andi swallowed the lump in her throat and stared up at Gwen, not sure what she was supposed to do.

Gwen met her gaze and Andi was surprised by the warmth and compassion in Gwen's eyes. Andi's breath caught at the sight of such unguarded emotion.

"We'll need to get this cleaned up. You have some small pieces of gravel under the skin there. Come inside and let me have a better look."

Andi was suddenly very aware of the warmth spreading through her body. The tingling sensation in her skin beneath Gwen's touch was beginning to make her uneasy. She didn't like to be touched by strangers, but there was something oddly alluring about Gwen that Andi couldn't quite shake. She couldn't take her eyes off her face and struggled to put together a coherent thought. When Gwen looked up from her inspection of Andi's hand, Andi took an involuntary step back. She was afraid Gwen would hike up the leg of her shorts and begin a close examination there like she had done with her hand.

"No. It really isn't a big deal. I'm sure it's fine. I'll take care of it when I get home," Andi stammered.

"I insist. Please. It's the least I can do to make up for you being flattened by my dog."

Andi studied Gwen's face and took in the feel of the soft fingers against her palm and was once again speechless as Gwen stroked the edges of the cut, trying to free the stones from the torn skin on her hand. She couldn't remember the last time she had been touched so tenderly, and the loneliness that had been haunting her for the past few weeks became a dull ache, punctuating the longing she had denied for years. She knew she should pull her hand away, but something kept her frozen in place. She couldn't bring herself to separate from even this minor connection.

Finally finding her voice Andi spoke. "I'm pleased to meet you, Gwen. I'm Andrea Massey. Most people just call me Andi."

Gwen smiled. The smile transformed her features from alluring to arresting, and Andi found herself captivated by the contrast of uncertainty and unguarded pleasure. Gwen gave Andi's hand a gentle tug. "Well, Andi, let's get you patched up. Come on, I insist."

Andi followed Gwen into the house. She was surprised when Gwen took her hand again and led her to the kitchen sink.

"Sorry about the mess, I only arrived last night, and as you can see I haven't managed to get much done yet," Gwen said as she ran cool water over Andi's hand, gently massaging the tattered red skin. She blotted the area with a towel, then turned and opened a box on the floor and retrieved a first-aid kit. She returned with peroxide, Neosporin, and a bandage. The peroxide burned when it hit the wound, and Andi flinched and hissed in a breath. To her amazement, Gwen leaned toward her and blew cool breaths across her palm, soothing the sting.

Andi watched Gwen's lips purse as if offering a tender caress. When the air hit her skin, Andi felt it crawl up her veins until her whole body responded to the pull of Gwen's breath as if she was tethered to her by an invisible string. Andi stiffened at the unusual response and hoped Gwen would think it was because of the discomfort from the abrasion. She was shocked to find she couldn't stop staring at Gwen's lips.

Gwen glanced up at Andi. "Does that hurt?"

Andi shook her head. "It just stings a little."

Gwen studied Andi's smooth soft hand, holding it gently as she worked the debris from the wound. The shock of seeing Andi splayed on the ground beneath Zeek was slowly subsiding. Zeek wasn't usually aggressive, but by nature her breed was territorial, and with the move Gwen had been afraid Zeek might struggle with the newness of the neighbors and foot traffic around the house. She was relieved the injury hadn't been worse and had been the result of a silly accident. Zeek was like her child, and she couldn't imagine her hurting anyone.

Gwen heard Andi hiss and felt her stiffen when Gwen tried to coax a bit of gravel out of the wound. Gwen eased on the pressure and glanced up, meeting Andi's eyes. She could see the discomfort written in the lines around Andi's mouth. She felt a sudden desire to touch Andi, to smooth out the lines of pain that strained her lips into a taut line.

"Sorry. I know that has to hurt."

Andi nodded, and Gwen saw the muscle at the side of Andi's jaw jump as she clenched her teeth.

"Just a bit more, I promise."

Gwen grew increasingly aware of the closeness of Andi's body next to her and the tender skin of Andi's hand lying submissively in hers. Andi was very attractive. She was athletic, yet soft in all the right places. Gwen recalled raking her hands over Andi's body searching for injury, the evenly toned muscles in her arms and legs, her skin tender and smooth. Gwen guessed Andi was a few inches shorter than her own five foot eight inches. She liked the way Andi's short chestnut hair curled slightly at her collar, the tips wet with sweat and clinging to her neck. Gwen imagined what it would be like to run her tongue along that long slender neck and taste the salt on Andi's skin. Gwen licked her lips in response and continued her assessment. Andi's build suggested she spent a lot of time in activities suited to tone her muscles while leaving her with all the right curves and softness that were unique to a woman. In short, Andi was captivating. Gwen liked what she saw, and she felt the muscles in her lower abdomen tighten in response.

Gwen looked up at her patient. Andi's cheeks glowed, and Gwen hoped this was from the exertion of her run and not from the incident with Zeek. Gwen pushed her attention back to the wound and drew in a long slow breath as she worked, detecting the scent of sweat and a hint of coconut and maybe something wild that reminded her of honeysuckle. The smell was intoxicating. She couldn't believe she had spent the morning thinking she would be surrounded by geriatric women with blue hair, and now the most exquisite, beautiful woman she could have imagined was standing in her kitchen. Gwen stroked the soft skin, lingering a bit longer than necessary. She could hear Andi's soft voice brushing over her senses like a cool breeze.

"Norris is a great place. I think you'll enjoy it here. This is a great house."

"Thank you," Gwen answered, her own voice seeming heavy and far away. She held on to Andi's hand despite being finished with the first aid. "There you go. That should do for now. How about your hip?"

The blush in Andi's cheeks darkened. "It's fine. I can take care of it when I get home."

Gwen smiled, acknowledging the awkwardness. "I really am sorry for all this."

Gwen looked down at her hand still holding Andi's. Heat rose to her face as her body responded to her attraction to Andi. She wanted to reach out and touch her. She let go before she made a complete fool of herself. Gwen's skin cooled in the absence of Andi's touch, and she instinctively closed her fist, trying to hold on to the lingering sensation of the touch. This was turning out to be a very good day.

"No harm done really." Andi looked around the room, taking her eyes away from Gwen for the first time. She needed a distraction so she could get a grip on herself. She searched for a way to put more distance between her and Gwen so she could think more clearly and settle the stir of attraction that had her out of sorts. Andi spotted Zeek lying sprawled on the floor at their feet, her big brown eyes looking apologetically from Gwen to Andi, making her eyebrows dance up and down.

"What kind of dog is Zeek?"

"Neapolitan mastiff."

Andi knelt beside Zeek, taking the big muzzle into her hands. Zeek raised her head, and Andi planted a kiss on top. "I'm sorry too, Zeek. I hope we can be friends."

These seemed to be the magic words. Zeek jumped up, tail wagging like a giant propeller as she lumbered out the back door.

"Guess it's back to squirrel patrol," Gwen said with an exasperated laugh.

Andi laughed too. "Guess so. Well, I really should get going. I still have to finish my run, and it looks like you have your work cut out for you."

Gwen winced and looked around at the mess. "Unfortunately, you are correct."

"Do you need any help?" Andi asked, and then looked away regretting the words. What was she doing? She didn't know Gwen, and it wasn't like her to offer to spend time with someone she didn't know.

"Thanks, but I think right now I just need to return the truck and make a plan. But I'd love to get together for a drink or dinner later."

Andi's eyes widened in surprise. "Thank you, but I can't." She was still trying to make sense of the feelings Gwen had stirred in her, and the thought of spending even more time with Gwen was both exciting and terrifying. Part of her cried out for some connection, but Andi knew better than to follow those feelings. She reminded herself that her life was much simpler if she didn't allow anyone close.

"Are you sure? I'd like to make this up to you." Gwen gestured to the bandage on Andi's hand.

Andi could feel Gwen's gaze as if she had been touched. She recognized the interest lingering in Gwen's eyes and felt increasingly uncomfortable with the closeness of Gwen's body. "You don't even know me," Andi said with an edge of distrust in her voice.

"That's the point in getting together, isn't it? So we can get to know each other."

Andi couldn't believe this was happening. She hadn't had time to understand her feelings and felt at a loss to explain. She wasn't used to being thrown off balance by anyone, and her words came out sharper than she had intended. "Thanks, but I'll have to pass."

"Why?" Gwen asked, moving closer. "It could be fun."

Andi swallowed, trying to clear the lump that was forming in her throat. She felt a stab of disappointment at the aplomb of Gwen's gesture. She wasn't used to women asking her out, and she certainly wasn't used to being so affected by anyone. "I'm sorry, I really can't. I need to go."

Gwen smiled playfully at Andi. "Okay. Maybe another time then."

Andi looked away, caught off guard by Gwen's apparent interest.

Gwen shrugged, unused to women saying no. "Fair enough." She'd noticed the sudden change in Andi's behavior and realized Andi was uncomfortable with the conversation, but she wasn't certain why. She was disappointed by Andi's rejection. She knew she had seen interest in Andi's eyes. It was one thing for a woman to say no to a date, but Andi's response had been defensive, and Gwen couldn't figure out what she had done wrong. A familiar pain stung the back of Gwen's throat as the memory of Miranda's words came back to her. *Really Gwen, you couldn't possibly think this could go anywhere. What could you possibly offer me other than a good roll between the sheets?*

Andi turned and headed toward the door, and Gwen followed her.

"Hey, I'm sorry if I made you uncomfortable. I just want to make up for what happened, and I thought we could have a good time together."

The look on Andi's face told Gwen she had said the wrong thing again. Andi looked as if she could shoot daggers at her with her eyes.

Gwen put her hands up stopping Andi's comment. "Look, we seem to be getting off on the wrong foot here. I didn't mean to offend you. Everything I say seems to come out wrong."

Andi paused, and for a moment Gwen thought she would reconsider.

"Thank you for taking care of my hand," Andi said and stepped out the door.

"Andi?"

Andi stopped. She turned and faced Gwen, her expression guarded.

"It was nice meeting you. I really am sorry."

Andi nodded. She heard the sincerity in Gwen's voice and caught the flicker of sadness in Gwen's eyes. All the irritation she had felt moments before seemed to melt away. She was just overreacting, and it wasn't fair for her to take it out on Gwen. "I'm sorry too. Have fun with the house. I'm sure I'll see you around town." Andi waved a good-bye and took off at a jog.

She heard Gwen's voice trail off behind her. "Looking forward to it."

Andi didn't respond. Her fingers closed against the bandage Gwen had applied to her injured palm, reminding her of Gwen's long tender fingers stroking her hand and Gwen's cool breath against her skin.

She picked up the pace, trying to run the thoughts of Gwen Palmer out of her mind. She had learned long ago that she couldn't allow herself to get close to anyone. No matter how alluring Gwen was, she couldn't take the risk. She wouldn't dare put anyone in danger that way ever again.

Chapter Three

The next day, Andi was still plagued with frequent thoughts of Gwen. She replayed the incident over and over in her mind, focusing on Gwen's touch and imagining her soft fingers caressing her body. She had been shocked when Gwen invited her for dinner or drinks, and she had meant her answer. But looking back on the situation now, she knew she had overreacted. She had been shaken by her physical response to Gwen, and the idea of spending time with her had sent Andi over the edge. She knew she was projecting her issues with the past onto Gwen and had lashed out at her because she offered exactly what Andi wanted, exactly what she couldn't have. Her life was way too complicated to get involved with *anyone*.

Still, Andi had felt anxious when she passed Gwen's house that morning—and she had deliberately driven by while out on errands for the shop and when she made deliveries for some of the elderly clients, just to see if she might see Gwen out. She was disappointed each time she failed to see Gwen. Andi ran her hands through her hair in frustration. Was she going crazy? Nothing was going to happen between her and Gwen, nothing *could* happen between them. So why was she torturing herself like this? It didn't matter how attractive Gwen was. *I can't go there.*

On her last pass by the house, Andi had already seen subtle changes, and she was happy knowing Gwen had given the old house a new purpose. A large Dumpster had been moved into the driveway and was slowly being filled with the debris from the renovation. She wondered what Gwen was doing. Did she need help?

Andi chided herself for the third time that day for allowing her thoughts to drift toward Gwen. She reminded herself of the things she loved about her quiet life, and that there was no need to entertain futile thoughts of this woman. She had good reasons for her solitude.

The bell above the door rang as someone entered the store, startling Andi from her thoughts. She felt her heart stop as she looked up to see Gwen standing at the counter.

"Oh, hi." Panic gripped Andi's chest and she wrapped her fingers tightly around the edge of the counter. She was thankful Gwen couldn't read her thoughts. The sudden appearance of the very woman she had been obsessing over embarrassed her. "How are things at the house? Are you getting settled in yet?" Andi asked. She tried to make her voice sound casual, but her words came out in a rush.

Gwen looked almost as surprised to see Andi as Andi felt to see her.

"Hi. I wasn't expecting to run into you." Gwen's smile quickly shifted from surprise to cool confidence. "I guess I'm out of the habit of seeing a familiar face, and you caught me off guard. The house is going great. I'm really enjoying the whole process. You'll have to stop by sometime and check it out."

Andi noticed the subtle rise in Gwen's eyebrows when she offered the invitation. What did that mean? Was Gwen flirting with her? Oh God, she couldn't be flirting with her.

"Sure. I'll do that," Andi answered, knowing she would do no such thing. "So, what can I help you with today?"

"Um, you work here?" Gwen asked with a hint of surprise in her voice.

"Actually, I'm the owner," Andi replied. "So yes, that means I spend a great deal of time here."

"Oh. Well, in that case, I'm looking for a refill on Zeek's flea preventative. The last thing I need is a flea infestation in the house."

Andi laughed. "Sure thing." She shuffled out from behind the counter and located the preventative for Gwen, who followed her through the store and stood so close Andi imagined she could feel the heat emanating from her body.

"There you go. That should do it," Andi said, handing Gwen the box.

"Thanks," Gwen said, stepping even closer and placing her hand lightly on Andi's arm.

Andi tensed, unsettled by the contact and the sudden rush of adrenaline coursing through her as every nerve ending in her body went on high alert. She was still keyed up from musing about Gwen, and having her actually touch her now was enough to spark a gentle thrum of desire.

"Have dinner with me. I know you don't know me, but I could really use some company. Zeek is a good listener and all, but the one-sided conversation gets a bit old after a while."

Andi chuckled and shifted uncomfortably. The sudden tightening in her belly shook her, and she became hyperaware of Gwen's hand on her arm. Andi shifted away from Gwen.

"I thought we already covered this. I'm not going to go out with you."

Gwen smiled as if she'd expected the response. "We wouldn't be going out. We could stay in."

Andi felt heat rise up her neck at the thought of being alone with Gwen and was irritated by her physical response and her irrational desire to say yes. She squared her shoulders and took a deep breath to regain her composure. "Definitely not."

"You misunderstood. I just want to have dinner. No strings. No expectations."

The bell above the door rang again, interrupting Andi before she could give a retort. "I'm sorry. Could you excuse me for a minute?" She was happy for the distraction as she hurriedly brushed past Gwen, intercepting the family of three that had just come in with their new puppy.

Gwen let out a forced breath. She stood back next to a box of dog toys and watched Andi. She couldn't figure out why it was so hard to talk to her. She thought she had picked up a hint of interest from Andi and she was definitely attracted to her. But Andi seemed almost offended by her offer for dinner. Gwen was confused by the mixed signals. When the family left she brought her items to the front.

Gwen decided to try again. "So…dinner?"

"Thank you, but my answer is still no," Andi answered frankly.

Gwen sighed. "Look, I know I came on a little strong the other day. It's fine if you don't want to go out with me, but I was hoping we could be friends. I wasn't kidding about needing the company. I don't know anyone else in town, and as far as I know you're the only other person here under the age of sixty. I'm not looking to hook up. I just like you and want to be friends."

Something in Gwen's tone penetrated the emotional barriers Andi had erected to keep people at a distance. Maybe Gwen's self-assurance and forwardness didn't mean she was a player. Andi knew she was being hard on Gwen, and it wasn't fair of her to put all the blame on Gwen when she was the one with the messed up life. But she wasn't ready to trust her. Most of all, she couldn't trust herself.

"You don't seem like the shy type. I'm sure you'll make plenty of friends quick enough."

Gwen's expression hardened. "What's that supposed to mean?"

Andi sighed. "Nothing." She knew she was being rude to Gwen. "I'm sorry. I'm not usually so rude. I guess I'm not used to this." She reached under the counter and pulled out a stool and sat as the fight drained out of her. "I'm not a very social person. I don't like to go out. I don't hang out with friends." She felt bad—she wasn't the kind of person who was rude to anyone on purpose. Maybe Gwen really was lonely. Just because she had isolated herself from personal relationships didn't give her the right to be rude to Gwen.

Andi reached out and laid her hand across Gwen's. She wanted to soothe some of the hurt she had caused. "You're right. I'm being rude and you don't deserve that." Andi sighed. "It isn't you. I just don't socialize much and I'd rather keep it that way."

"You do eat don't you?"

Gwen's teasing tone surprised Andi, and she couldn't hold back the grin that pressed at the corners of her mouth. She pursed her lips to suppress the smile. "Of course I do."

"So, since you're going to be eating anyway, why not do it at my place. You can have your own plate and everything."

Unconsciously Andi curled her fingers around Gwen's hand. "You don't give up, do you?" As much as she hated to admit it, Gwen was getting to her. Just because she had dinner with a woman didn't mean she had to get involved with her. Maybe they could be friends. The thought sent a thrill through her. She had been so lonely for so long it hurt. Could she risk it? Was it too much to hope for? Was it too much to ask of Gwen?

"If you're really just looking to make friends around here, maybe you should go to the Concert on the Commons this Friday night. Everyone in town will be there. I'm sure you can meet some new friends there." It was her last effort to push Gwen away, and the cold stare that eclipsed Gwen's gaze was like a punch to Andi's midsection. She instantly regretted the words. She hated hurting Gwen and found it was getting harder to say no.

Gwen pulled her hand away. She clenched her teeth and held her breath as the rejection hit its mark, making spots dance in front of her eyes. She tried to get a grip on her emotions. Andi's words were like a slap in the face. What had she been thinking to come here and ask Andi out? Andi obviously didn't think she was good enough for her. Well, she wasn't about to waste any more time trying to be friends with Andi.

"Yeah, sure, I'll do that," Gwen said in a flat tone. She signed the receipt slip and picked up her purchase. "This was obviously a mistake. It won't happen again."

Gwen shut the door without a sound on her way out. She wasn't sure why Andi's rejection bothered her so much. But for some reason, she cared about what Andi thought of her. Andi had tried to tell her she didn't have friends. But who didn't have friends? Was Andi just brushing her off or did she really isolate herself? The whole thing was frustrating as hell, and Gwen wanted to wash her hands of the mess. But she had seen something else in Andi in those first moments when they met, something Andi tried to hide. And that something had stirred Gwen in a way no other woman ever had.

CHAPTER FOUR

G wen made her way through the crowd gathered in front of the post office. She had hesitantly volunteered for the watershed cleanup when Glenda had insisted she help out with the annual event the town put together, to pick up trash and other detritus along the hiking and off-road vehicle trails through the park. She had so much she needed to be doing with the house, but if she was going to become a part of this community, she had to do her part. Besides, this was the perfect opportunity to meet people.

She spotted Glenda standing with a group of regulars from the diner and made her way over. Glenda looked up just as she reached the group.

"Hey, there you are. I was beginning to think you weren't going to make it," Glenda said cheerfully.

Gwen shrugged. "No way. I couldn't let you have all the fun."

Glenda smiled and then started as if she had forgotten something. "Oh, I have someone I'd like you to meet." She turned to a petite blonde standing next to her. "Gwen, this is my niece, Pria. She's spending the summer with us."

Gwen took Pria's hand. "Nice to meet you, Pria."

Pria smiled at Gwen with a hungry look in her eyes. "Hmm. Yes, it is."

Gwen dropped Pria's hand, aware that Glenda was watching the exchange. Pria had certainly telegraphed her interest to everyone within a mile radius of the group. There was also no doubt that everyone in the group was aware of how attractive Pria was, but she couldn't be more than twenty-three years old, and the delicately manicured nails and designer T-shirt and jeans sent warning bells ringing in Gwen's ears. In her experience, this girl spelled trouble. Gwen cleared her throat. "So, what's the plan?"

Glenda immediately took charge. "We're all meeting at the watershed in an hour. The groups will be assigned before we leave. We'll spend the day picking up trash and other stuff that's collected along the trails over the winter. After that we'll all meet up at the pavilion for dinner and music. It's a great time for everyone and a good way to get some much-needed work done in the park."

"Sounds good to me." Gwen smiled and rubbed her palms together, ready to get the day started.

They were directed to a line of Jeeps and trucks that were to be used to transport the volunteers to the work site. Gwen followed her group and was startled when she felt a hand slip around her biceps. She paused and looked around to find Pria smiling back at her.

"Want to share a seat? If I'm going to spend all day picking up trash, I'd at least like to enjoy the view." Pria let her eyes travel down Gwen's body with the look of a starving lioness.

Gwen's mouth went dry. Pria was making it very difficult for her to keep her mind on the day's task. She took a deep breath to steady herself. Pria was beautiful and her intentions were clear, but Gwen didn't feel the familiar desire to see anything come of it. She knew what Pria was after, and although a night of sex would be fun and was damn tempting, she really didn't want to pick that lifestyle up again. She had left that life behind. She wanted to believe she could have more, *be* more to someone. She had to believe there was someone out there who would share her dream of forever. This was going to be a very long day.

❖

Andi leaned against the massive maple tree and watched the crowd gather. As if drawn by a magnet, she caught movement in the crowd and recognized Gwen making her way through the crowd, her head held high, shoulders squared. Although she walked with purpose, her stride was graceful and confident. Andi couldn't look away. She was mesmerized by the subtle power that resonated from Gwen. Andi studied her quizzically and realized what Gwen exuded was pure raw sex. She shifted to relieve the pressure gathering between her thighs as the now-familiar hunger for Gwen grew more insistent. Andi pushed the thought out of her mind, not wanting to acknowledge the stir of arousal coiling beneath her skin.

She watched as Gwen became acquainted with her group. Andi's shoulders tensed and she found it difficult to swallow when Glenda's niece stepped close to Gwen, a hungry expression on her face.

Andi was very familiar with Pria and her summer affairs. She felt a twinge of jealousy at the thought of Gwen and Pria together. The thought both irritated and unnerved her. What did she care who Gwen spent her time with? But Pria, of all people, really? Andi sighed. Wasn't this what Gwen had been looking for? Wasn't that exactly why she had made sure to distance herself from Gwen? Then why did this bother her so much?

Exasperated, Andi pressed her shoulder into the tree and pushed off, heading toward the caravan. She would just make sure she wasn't in Gwen's group. It was none of her business who Gwen spent her time with, slept with, or dated. It was time she got Gwen Palmer out of her head.

"Hey, Andi," a gravelly voice called just as she was making her way past the picnic tables. Andi couldn't believe her luck. She took a deep breath before she turned to face Earnest McNeely, the leader of this little tribe of do-gooders. She knew that when she turned around, she would be facing Gwen and her group, and there would be no way she could escape unnoticed.

"Yeah, Earnest, what's up?" Andi tried to keep her eyes focused on Earnest, but Gwen stood directly behind him. Gwen turned toward her, and Andi watched Gwen's expression morph from gentle and playful to wistful and guarded the instant her gaze fell upon Andi.

The cold stone of regret that had settled in Andi's stomach seemed to expand, and she fought the urge to cough. For a moment she had the urge to go to Gwen. She wanted to reassure her, apologize for hurting her, anything to take away her look of disappointment.

Earnest stopped in front of Andi. "Hey, you all right? You look a little green around the gills."

Andi shook her head. "No. I'm good. What can I do for you?"

Andi kept her gaze steady as Earnest eyed her warily. Every second seemed like an eternity as she stood there, knowing Gwen was watching her. She wished Earnest would get on with it, so she could get as far away from Gwen Palmer as possible.

"Well, if you're really up to working with us today, I need you to lead a team up to the old cemetery. Stevens can't make it. His wife fell last night and broke her ankle, and he has his hands full with her and the kids."

"That's rough. Sure, I can lead a group. No problem."

A look of relief settled over Earnest's features. "Thanks, Andi. You're a real lifesaver. I'll give you truck number nine. They seem to be the youngest group—without giving you the kids, and they should be able to handle the climb a little better than some of the others. Grab your radio from the fire chief, inside the diner." Earnest slapped Andi playfully on the shoulder. "Better get going if we're going to make it through the watershed before dark."

Andi nodded, and in a flash Earnest turned and headed for a group of kids from the middle school. Andi gave a sigh of relief. At least she wouldn't be responsible for a troop of preteens all day. She gathered her gear from the fire chief along with her route map and located her truck. Everything seemed pretty straightforward, and Andi was looking forward to the day on the trails. She stored her gear under the seat at the back. Tall water coolers were already on board, and she was happy to see that this year the city had thrown in a large box of snacks. Andi had just finished going through the first-aid kit and putting everything away when her group began to board. Her heart plummeted on a surge of disappointment and dread when she looked up to see Pria slide into the Tahoe, followed close behind by Gwen.

"Shit." Andi closed her eyes. This could not be happening. She was already finding it difficult to stop the thoughts of Gwen that had taken up residence in her mind since the day they'd first met.

Despite her assertions that she was not interested in having any sort of relationship with Gwen, she had the uncontrollable desire to be close to her, to talk to her, to watch the way she moved. The idea of watching Gwen fall under Pria's spell made her irrationally angry and, to her irritation, jealous. This was going to be a *very* long day.

❖

Andi passed out the assignments to her team, making sure not to make eye contact with Gwen. She had managed the ride without throwing up, but Pria was making it difficult for Andi to ignore her, and the more she saw, the more irritable she became. Pria was practically sitting in Gwen's lap and giggled like a teenager every time the SUV hit a rough spot. Even worse, Gwen didn't seem to mind the attention and had put her arm around Pria when they went over a particularly rough section of road.

Andi directed Gwen's group to cover the cemetery and surrounding field that was a popular hangout for the local teens. The area was riddled with discarded beer bottles and fast food trash. She instructed the group to make their way down the slope to meet up with the second group that would start at the bottom of the valley and follow the dirt road back to the truck. Andi and two others would work their way up one side of the road farther up the mountain, and then backtrack down the other side to meet back up at the original start.

This was a good plan. It allowed the strongest hikers to work the toughest parts of the grid, and as an added bonus allowed her to keep her distance from Gwen and Pria. Maybe she would be able to enjoy this day after all.

"Does everyone understand their group assignment?"

Murmurs of agreement filtered in from the various members of the group with many nodding their heads in agreement.

"One last thing," Andi said, opening a small brown paper bag. "Everyone needs to take one of these whistles. If you have any problems or need help, blow the whistle. If you hear a whistle, the nearest group should answer. Everyone should meet up at the truck in case there's an emergency and we need to get back down the mountain." She looked around the group, making sure she hadn't missed anyone. She passed Gwen and Pria, making sure not to let her emotions betray her, handing out the whistles without any acknowledgment as if Gwen were just another member of the group…which she was.

"Okay, that's it, have fun, everybody."

When the group split up, Andi let her gaze slip to Gwen, and to her chagrin, Gwen was looking straight at her, a curious look on her face. Andi froze, unable to read what was in Gwen's eyes. She knew she should look away but couldn't bring herself to break even this minute contact. Gwen's lips parted as if she was about to say something, and Andi found herself staring at Gwen's lips. Gwen took a step forward but was cut off when Pria came running up and grabbed her around the waist, breaking the connection.

Andi quickly averted her gaze and walked away.

Gwen stumbled when Pria pushed into her and she caught hold of Pria as she righted herself. When she looked back to where Andi was standing only a moment before, she was gone. Gwen watched Andi walk up the rocky dirt road, her pack riding high on her back and her head down. She stopped to help another member of the group settle their pack more securely on their shoulders, offering a gentle pat on the back, and then pausing to answer another woman's questions about the path, pointing across the field and back along the Jeep road. Gwen watched with wonder as Andi engaged the members of the group and took command with confidence. Andi smiled warmly and said something that made the other woman laugh, and Gwen wished she had been the recipient of that smile. She wished she could hear what was said. She wanted to share those simple connections with Andi.

Gwen sighed as she watched Andi fade into the foliage along the mountain road. Part of her wanted to go after her, but she wasn't up for another shutdown. Andi had made it clear she wasn't interested. Gwen just couldn't figure out why it mattered so much what Andi thought of her. But there was something different about Andi, and she just couldn't let go.

"Come on, sweetie, let's start over here." Pria tugged on Gwen's arm.

Gwen took one last glance at the spot where Andi had disappeared from sight. "Sure. Let's go."

❖

Andi stood at the edge of a rock cliff gazing out over the miles and miles of mountains and valleys. A blue haze hung over the mountains in the distance, giving the appearance of a never-ending landscape. Andi imagined if she walked far enough, she would walk right into heaven. A light breeze ghosted through the trees, lifting the hairs at the back of her neck, sending a chill across her skin. She took a deep breath and drew the fresh mountain air into her lungs, pushing out all the stress and worry she had been swallowing all morning. She let her muscles relax and closed her eyes, lifting her face to the warm rays of the sun.

The screeching sound of a whistle caught Andi's attention and she jerked, turning toward the intrusive alarm. Without hesitating, she grabbed her bag and ran. The distance between her and the distress call seemed too vast to measure. Every step of her feet pounded into the dry earth, mocking her. She swallowed the panic rising from her chest and tried to keep her focus on the task ahead of her. She knew it wouldn't do anyone any good if she couldn't keep herself together. A million terrible scenarios played in her head, and each one involved Gwen.

Andi cursed her own impotence. She shouldn't have broken the groups up so far apart. She should have been closer. Sweat and dust filmed her skin, and the very air seemed too thin to breathe. Fear clutched at her throat as old memories surfaced, and she found herself defenseless in another forest, fighting for her life. The piercing shrill of the whistle morphed into her own anguished cries, and she could almost see the figure of the man looming over her.

Her foot rolled as a stone shifted beneath her boot, sending her sailing face-first into the dirt. She rolled, catching herself before she slid into a tree. She heard footsteps thundering down the path and tasted blood and dirt. Her chest tightened with growing fear. She slid her tongue over her lips and spat into the dry earth. She shook her head, trying to clear her muddled thoughts, reminding herself where she was. The blood was from her fall. She hadn't been struck with a fist. That was another time. She jumped to her feet and wiped the dirt from her mouth with her hand. The whistle kept her grounded in the present, reminding her she needed to get back to the cemetery.

Andi was one of the first to reach the Tahoe. Glenda was the one blowing the whistle, and Andi could see Gwen and Pria writhing on the ground. Her first thought was that Gwen was striking at Pria, but as she grew closer she could see Gwen feverishly trying to strip off Pria's shirt. Pria was slapping at her own arms and face and screaming.

"What happened?" Andi asked as she ran up to the small group.

"Yellow jackets," Glenda wheezed. "They must have stepped on a nest."

"Does she have an allergy to stings?"

Glenda stammered but didn't seem to know the answer.

Andi didn't wait for Glenda to figure it out. "Pria—are you allergic?" She joined Gwen in trying to free Pria of the clothing and the bees trapped inside. Pria was crying, the pain no doubt amplifying her terror. Andi placed her hands on either side of Pria's face, forcing her to look at her. "Pria. Sweetie, I need you to try to calm down. I need to know if you're allergic to the bees." Andi tried to keep her voice calm as she spoke to Pria. She knew if she could get Pria's attention, the tone of her voice and her own lack of fear would help Pria relax.

Pria shook her head. "I don't think so. I've never had a reaction before."

"Good girl." Andi swatted away a yellow jacket that appeared on Pria's side. She felt a sting catch her little finger and she jerked her hand away, dislodging the tiny invader. Andi looked around the group. She needed to treat the stings, and she needed to get Pria back to town where she could be monitored. Despite the frantic search, Pria seemed to have only three stings that Andi could see.

"Glenda, go to the back of the truck and bring me the first-aid kit." Andi looked over at Gwen who was steadily searching Pria's back and arms for more stings. She noticed Gwen had several welts along her neck, arms, and hands and felt a new wave of anxiety rush through her.

"Gwen, are you allergic to the stings?"

Gwen looked at her blankly. "What?"

"You've been stung. Are you allergic?"

Gwen shook her head. "I don't think so."

Andi felt only slightly relieved. The stings to Gwen's neck could present a threat to her life if she had even a mild reaction, especially if the swelling cut off her airway. Andi jumped to her feet and grabbed the hem of Gwen's T-shirt. "Take this off, now!"

Gwen didn't hesitate. She grabbed the shirt and pulled it over her head.

As Andi feared, several more stings decorated Gwen's back and stomach. Andi felt light-headed and fought the wave of fear that rolled over her, making her feel faintly dizzy. Oh God, not Gwen. How did she let this happen? Why hadn't she kept the group closer together? She'd been so wrapped up in herself, she'd put Gwen in danger. Andi flinched at the thought. Hadn't that been what she was trying to avoid?

Glenda returned with the first-aid kit and handed Andi the sting kit. Andi opened the pack and handed some of the ammonia swabs to Glenda.

"Use these. Make sure you cover every sting."

Andi tore open the swabs. She hoped the ammonia would ease some of the pain and deaden the formic acid that continued to be pumped into Gwen's body in places where the stingers had detached from the hosts. Andi took her keys from her pocket and flipped to her grocery discount card. She used the stiff plastic to scrape the stingers off Gwen's neck and stomach without pressing more venom into the wounds.

Andi pressed her fingers into Gwen's hair as she cradled Gwen's neck, trying to locate each sting. "Hold still." She brushed her fingers gently over the swollen wounds, applying generous amounts of ammonia. When she began to work on the stings on Gwen's stomach, Gwen's breathing changed. Andi could hear each husky intake of breath, and she felt the first ping of panic. "Are you having trouble breathing?"

Gwen tensed when Andi's fingers played across her stomach. She hadn't really registered the stings as long as she was focused on Pria. Now they were becoming torturous pinpoints of fire and pain. She relinquished control to Andi, hoping for some relief from the pulsing heat that seemed to swell beneath each sting. But as soon as Andi's fingers touched her, she forgot about the stings. Each stroke of Andi's fingers across her skin felt like a thousand teasing kisses, and her focus was directed to the soft sound of Andi's voice, the heat of Andi's breath on her skin, the tender press of Andi's fingers in her hair. Andi was so close to her she could once again smell the lingering scent of coconut and honeysuckle.

Andi's hand flew up to Gwen's face and cupped her cheek.

Gwen thought she would melt when her eyes met Andi's. They were wide and fearful and reminded Gwen of an ocean storm. She was sure if she could hold Andi's gaze long enough, she would see lightning flash. Andi's cheeks were flushed and her lips were pressed into a worried line. They were so close Gwen knew she only had to lean forward a couple of inches to taste them.

"No," Gwen said, her voice raspy. "I think I'm okay."

Andi moved her hand away and went back to tending to the stings. Gwen closed her eyes for a moment trying to get a grip on her arousal. The last thing she needed was for Andi to recognize that what was happening to her had nothing to do with the stings and everything to do with Andi's hands on her body.

"I think that'll do for now. I really am okay." Gwen sat forward and ran her fingers over the welts on her neck.

Andi looked around the group, counting each person out loud. "Okay, that's it everybody. Let's load up and get back to the station."

Pria climbed into the truck and sat slumped in the seat with her head on Glenda's shoulder.

Gwen shook out her shirt to make sure no strays were still hiding in the folds. She was glad Pria was okay and equally glad she seemed to have lost interest in her. Then she saw Andi rip open another ammonia swab and rub it over her own hand.

"Did one catch you too?"

Andi nodded.

"Let me see." Gwen stepped forward, slinging her shirt across her shoulder. She reached out and took Andi's hand which had swollen to double its normal size.

"Oh shit, Andi. Are you allergic to these things?"

"Yeah." Andi slid the EpiPen into her pocket. "But I think I'll be okay."

"You going to need that?" Gwen gestured toward the EpiPen.

"I hope not." Andi brushed past Gwen. "Let's get going."

Gwen felt a wave of concern wash over her. Andi had put herself in danger for her and for Pria without any hesitation, knowing the danger to herself. Gwen watched Andi toss the first-aid kit back into the truck, and Gwen wondered what could make someone so selfless be so distant.

Chapter Five

Gwen let the paramedic check her vitals. She hadn't had any reaction to the bee stings, but Andi had insisted that everyone who was stung be checked out at the fire station. She watched Andi take care of Pria and Glenda and make sure everyone in her group returned from the mountain safe and sound. She noticed how Andi downplayed her own discomfort despite her obvious reaction to the sting. The medic had given Andi some kind of injection, and Gwen heard him tell Andi to take the Benadryl he was sending home with her. She couldn't quite shake the discomfort growing in her chest when she thought of something happening to Andi.

When Andi walked out of the fire station, Gwen followed her.

"Hey, are you doing okay?"

Andi stopped and looked at her swollen hand. "It's not as bad as it looks. I'm fine."

"You did a great job today."

Andi sighed. "Thanks, but I think you did most of the work. You took most of the hits too." Andi stepped close to Gwen and cupped her chin in her hand. She tilted Gwen's head to the side and studied the welts still visible on Gwen's neck. "Looks like the swelling is going down." She let her fingers brush lightly across Gwen's face as she released her.

"Thanks for helping me out today. Those things really pack a punch," Gwen said.

Andi smiled. "I'm just glad everyone's okay."

Gwen looked across the street toward the pavilion where the band was playing. The music echoed off the surrounding hills and buildings, amplifying the sound and filling the air with energy.

"Do you want to get a bite to eat?" Gwen asked, wanting to prolong the contact with Andi. The feel of Andi's fingers on her skin was intoxicating and she was desperate for more.

Andi cupped her swollen hand in the crook of her arm. "I think I'll head home and get some rest. That Benadryl will knock me out in no time and, I'd really like to be home when it kicks in."

Gwen nodded, understanding Andi's need to rest. She had the unsettled need to make sure Andi was okay. "Sure. I just thought you might need something in your stomach. You had a big day and the adrenaline had to wear you out."

"Don't you have plans with Pria?"

Andi's tone was clipped and Gwen grinned despite the obvious stab. "No. She's sweet, but not what I'm looking for."

"Hmm. That's not what it looked like earlier."

Gwen took a deep breath and didn't let herself be baited. "I'm sure there are a lot of things that aren't exactly as they seem." She realized that every time they got close, every time Andi let her guard down in the slightest, she immediately became defensive and started an argument.

Andi frowned. "What's that supposed to mean?"

Gwen put her hands up, signaling a truce. "I'm just saying that I think we got off on the wrong foot." God, this woman was stubborn. "Can't we just be friends? Let's just pretend I never asked you out. If I'd known it would cause this much trouble, I wouldn't have."

Andi stared at Gwen without responding. Gwen began to feel self-conscious. "What? Say something."

"Why are you so nice to me? Why act like it matters?"

Gwen was stunned. "It matters to me," she said softly, surprised by her own honesty.

Andi drew in a deep breath, letting it out as a sigh. "Gwen."

"No. I've put a lot of thought into this, and I can't put my finger on a single thing I could have done to make you dislike me so much."

A flash of pain marred Andi's expression and she closed her eyes. When she looked back at Gwen her eyes were glassy and mournful. "I don't dislike you, Gwen. I'm just not very good with people."

Andi's voice was but a whisper, and Gwen had the urge to reach out and touch her, but instinctively Gwen knew if she did, Andi would retreat again.

"I watched you all day today. I saw how you took care of everyone, even when it put you at risk. I get it that you're trying to push me away, I just don't understand why," Gwen said gently.

All the fight seemed to go out of Andi and her shoulders slumped. "You're right," Andi said. "I've been trying to push you away since the first time we met. I don't want to complicate your life. And my life is definitely complicated."

Andi's voice was sad. She was clearly getting upset and Gwen was following suit. The idea of Andi hurting grieved her. She would do anything to take that sadness away.

Andi continued to explain. "It isn't anything you've done, Gwen. It's me. I can't risk letting anyone into my life right now. It's the best for both of us. I'm sorry."

"Okay," Gwen sighed. She felt defeated. "I guess I've been a little raw myself. My last relationship, if that's what you can call it, didn't end so well. I'm still a little sensitive about the rejection thing. I took it personally when you pushed me away because I felt like I wasn't good enough for you."

Andi stopped walking. She looked at Gwen, stunned by what she heard. She knew it had to be hard for Gwen to share that hurt with her, and it warmed Andi that Gwen had shown her that vulnerability.

"How can you think that? I can't imagine anyone feeling that way about you. Whoever she was, she was a fool. I'm sorry I made you feel that way."

Gwen's head was pounding now, and she wasn't even sure where all this emotion was coming from. She felt as if years of disappointment and hurt were being channeled into this one moment, and she couldn't stop the release once she started. Her eyes burned with unshed emotion. Andi's sudden kindness confused her and made her want to wrap her arms around Andi and weep like a child. God, what was happening to her?

"I haven't been fair. I really am sorry, Gwen."

"Sure." Gwen started to walk away but Andi grabbed her hand. When she looked down, Andi's eyes were soft and gentle.

Andi squared her shoulders, drew in a deep breath and looked directly at Gwen. "How about Friday?

Gwen blinked, confused by the question. She wasn't certain she had heard correctly. "How about what Friday?"

Andi shrugged. "I really don't feel like hanging around here for dinner tonight, so how about dinner Friday night?"

Gwen hesitated. She hadn't been prepared for this sudden change. Reluctantly she answered, "Okay, sure."

Andi smiled. "Friday it is. What should I bring?"

Gwen was still trying to get her head around the sudden change in the conversation but was afraid to say much, for fear of jinxing herself. She stood there, madly trying to formulate a plan.

To her relief Andi rescued her. "How about you order the pizza and I bring the beer?"

Gwen tried to keep up. "Okay. Deal."

Andi smiled. "Your house at six o'clock, okay?"

"That's perfect." Gwen relaxed a little and smiled.

Andi started walking again and Gwen walked with her. Andi hadn't let go of her hand, and she liked the feel of Andi's long slender fingers laced in hers. All too soon Andi stopped outside a modest Craftsman-style house with pale green siding and white trim.

"This is me," Andi said, gesturing toward the house.

Gwen looked to the house and back to Andi. "Oh, yeah. Okay. Good night then. I'll see you Friday."

Andi gave Gwen's hand a slight squeeze before letting go and walking away.

Gwen watched until Andi was safe inside. She wasn't sure what just happened, but she was grateful that Andi was finally willing to give her a chance.

Once inside the house, Andi leaned her back against the cool wood, relieved to be safe at home where she could finally let go of the storm of emotions she had warred with all day. She was tired. She stood there replaying the events of the day—her fear when Gwen had been stung, the wounded look in Gwen's eyes when she talked about her past, and the feel of Gwen's hand holding hers on the walk home. She had been unfair to Gwen and had to admit she had been projecting her feelings. It had felt good to stop fighting and just enjoy spending time with Gwen without the angst that usually accompanied their conversations.

Gwen had surprised her with the way she had cared for Pria despite her own pain. The memory of seeing the stings riddling Gwen's body made her shiver. Gwen hadn't even flinched. She had been totally focused on helping someone she barely knew. That alone was enough to make Andi rethink her assessment of Gwen. And the fear that had twisted Andi's stomach when she thought Gwen might be in danger had been overwhelming. Gwen's raw emotion had been heartbreaking, and Andi hated that she had added to that pain.

It was time for her to grow up and stop punishing others for her past. She was friendly with lots of people in town. Why should Gwen be any different?

Andi pushed away from the door. She wanted a shower, but her need for sleep was more pressing. She stripped off her clothes as she went through the house. When she reached her bed she was completely naked. She tossed back the covers and slid between the cool sheets, letting the weight of the covers comfort her.

The medication made it difficult for her to think. She prayed that tonight, for once, she wouldn't dream of the past, or the fear. She just wanted to shut off the world and sleep. Her last thought as she closed her eyes and drifted off was of Gwen holding her hand.

A clear blue sky offered not a single cloud to block the punishing rays of the sun. The dull thud of the mattock marked the rhythm of the strokes assaulting the ground around the old tree stump. Andi's arms ached as they absorbed the vibrations from every strike into the hard earth. Sweat trickled down her neck in rivulets, and her shirt stuck to her wet back. The heat of the bright sun beat down on her with punishing intensity, scorching her skin. Her mouth was parched and her lips felt dry and rough. But not even the heat or the strain of her labor could soothe her today. She had come out to work off her anxiety and had found her thoughts drawn into the past. It was not a place she liked to visit. Nothing good lived in her memories. But something about Gwen had stirred her and she knew that was a bad sign. She could no longer deny liking Gwen. What was there not to like? She'd settled it. She would try to be friends but there would be nothing else. There was no way she was going to go there. Never again.

"Whose dog shit in your daisies today?" The familiar weathered voice barked, startling her.

She'd been so lost in her thoughts she hadn't heard Mrs. Peterson approach. Andi stopped, only now assessing the damage she had managed to inflict on the old stump. She looked around. "What do you mean?"

Mrs. Peterson stood on the sidewalk, her hands perched petulantly on her hips. "I mean that you've been out here whaling on that old stump for the past two hours like you're trying to pay it back for some terrible crime. Clearly, something's bothering you."

Andi opened and then closed her mouth several times, feeling very much like a fish trying to breathe out of water. Exasperated, she pulled off her gloves and tossed them at her feet before sitting roughly on the ground.

Mrs. Peterson studied her thoughtfully. "Looks like you're trying to work something out of your system. Do you need anything, dear?"

Andi looked up into the old gray eyes, surprised by the sudden gentleness she heard in the usually rough voice. For the first time, Andi wanted to explain, to finally tell someone her story. But the moment passed quickly and she just couldn't bring herself to do it.

"Thank you, but no. I'm fine." Andi fought back the swell of emotion that gathered into a lump in her throat. She drew up the neck of her T-shirt and wiped at her face, using the sweat as a cover for her emotional lapse as she tried to pull herself back together. "Thank you for checking up on me."

Mrs. Peterson peered at her as if she wasn't fooled by Andi's attempts to hide her feelings. But after a moment she straightened her posture, and the gentleness was suddenly gone.

"Well then, you best take a bit of a rest and get a drink before you have heatstroke."

Andi smiled. "You're right. Good thing I have you looking after me, or heaven knows what trouble I might get myself into." Andi was relieved the old woman hadn't pried any further. She needed to keep her barriers in place, and it wouldn't do any good to bring up the past now.

The corner of Mrs. Peterson's mouth twitched into a faint grin. She squinted at Andi and pointed a twisted arthritic finger at her. "If you ask me, you could do with a little trouble, might even be fun."

Andi gaped at the old woman who had already turned and was making her way back across the street, mumbling something that Andi couldn't quite hear. She wondered what Mrs. Peterson had meant. She shook her head, confused by the unusual encounter.

Andi looked again at the stump and decided she had battled enough memories for one day. She gathered her tools and cleaned up her mess and made a retreat to the backyard. She stripped off her T-shirt and shoes and dove into the pool. The water was cool and refreshing as she felt it wash away all the heat, sweat, dust, and worry that had accumulated on her like a heavy blanket that threatened to suffocate her.

After the brief swim, she made her way to the small refrigerator at the edge of her covered porch. She opened a beer and fell into her favorite lounge chair. Her shoulders eased and she let out a long breath. Mrs. Peterson's words played over in her mind. *You could do with a little trouble, might even be fun.* Andi's thoughts drifted to Gwen. She remembered the gentleness of Gwen's fingers in her hand. She thought of the openness she had seen in Gwen's eyes when she looked at her. She thought of the tall, lean body standing over her, caring for her with a tenderness Andi had longed for her whole life.

The warmth that began to build in her middle and spread through her skin had nothing to do with the sun. Andi imagined what it would be like to have Gwen's gentle fingers caressing her, to have the length of her body pressed against her. She took a long draft from her beer and sighed. "This is definitely trouble."

Chapter Six

Gwen swept up the last of the debris from the latest construction. She had managed to refinish the kitchen cabinets and had installed a subfloor but wasn't quite ready to begin the tile job. She wasn't looking forward to laying out the two-foot rectangular tiles over the 200 square feet of kitchen floor. The granite countertops were being installed in three days, and the appliances were scheduled to arrive the day after that. She sighed at the amount of work she needed to do before then. But it wasn't something she couldn't manage.

She had already stripped the bathroom of the tub surround and installed a walk-in tile shower, a new toilet, a new sink, and a double slipper tub. She still had work to do on the shelves for storage, but the room was usable. She picked up the drop cloths in the living room and stored the paint cans in the hall closet. That was as tidy as she could make the place in its current condition.

She checked her watch. She had just enough time to shower, change, and order the pizza before Andi was scheduled to arrive. It was exciting having someone visit her in her new house. It made her feel like she was officially home. She thought of her encounters with Andi, and a knot of worry began to form in her stomach. They hadn't exchanged any personal information at all. She didn't even have a way to contact Andi. What if she changed her mind and didn't show?

Gwen frowned thoughtfully as she stepped into the shower. Andi was difficult to figure out. Gwen seemed to have a knack for saying the wrong thing to Andi, and she knew she needed to be careful if she wanted Andi to take her seriously. She couldn't explain why she felt so compelled to be around Andi. Something about her just felt familiar, right somehow. Gwen's insides twitched at the thought. She definitely wanted to know more about her. The moment she had laid eyes on Andi, lying in her front yard half-terrified of Zeek, Gwen had been stunned by her beauty. She had enjoyed the warmth of her hand and her tender soft skin in those first few moments before everything seemed to fall apart.

Gwen sighed. Then things had gone to hell. She could only hope tonight wouldn't be a replay of their disastrous encounters. But Andi had seemed sincere about the dinner date. Gwen just hoped she hadn't had a change of heart.

Gwen stuck her head under the shower spray, allowing the hot water to thrum against her skin. As she hurriedly rinsed, stepped out of the shower, and dried herself, she became increasingly anxious that Andi wouldn't show up at all. The thought made her chest tighten with disappointment. She wanted to have the chance to see Andi again, a chance to show Andi she wasn't who she thought she was. Gwen felt hollow and ached at the thought that she wasn't good enough for Andi. Andi had as much as said so, and part of her believed it. But Andi wasn't like any of the other women she had known. There was something special about her that made Gwen want to be better, made her want more than just a transient liaison or a convenient physical relationship. She hoped Andi felt the same. She couldn't handle having her feelings thrown away again, the way Miranda had. Gwen needed to prove to Andi that she was worth taking a chance on. Perhaps then she could believe it herself.

She dressed and ordered the pizza, watching the clock anxiously. Andi would be arriving soon. Gwen looked around the room one last time. She felt like she was standing on the edge of a cliff, unable to see what lay before her. When the doorbell rang, she jumped. Although she had anticipated the sound, it startled her and her nerves frayed with insecurity. She took a deep breath to calm herself.

Ready or not, she took a tentative step forward and opened the door.

❖

Andi paced the floor of her living room, her keys gripped firmly in her hand. Her stomach ached as it tied and retied itself in knots. The hair at the base of her neck was damp with perspiration. She looked at her watch and considered not going to Gwen's, but she couldn't allow herself to just not show. How had she gotten herself into this? Not only had she agreed to a friendly social dinner, something she never did, but she would be spending the evening with a woman who seemed to ignite feelings and yearnings she couldn't afford to entertain. Despite all her attempts to push Gwen out of her life, out of her mind, she longed for the promise she saw in the way Gwen looked at her. It was a promise she dreamed of but couldn't keep.

Her cat, Goliath, lay in his spot on the sofa, eyeing her quizzically. His tail twitched irritably each time she passed. Suddenly he reached out a paw and snagged her shorts with his claw. She stopped.

"Sorry, boy, I'm getting on my nerves too."

The cat blinked up at her. When she reached down and rubbed his ears, he began to purr, making her feel better. She blew out a long breath, feeling somewhat calmer, picked up the small cooler she had packed earlier, and went out the door.

As Andi pulled into Gwen's drive, Gwen was standing on the front porch, paying the pizza-delivery guy. Gwen looked up with a bright smile and waved to Andi, motioning for her to come inside. Andi was simultaneously scared to death and exhilarated at the sight of Gwen. She tried to pull herself together and reminded herself this was only dinner. She had nothing to be worried about.

Gwen waited for her at the door. "Thank you for coming. I was afraid you might change your mind."

"I almost did," Andi said honestly. She wondered if her voice sounded as shaky to Gwen as she thought it did. Her heart had started pounding in her chest the moment she pulled into the drive. No matter how much she tried to tell herself she wasn't interested in Gwen Palmer, her body told her differently.

Gwen stopped and looked at Andi for a moment to see if she was serious. Nothing in Andi expression indicated she was joking, but her eyes were kind, although slightly fearful, and Gwen noticed the subtle tension as Andi stood not quite facing her, and how she dropped her gaze when Gwen tried to meet her eyes. Andi seemed so vulnerable. Gwen had the urge to reach out and touch Andi but thought better of it. That would surely send Andi running.

"I can't say I blame you. I mean, we don't really know each other, and I've been a little pushy. But I promise I'm completely harmless," Gwen teased.

This seemed to ease some of the tension from Andi's shoulders, and she glanced nervously at Gwen.

"It's nothing personal. I just don't want you to get the wrong idea about this."

Gwen shrugged. "Like I said before, it's just dinner with a new friend." She didn't really want to believe that, but the frightened look in Andi's eyes had surprised her. The thought of Andi being afraid of her was even harder to take than Andi thinking she was trying to play her.

They walked into the kitchen together. Gwen placed the pizza on the makeshift counter, and Andi opened the cooler to retrieve a couple of beers.

"The house looks wonderful."

"Thank you."

"Where did you learn to do this kind of work?" Andi asked, handing Gwen a beer.

Gwen reached out for the beer and felt the tips of their fingers brush lightly as their eyes met. She caught a fleeting look of need ghost across Andi's face before she masked the expression and pulled away. Some of Gwen's own fear subsided, but she could still feel the uncertainty in Andi's posture that gave away her vulnerability.

Gwen tried to act nonchalant even though her stomach clenched as her body reacted to the touch. Realizing she hadn't answered

Andi's question, she cleared her throat and stepped away. "I worked with a small construction company when I was in college. It was hard work, but the pay was good and it allowed me to work with my hands. I found that I really enjoy it. I spent a couple of years at a local community college getting the basics, and after I managed to save enough money, I transferred to Montana State University and finished my degree in environmental biology. I worked for a few years after that, and then got my master's in environmental engineering and went to work."

"Wow. That sounds like an interesting field. What brings you to Tennessee?"

Andi sounded genuinely interested, and Gwen couldn't help but want to tell Andi everything about herself. "It's hard to explain, but mostly I wanted a change. I needed a fresh start. I felt like I settled for the first job that came along and I became complacent in my life. My family was in Chicago, but if I'd been honest with myself, the job wasn't really what I wanted. Things weren't working out in my personal life, and company cutbacks solved the problem for me. I found myself single after foolishly thinking I was in love with someone who didn't feel the same way about me, and unemployed because the affair created a conflict with my job. After so many bad choices, it seemed the perfect time for a fresh start, and I wanted to see what I was missing in the big wide world. I managed to land a job here so it seemed like a good place to start."

Gwen hoped Andi wouldn't ask her more about her personal life. She didn't want to have to explain that she had an affair with her boss's wife, and when things got sticky, she had been terminated from her position.

Laughing softly, Andi looked at Gwen. "So you chose to run away to a small, secluded town in East Tennessee?"

Gwen smiled. "I guess it does seem a bit odd, but I was tired of the city. I wanted to have a chance to walk outside my door and not have car alarms, sirens, and all the other chaos going on around me." She casually glanced at Andi as she talked, noticing how Andi was beginning to relax. More of the tension in her shoulders had eased, and she faced Gwen when she was talking now. That was progress.

"What do you think of the area so far?"

"I love it here. I don't think I've ever encountered a town quite like it. It's beautiful and I can't believe how friendly everyone has been. To be honest, the first day I thought I had moved into a retirement community. Everyone I met was at least sixty-five—until I met you of course."

Andi met her gaze and Gwen warmed. Other than a few close friends from college and Peter from work, she didn't usually disclose so much about herself to anyone. And most of the women she had dated weren't really into getting to know her beyond the bedroom. The easy conversation with Andi was refreshing.

"Enough about me. It's your turn now," Gwen said. "Tell me about you. Have you always lived in Norris?"

Andi looked out over the yard and toyed with the label on her beer. "No. I moved here from Chattanooga around three years ago. I was drawn to the simple, quiet life." Andi shifted in her chair, and Gwen thought she seemed uncomfortable with the question.

"Once I opened the store, I became very invested in the people here. As you noticed, there are a lot of elderly people, and many live alone. It's nice to be able to help them keep their four-legged companions, when they can no longer get out and do things for themselves. It's simple work, but very rewarding."

Gwen liked the sound of Andi's voice and wanted her to keep talking. "What made you decide to open a pet-supply store?"

Andi laughed. "That was easy. For the first few months after I moved here, it seemed I met all the neighborhood pets before I met their owners. And it seemed everyone had a pet. I knew most of the dogs in town by name, but not their owners. People became Cookie's mother, or Fido's dad. A supply store just seemed to make sense."

Gwen leaned forward in her chair, resting her elbows on her knees. "I guess Zeek fits right in then."

Andi chuckled, the smooth and lilting tone resonating in her chest in a way that made Gwen want to place her hand there and feel the tremors with her fingers.

"Yes, she certainly does."

Both women laughed hard as Gwen recalled the look on Andi's face the day Zeek had plowed her over. "You looked like you weren't sure if she was going to eat you or lick you to death."

"Actually, I was trying to figure out why a bear would be chasing a squirrel."

Andi laughed even harder now, and wiped tears from her eyes. She liked to laugh and hadn't done it enough lately. And she liked Gwen's laugh. It was the kind of rich, deep laugh that resonated from inside and filled the room with warmth and comfort. And Andi found it refreshing. She realized with every passing moment how much she had missed the companionship of a friend. And Gwen had been true to her word. She hadn't made any overtures toward her since she arrived. Gwen seemed more grounded than Andi had expected, and she found herself warming to her a little more.

Realizing there was something missing in the evening she looked around and asked, "Where is Zeek?"

"Oh, she's sulking."

Andi was confused and intrigued.

As if reading her mind, Gwen answered. "She had a bath earlier and has decided to punish me by refusing to come out of the bedroom. She does that sometimes. I think she does it so I'll have to sleep with the smell of wet dog all night."

Andi thought of the giant dog, soggy and wet, with her giant head lying on Gwen's pillow.

"Honestly, I'm surprised she hasn't come out to investigate. She must really be angry with me. It could be she didn't like the flea treatment. That's always an added insult."

"Has she ever had any problems with the medication before?" Andi was a little nervous. Some dogs did have a reaction to the medication, and she wanted to see if Zeek was okay, but she didn't want to act like she didn't trust Gwen's judgment.

"No, don't worry. She just likes to punish me. But if it'll make you feel better, I can go check on her."

"That's okay. I'm sure you're right."

The sound of padded feet and toenails on the wood floor got Andi's attention, and she looked through the open french doors to see Zeek standing in the kitchen, appraising her.

Gwen shook her head, grinning. "She must have heard her name and had to see who was talking about her."

"Hey, Zeek. How are you doing, girl?" Andi said, relieved to see the giant dog.

Zeek's ears perked up, and she came sauntering out onto the deck, doing her best John Wayne impression, which was quite cute on a dog. She gave Gwen a cursory glance before laying her giant head in Andi's lap with a moan.

"Guess I'm still in the doghouse," Gwen said, sounding amused.

Andi rubbed Zeek's ears. "You smell good, Zeek. No bugs on you."

The dog moaned again and Andi wasn't sure if that was exasperation or pleasure.

Night had fallen, and the stars blanketed the sky like diamonds. The cool night air was a welcome reprieve from the heat of the day. It was a perfect evening. Andi couldn't remember the last time she had enjoyed talking and listening to another person the way she had with Gwen. She knew most of the locals, but only in a superficial, neighborly kind of way. This seemed personal, like she was looking into a page of Gwen's life, and the feeling made her want to know more. The thought unsettled her.

"Thank you for having me over tonight. I've really enjoyed the company," Andi said, thinking it was time for her to go.

"I should be thanking you. I love working on the house, but I guess I've been a little lonely. It's good not to eat alone. And I wanted to make up for my earlier behavior. I'm afraid I gave the impression of being a bit too eager when I asked you out. But I could really use a friend. I really wanted to get to know you, and tonight was perfect."

Andi regarded Gwen for a moment, very aware of how tender her voice was. Gwen wasn't at all what she had expected. She had convinced herself Gwen was cocky and looking for a fast hookup, but tonight Gwen had been different. She was confident and self-assured, but not arrogant. She seemed warm and open and something about her made Andi feel safe. She watched Gwen's smooth gestures as she lifted the beer to her lips and took a drink. Andi stared at a bead of the golden liquid clinging to her lips and watched as her lips parted and her tongue moved across the surface to wick away the moisture.

"I've enjoyed it," she said, realizing it was true. "I should be going though—Zeek here is looking a bit tired."

"Are you sure? I think there's another beer left, if you'd like to stay a while longer."

Andi hesitated, hearing only sincerity in Gwen's voice. "I appreciate it, but I should call it a night. I'm already over my two-beer limit." Andi lifted Zeek's head and pushed back her chair as she stood. "It really was a nice night. Thank you."

Gwen followed Andi through the house and out to her Jeep. "Are you okay to drive?"

Andi turned to face Gwen, her hand resting on the top of the small half door of the Jeep. She looked up the street and considered her options.

"Well, I could walk home, but then I'd have to retrieve my Jeep tomorrow, and the neighbors would have a scandal brewing by morning. Or I can just take it easy. I only live one mile from here, and I'm sure I'm okay to drive. I only had three beers in"—Andi looked at her watch—"oh my goodness, four hours," she said, surprised by the time. "How did it get so late?"

Gwen was still smiling at her. "Well, if you're sure you're okay." She placed her hand over Andi's for a brief moment, her fingers brushing across Andi's skin, a featherlight touch that made Andi shudder. Andi's eyes drifted to Gwen's lips, which were slightly parted, and she imagined how they would taste.

"I promise I'm okay," Andi said, drawing her hand away. "Thank you again for dinner."

"You're welcome. Have a good night," Gwen said, taking a step back from the Jeep.

❖

Andi could barely make out Gwen's silhouette standing at the end of the drive as she looked back through her rearview mirror.

But she could tell Gwen was watching her drive away. She rubbed her fingertips across the back of her hand, savoring the feel of Gwen's touch against her skin. It had only been a moment, but she had trembled at the connection. She had felt the heat melt into her own skin, and she realized they had touched only twice the entire night. Gwen had more than kept to her promise—dinner, friendly conversation—and regret needled at Andi. A gentle prick had started at the back of her mind, and something within her knew she would continue to crave Gwen's closeness.

What am I doing? Andi sighed and ran her fingers through her hair. She was confused. Her life was too complicated to even entertain thoughts of Gwen, but here she was, letting fantasies and images flood her mind. She had known better than to come tonight, but she didn't know how to keep pushing Gwen away.

Chapter Seven

The next morning, Andi tightened the straps of her PFD and walked her paddleboard into the water. The sun was just beginning to crest over the mountain, and the sounds of morning stirred in the air as the birds sang out like the voices of angels.

She loved the lake in the morning. The water was so still it was like glass. Not many boats were out this early, and she had the lake to herself for the most part. Holding the paddle firmly in her hands, she focused on the feel of her stroke, keeping her balance centered over the board as she focused on the glide of the flat craft across the water.

Thoughts of Gwen had played through her mind all night, and she had slept restlessly. Even now images of Gwen swept across her vision. She could conjure the perfect image of Gwen's lips, the glint in her eyes when she laughed, the subtle way she gestured with her hands when she talked. It seemed Andi had memorized every movement of Gwen's body, and now her own invented new thoughts of what it would be like to touch her, to hold her long lean form next to her and taste her sweetness on her tongue.

Andi pushed her board through the water with increasing effort as she tried to use the rhythm of her body and the stroke of the paddle to calm the restlessness she felt growing under her skin. She focused on the lake, allowing the smooth surface and gentle lap of the water to sooth her. She drew in a deep breath of the fresh mountain air, trying to clear the restlessness from her mind.

It wasn't unusual for her to have difficulty sleeping. She often welcomed the dawn, anxiously waiting to shed the weight of memories that haunted her each night. But last night had been different. She wasn't running from fear or hurt, she was running from the stirring within her that craved the closeness of a woman.

That was a pain she couldn't flirt with. Women had been both the nectar of life and the kiss of death for her. As sweet as the beginning heat could be, the pain at the end would be too much. For the first time in months, Andi thought of JC. They had been lovers for two years, and JC had made it clear from the beginning that her job was more important to her than Andi. And when Andi had really needed her, when she was in real trouble, JC had turned her back on her. That was a pain she still couldn't put to rest and something she didn't think she could survive again.

As Andi turned into one of the many coves that made up the intricate pattern of the lake, a great blue heron took flight in front of her, its giant wings gliding gracefully as it maneuvered its long, stork-like body no more than a foot or two above the water, the tips of its wings brushing lightly across the surface.

Andi shifted her weight and slowly lowered herself until she was sitting on the board. Giving in to her fatigue, she lay back and gazed up into an endless blue sky. The sun was fully up now, and the brilliant, cloudless sky reminded her of the tender blue of Gwen's eyes and the way they made her feel as if they looked into her soul.

Andi closed her eyes for a moment as if she could shut out the image her mind had conjured. She didn't quite know what to think of her new preoccupation with Gwen Palmer. She hadn't entertained thoughts of a woman in so long, she had thought she would never again crave that closeness. She had chosen solitude and had committed herself to a single life. It was easier that way, less complicated, safer.

Andi thought over her life. In all her relationships, she had never really been loved in return. It seemed she always found herself with people who didn't want to accept her past, or life would intervene and pull them apart before any real feelings could surface. Her thoughts drifted to Melissa, and a terrible pain ripped through her chest. No. She wouldn't think of that time in her life. She pushed the memories aside and swore at herself for her weakness.

Since meeting Gwen, she had grown restless and the once-peaceful solitude had become too still, too quiet. But she wasn't ready to open up her heart again. She wasn't ready to trust someone enough to try. Her brain felt heavy as too many thoughts warred in her mind at once. Nothing had happened last night. Gwen hadn't said or done anything throughout their evening together to suggest anything other than friendship. The thing that troubled her was that she had been disappointed that Gwen had kept her word. But it was for the best. Gwen was her ultimate dream woman, the perfect combination of softness and strength, confidence and empathy, and Andi knew just how dangerous that was for her. And maybe more important, just how dangerous it could be for Gwen. As much as she needed to protect her own heart, she wouldn't risk another person she cared about. And that meant staying away.

Andi's arms were heavy and tired from the workout, and her core muscles began to protest from fatigue as she made her way to shore. She stored her gear and carried the paddleboard to the Jeep, securing it tightly to the roll bars above her head. It was a familiar pattern. Most of the summer, the board would remain tied to the roof with almost daily trips to the lake.

Andi sighed as she sat in the old Jeep, looking out over the lake. She had her answers. Her memories had resurfaced to remind her that she couldn't afford to complicate her life by getting involved. They would both only end up getting hurt.

Gwen slid into her now-familiar spot at the counter of the coffee shop and breathed in the soothing aromas of fresh coffee and bacon. "Good morning, Glenda."

"Good morning, Gwen. Be right with you, sweetie. The usual?"

"You bet. How's Pria?" Gwen had quickly established herself among the local morning chatter and loved the way the people of the little town had opened up to her.

"Oh, she's fine. Nothing keeps her down for long."

"Well, that's good."

Glenda smiled as she set a steaming cup of coffee in front of Gwen and went to clear off a recently vacated table.

Gwen inclined her head to an older gentleman at the end of the counter, slowly turning his cup back and forth between his large weatherworn hands. His big white cowboy hat and old faded overalls were a familiar sight. "Hey, Ward. How's Millie?"

The old man looked up from the cup he had been peering into and smiled, a Santa Claus twinkle lighting up his eyes.

"Good. Real good. Slept easy last night. That girl that helps out came by early this mornin'. She's looking after her now."

His eyes clouded again after a minute and he went back to staring into his cup. Gwen's heart went out to the old man. Through the diner chatter she had learned that Ward's wife was suffering with Parkinson's disease, and Ward was her primary caregiver—although he usually seemed hardly able to care for himself.

Glenda passed by and stopped to top off Gwen's coffee, bringing her back to the present. Gwen pondered the list of things she needed to work on this week and dreaded the daunting task of clearing the front yard of some of the debris. The front yard was a partially unearthed slab of rock that made it impossible to landscape. She had also noticed the one plant that did grow around the stone was poison ivy. Knowing she could rouse some advice around the diner, she opened up the topic to Glenda.

"Hey, Glenda, do you know anyone locally who does landscaping?"

Glenda turned to look at her. "What kind of landscaping?"

"Well, I need someone to help me figure out what to do with that giant rock in my front yard. I haven't got a clue what to do with it, and right now it's just an eyesore."

"Well, for that kind of stuff, I'd recommend Andi. She has the best gardens in town. But I don't know if she does any work for hire—you could ask her though, here she comes now."

Gwen couldn't help but look over her shoulder toward the door when she heard the familiar chime. Every head in the room turned to see who had arrived.

Gwen's heart skipped as she watched Andi stride through the door.

"Mornin', Andi." Glenda called from the counter. "Were your ears burning?"

"No. Should they be?" Andi answered with a smile.

Gwen watched as more than one of the men at the counter got up to pat Andi on the back, shake her hand, and say a word or two. Even old William McGuire was friendly with Andi, and Gwen had never heard him say two words to anyone else. He would mostly offer a slight nod or a grunt to Glenda if he wanted more coffee, but that had been the extent of it.

Andi seemed to bring out the best in everyone.

When Andi finally made it to the counter, Gwen smiled and said hello.

Andi nodded and smiled in return but didn't say anything, and Gwen noticed the absence of the warmth she had seen in Andi's eyes over dinner.

"So what were you saying, Glenda? Who's been talking about me?"

"Well, Gwen here was asking if I knew anyone who could help her landscape that old rock in front of her house. I recommended you and told her she should ask you to help, but I didn't know if you would take on the job."

"Oh." Andi's smile faltered. After a moment she looked to Gwen again. "That's a tough one. That old rock probably covers most of the property. Sorry, Gwen, but I don't think I'm the right person for the job."

Gwen was disappointed. "Oh well, I guess I can just look through the listings. Maybe one of the nurseries can help." Gwen shrugged, letting the issue go. The distance she felt from Andi seemed foreign to her after the evening they had shared. Why the change? Would she and Andi have to go through this breaking-the-ice every time they were together?

The silence seemed to drag on as Andi waited for her coffee and Gwen sat staring into her cup. The longer Andi waited the more unease she felt. She was being deliberately distant and that wasn't fair to Gwen. She had to find a way to be around Gwen without letting her hormones take over or turning into Cruella De Vil. Surely she could be friendly with Gwen. It was just a crush. In time she wouldn't feel so out of sorts around her.

"You know, I could give the yard a look and draw some ideas up for you, but you would probably still have to hire out some of the work."

"That's okay," Gwen said, no warmth in her voice, "I appreciate the offer, but I'm sure you have enough to do without trying to figure out my mess."

Andi knew she should take the out that had been offered, but she found she just couldn't say no to those heart-melting blue eyes. And the look of disappointment she had seen flash across Gwen's face made her feel guilty.

"I can drop off some sketches in a few days, if that's okay? I'll need to stop by and look things over first."

"Really, Andi, I don't want you to feel like you have to do this."

"It won't be a problem as long as you don't mind giving me a while. Are you in a hurry?"

"No, just trying to set things up so I don't get in the habit of procrastinating and find myself avoiding the tasks I'm not good at."

"It's settled then."

Gwen's smile didn't reach her eyes, and Andi felt a stab of pain. It was the first time she had seen Gwen so closed off, and Andi knew she was the cause. She should leave this alone. Anything she did would just make things worse. Andi picked up her coffee and thanked Glenda as she stepped away. "See you soon, Gwen."

Andi placed a hand on Gwen's shoulder as she passed, feeling the inexplicable need to touch her. Her face warmed at the slight touch as she brushed past. She didn't know what was happening with her, but the mixed emotions she had been experiencing since meeting Gwen were driving her crazy.

When Andi stepped away, Gwen couldn't help but turn toward her. The light touch on her shoulder felt warm, and she had wanted to lean into it. She didn't get it. One minute Andi was cold and distant and the next she seemed to invite Gwen in. She watched Andi move down the counter to Ward, who still sat staring at the same cup of coffee. Andi leaned next to him, pulled a small package from her pocket, and slid it in front of him. His eyes seemed to mist over for a moment, and then he placed a heavy hand on Andi's shoulder and gave her an affectionate pat. Andi nodded, stepped aside with a smile, and walked out of the diner.

Gwen was curious about the exchange. Whatever Andi had left for Ward seemed to make all the difference in his mood. He sat looking out the window after Andi with a faint smile on his face and the twinkle back in his eyes. What was it with that woman? It seemed the whole town was enamored of Andrea Massey, including herself. Why was that? Andi seemed so private, so elusive. But every time Gwen had been close to Andi, she felt a need wash over her. Andi had awakened something within her. When Andi wasn't being guarded and defensive, there was a gentleness about her that put everyone at ease. But Gwen knew she hadn't imagined Andi's distance only moments before. Was it just her? Maybe she should just take the hint. Andi just wasn't into her.

CHAPTER EIGHT

The rapid tapping on the front door was met with a deep moan from Zeek, who shot to her feet and lumbered through the house to inspect the potential intruder. Gwen laughed. One of the reasons she had chosen Zeek was her breed didn't usually bark at intruders, instead preferring to sneak up on their prey. It made for a much quieter existence not to have her barking her head off at every sound. Gwen dropped her paint roller into the pan and wiped her hands across her faded jeans. The wood floors were cool beneath her bare feet and the smooth finish made her smile. Refinishing the floors had been a huge undertaking, but she couldn't have been happier with the results. As she made her way across the foyer, Gwen glanced toward the door to see who Zeek was so eager to investigate. Her tail was wagging expectantly. An unusual occurrence when someone was at the door.

A pulse of excitement jolted her as she recognized the short dark hair and sun-kissed skin. She wasn't expecting visitors, but she was pleased to see Andi waiting anxiously by the door. Gwen's breath caught at the sight of Andi gazing off into the yard looking thoughtful. Gwen felt a thrill of excitement grow in her belly as she took in Andi's long lean figure and her pensive expression. It had been three days since she had seen Andi at the diner and she wondered what had brought her by. She had convinced herself Andi had only said she would come by because she hadn't wanted to say no after being put on the spot in front of everyone at the diner.

Andi turned to leave just as Gwen turned the latch.

"Hey," Gwen said as she swung the door open.

"Hi. I'm sorry to stop in without notice, but I still don't have a number for you, and I wanted to check in and see how you're doing. I hope I'm not interrupting anything."

"Not at all, come on in. I'm just doing some painting today. I'm glad you stopped by."

As Andi stepped inside, Zeek brushed past Gwen and pushed her giant head into Andi's hand.

Gwen laughed. Trust Zeek to break up any awkwardness. "Looks like I'm not the only one glad to see you."

Andi blushed, and Gwen couldn't help but wonder if Andi was pleased by the comment. Could Andi feel more than she was letting on, or was she embarrassed by the overture?

Andi cleared her throat, leaned down and scratched Zeek's head, and rubbed her floppy ears.

"Hey there, Zeek. It's good to see you too, sweetie." She glanced up at Gwen, melting her with a big smile. "I could get used to a greeting like this. The most I get from Goliath is a nudge toward the food bowl."

Gwen watched the exchange and felt the heat rise in her face as she imagined Andi's long lean fingers brushing through her hair and across her face, in a totally different greeting. She turned and made her way back through the living room that was still littered with drop cloths and paint cans. She was surprised by how happy she was to see Andi.

"Can I get you something to drink?" she asked as she led the way to the kitchen. She thought she could feel Andi's eyes on her as she went, and she smiled to herself. She found herself taking shallow breaths, not wanting to do anything to ruin the moment.

"Sure, that would be nice," Andi responded and followed her to the kitchen. Andi looked around and gestured to the new countertops and new tile on the floor. "The renovations seem to be going well. You've gotten a lot done in the last week—the house is beginning to feel loved again."

"Thanks. The countertops were put in yesterday and the appliances arrived this morning. Good thing too, I was getting tired of living out of a cooler."

Gwen strode over to the new refrigerator and opened the door. She'd felt like a storm was brewing inside her from the moment she had recognized Andi at her door, and she tried to hide the subtle tremor in her hand as she reached inside and pulled out two diet sodas.

"So, what brings you by?" Gwen wanted to believe Andi simply wanted to see her, but Andi's past reluctance made her doubt that.

"Oh, I put some thought into your landscaping project and brought by some drawings. I thought we could have a look and I could explain my ideas."

Andi pulled a folder from her bag and leafed through the contents.

"Wow, that's great. I really can't thank you enough for doing this." Gwen was grateful despite the underlying disappointment that Andi wasn't here just to see her.

Andi smiled faintly. "Well, don't get too ahead of yourself, you haven't even seen the drawings yet. You may hate them."

"I doubt that. Come on then, let's see them," Gwen said, excitedly rubbing her palms together.

Andi laughed and pulled the drawings out of a large folder.

"Oh wow." Gwen looked up at Andi in amazement. "How did you do all this?"

"It's nothing. Do you really like them?"

Gwen watched a blush rise in Andi's cheeks and heard a hint of uncertainty in her voice. "Like them? I love them. I hadn't imagined this was possible. Will it be difficult to do? And how will I maintain it?"

Andi laughed again. "Don't worry. I'll explain everything, and it'll be easier than you think to keep up with."

"If you say so."

Andi picked up a design and began pointing out the different uses of the natural elevation of the yard and the flow of the stone to incorporate many plants that were indigenous to the area and grew well in shallow, rocky soil. "This one is my favorite."

Gwen marveled at the way Andi read the landscape. She seemed so connected to the plants that she wondered how Andi had learned all this. Gwen worked with trees and issues surrounding erosion and water pollution and invasive insects and disease, but this was way outside her area of expertise. She was amazed at the way Andi had read the landscape and seemed to intuitively know what she'd like in her yard. She found herself staring at Andi, mesmerized by the layers of complexity she continued to discover. And the more she learned about Andi, the more she wanted to know.

"You really did an amazing job with all this. Have you ever thought of starting another business?"

"Thanks," Andi said, her blush deepening. "I thought about it, but I seem to have my hands full with the shop for now, and gardening is just something I do for fun."

"Well, I think you could really make a killing just drawing up the plans. You're really good. What do I owe you for doing this for me?"

"Oh, I couldn't charge you. Let's just call it a housewarming gift."

Gwen frowned. "I can't let you do that. You put too much into this. I need to give you something."

Andi watched the muscles in Gwen's arm flex as she pushed herself out of her chair. She felt a tightening in her middle, her body responding involuntarily to the movement and strength of Gwen's body. She imagined Gwen's arms pressed beside her head as Gwen hovered over her. Hurriedly, she looked away, trying to hide the flush of color in her cheeks as the heat surged to her face.

As soon as Gwen had opened the front door, Andi had been stunned by the sight of her in a tight-fitting sleeveless ribbed T-shirt, faded jeans, and bare feet. Now she took notice of the paint smudges that dappled Gwen's T-shirt, and it looked like her jeans had been the first line of cleanup, as they bore the unmistakable prints of Gwen's fingers brushed haphazardly across the worn fabric. She tensed as she ran her eyes appraisingly across the firm muscles of Gwen's arms and fought the urge to reach out and run her fingers along the corded muscle. She tried to avert her eyes when she found she was looking at the soft swell of Gwen's breasts. The T-shirt left nothing to the imagination. Andi felt the urge to touch and barely restrained herself. She glanced up and thought she caught a faint smile flicker across Gwen's face. She hoped she hadn't been discovered.

Andi tossed her bag over her shoulder. "I have to get going. Good luck with the rest of the work."

Gwen caught Andi's arm as she started to brush past. "Wait, don't go yet."

Andi froze as Gwen's hand gently gripped her arm, and another tremor ran through her. At the jolt, Andi jumped and pulled away.

Gwen took a step back, never letting her eyes leave Andi's.

"I need to go," Andi gasped almost painfully. A flashback to the past, but more. She'd known if she didn't pull away, she might not be able to keep from touching Gwen in a way that would leave no doubt of her desire. And that could never happen.

Gwen raised her hands in the universal I-won't-touch gesture. "I'm sorry. I didn't mean to upset you. I just wanted to do something to thank you. I don't know how I can repay you for this." She took a step closer to Andi, who immediately stepped back.

"Andi, are you okay?"

The look on Gwen's face was so gentle, so tender, it felt like a caress. In that moment, Andi wanted to fling her arms around Gwen, press her face against her chest and feel her strong arms wrap around her. But she would not be rescued, not now, not ever, and she knew that if she allowed herself to need that comfort from Gwen, she would be lost. In the deepest recesses of her soul, she wanted someone to rescue her, someone to love her, but that could never happen. It was too much to ask.

"I'm fine. I just need to go. I'll be late." Andi ducked her head and walked swiftly down the hall to the door. "I'll let you decide what to do about the plans. I'll be at the shop if you need anything else." Her heart broke at the look of concern she saw on Gwen's face. She didn't want to once again make Gwen feel she had done something wrong. But she couldn't tell her the truth either, that she was running because she wanted her. She had to get out of there before she did something she would regret.

She heard Gwen call out her thanks, again, as she almost ran out of the house. Then there was the knock of the screen door closing behind her and fresh warm air greeting her. Andi didn't stop until she was at the shop, where she went straight to her office and closed the door.

Her legs shook and her palms were sweating. Every inch of her body thrummed with desire. God, what was happening to her?

❖

Gwen stood shocked by Andi's reaction, not sure what she should do next. She was confused by Andi's sudden departure and the look of fear she'd seen in her eyes. One moment they had been having a perfectly wonderful conversation, and the next Andi looked as if Gwen were wielding an ax at her head. No matter how much Gwen thought about the interaction, she couldn't figure out what had happened to upset Andi.

She looked at the plans Andi had drawn up for her garden. She could see how much time and care Andi had put into the project. What could have made her bolt like that? She was very hard to figure out. One minute she was kind and friendly and warm, and then suddenly she would become evasive and distant. No. It wasn't just distance she saw in Andi, it was all-out fear. But what could Andi be so afraid of? The realization washed over Gwen like a chill breeze.

Gwen rubbed her hand across her face and let out a sigh. Well, something was up, and maybe this was just a sign that Andi was not the kind of woman she needed to be getting mixed up with. But for some reason she couldn't leave it alone. She wanted to know what had caused the pain she had seen in Andi's eyes. Did Andi think so little of her that she was afraid to even be close to her?

She looked back to the plans lying on the table. No, if Andi thought of her that way, she wouldn't have gone through so much trouble for her. What then? What could have elicited such fear? To her surprise, she felt an overwhelming urge to protect Andi—to show her she was safe with her.

❖

Gwen walked into the pet-supply store at ten minutes till closing, with a very excited Zeek in tow. She had been over this in her mind a hundred times and had finally decided she had to clear the air with Andi. At the very least, she needed to pay her for the plans she had drawn up for the garden. It was getting late, and she had deliberately waited so that she wouldn't have interruptions from other patrons. When the bell rang above the door, Andi's cool voice called from the back office.

"I'll be right out."

Gwen didn't answer but stood waiting by the counter. Her palms were sweating and her heart was pounding in her chest. She caught her breath when Andi appeared moments later.

"Oh…hello." Andi rounded the corner and stopped abruptly when she saw Gwen standing there.

"Hi." Gwen smiled. She knew she was about to go way out on a limb and risk pushing Andi even further away, but she just couldn't leave this alone. She needed to know Andi was okay and she needed answers. This tension between them was driving her crazy.

"What can I help you with?"

"I wanted to see if you were okay. I'm afraid I did something to upset you, and I didn't mean to." Gwen braced herself emotionally for Andi's answer. She didn't know Andi's story, but something was wrong and Gwen wanted to know. She needed to know it wasn't her.

"No, it isn't that. I just…I just realized I had forgotten an appointment and needed to go, that's all."

Gwen was certain Andi was lying. She wasn't really surprised, just disappointed. She decided not to push for the direct answers. Instead she would try to disarm Andi with good will. Perhaps if she didn't push, Andi would be less inclined to shut down. "Good. Then you won't mind taking this." Gwen produced a small envelope and handed it to Andi.

Andi took the envelope and looked inside. She pulled out two tickets.

"Umm. What's this?"

Gwen couldn't seem to stand still. Nerves. "Tickets—to the local performing arts center for their upcoming production of *The Little Prince*. I thought I'd ask you to go to the play with me, as a thank-you for the garden plans you made. I figured since you wouldn't let me pay you, this would be a good way for both of us to benefit."

Andi looked thoughtful as she studied the tickets for a moment. "Thanks. This is very thoughtful of you, but I can't accept." Andi handed the envelope back to Gwen without meeting her eyes.

Gwen was determined not to give up so easily. "Come on, Andi. It's just a play. I kind of hoped it could be a date." There was the big question and she totally expected Andi to turn her down flat.

Andi's eyes flashed up to meet Gwen's, her face turning red. "A date?"

"Yeah, you know, dinner, an evening out, time to get to know you better. A date."

"We've already been through this." Andi's tone was gentle, her eyes soft. "I'm not going to go out with you, Gwen."

Gwen's insecurity was like a fist around her heart, making it difficult for her to breathe, but she'd heard the faint hesitation—was it regret?—in Andi's voice, and she wanted to believe Andi wanted to say yes. "Are you seeing anyone?"

Andi bit her lip and looked away.

"I'll take that as a no. Come on, Andi. Say yes."

"No, I'm not seeing anyone and I'm not *interested* in seeing anyone," Andi said flatly.

Gwen didn't waver. "I know I haven't been imagining things, Andi. I know there's something between us, and I know you feel it too. I thought we could just see where this goes. I wouldn't ask if I wasn't committed to seeing where this could take us."

Andi sighed. "You're right. I think you're very nice and I like you, but I'm just not into dating right now. I told you my life is complicated. I can't afford to become involved."

"What are you so afraid of?" The question wasn't spoken as a challenge. Gwen was simply trying to understand. Something was hurting Andi, and Gwen wanted to make the pain stop. And this would have to be her last attempt—Gwen knew there was a fine line between caring and, well, stalking. And she cared too much about herself to continue to pursue someone who didn't want her.

"Gwen, please don't make this more difficult than it already is. I can't give you what you want. I just can't do this."

Gwen heard sincerity in Andi's voice and saw pain cloud her gaze. She wasn't going to get the answers she was looking for, but at least Andi wasn't shutting down this time.

"Okay. If you don't want it to be a date, we can keep it as friends but I still want to spend time with you. It was so nice having dinner with you the other night—I hoped we could do that again. Besides, I wouldn't feel right if I didn't do something to repay you for putting together those plans for me. Please? If you don't let me, I'll never be able to ask you for a favor again, and we *are* neighbors." Gwen flashed what she hoped was a charming—and nondesperate—grin to punctuate her plea.

Andi studied her and seemed to contemplate the idea. "When is the play?"

"Not until next month, but I thought the tickets would give me a reason to come talk to you." Gwen laughed. "I guess I'm striking out big-time today."

"Okay. You're right, there's no reason we can't be friends. I'm sorry I've been so rude lately, I'm just a very private person and I'm not used to meeting anyone who…" Andi stopped abruptly.

"Anyone who…what?"

Andi shook her head. "Never mind."

Gwen could tell this was the most she was going to get for the moment. "You don't have to explain. Friends it is." Gwen extended her hand in a playful gesture.

"Friends it is." Andi took her hand and they shook on the deal. But at Gwen's touch she felt her knees grow weak, and her body tingled at the slight connection between them. This wasn't going to be easy. She might be able to convince her mind that she and Gwen were only friends, but her body had other ideas.

"Listen," Andi said, no longer having the strength to keep pushing Gwen away. If they were going to be friends, she had to act like one. "Since we're going to be friends, I was wondering if you'd like someone to show you around, you know, check out the local trails and the lake and stuff like that."

"That would be great. With all the work I have been putting into the house and trying to gear up to start my new job, I admit I've been a bit out of the loop."

Andi cocked her head to the side curiously. "What is it you do exactly?" Andi felt more relaxed when she stopped fighting with herself, and now she didn't want Gwen to leave.

"I'll be focused on some research involving the emerald ash borer."

"The emerald what?"

"Sorry. It is a nasty insect that's been introduced to this country from Asia. It's destroying the ash trees. We're trying to learn more about how we can control the pest and will be tracking what areas it's moving into. I spend most of my time buried in data. So far the emerald has been found in a few counties near here but hasn't shown up here yet."

"I see," Andi said, genuinely worried about the trees. "Sounds serious."

"It is."

Andi was intrigued. She had no idea there were things out there killing her beloved trees. She was alarmed by the memory of the devastation the area had suffered from the pine beetle a few years earlier.

"Sorry if that was a mood killer," Gwen said, cutting off Andi's melancholy train of thought, "but what did you have in mind when you asked about my lack of local exploration?"

"I do a little kayaking on the lake and the Clinch River, and I thought you might like to go out on the water with me." Andi suddenly felt silly. She couldn't believe she was actually asking

Gwen out, sort of, and right after turning her down flat. But they had agreed to be friends, hadn't they?

Gwen took a moment before answering. The awkward silence and Gwen's appraising look made Andi nervous, and she shifted her gaze.

"I'd love to go out on the water with you. It would be nice to have someone show me around."

Andi smiled. "How do you feel about this weekend? I thought we could go out Sunday morning and then head back to my house and fire up the grill." Excitement surged through her as if every nerve ending was at attention. It felt good.

"That would be great. You tell me when."

They settled the details as Andi playfully teased Zeek.

Zeek suddenly stiffened, her giant head swinging around as the sound of two dogs barking outside caught her attention. She bellowed an answering bark, pulling at her lead and almost toppling Gwen over.

Andi brushed her hands through her hair and sighed. "Guess that's it for me today."

"Don't take it personally. I think she has attention deficit disorder."

"Maybe." Andi chuckled. "I think she's sweet."

Gwen grinned. "What are you doing for dinner tonight?"

"Nothing really. I just planned to heat up some soup or something and do a little baking for the shop."

"Well, I've been dying to get out of the house. Some local guys told me of a place to have dinner and play some pool. Would you like to go?" Gwen knew she was taking a risk, but Andi's guard was down and she wanted to take advantage of the moment. She tried to hide her nervousness by tugging Zeek's leash and messing with her collar.

Andi stiffened.

Gwen recognized the reaction and knew she'd overstepped, knew Andi was about to pull away. She had to do something to diffuse the tension. "Of course, if you know something about this place that I don't, we could go somewhere else. You can choose."

Gwen thought she could see every muscle in Andi's body relax just as abruptly as she'd tensed.

"Okay, I'll go. But you have to promise not to laugh. I don't normally play pool."

Gwen laughed. "Deal." Maybe Andi was finally letting her in. "You sure about this?"

"I'm sure. It'll be fun."

Andi smiled, and it warmed Gwen to her core.

Chapter Nine

Nick's Place wasn't crowded. This was Andi's first visit, although she'd heard of the local favorite, and she felt some relief as she took in the almost empty parking lot. It was only six o'clock, but perhaps she wouldn't have to deal with a crowd after all. She noticed Gwen watching her as they walked to the door and she tried to hide her trepidation. She hadn't been out anywhere with another woman in years. And she didn't like public places. Despite her unease, she wanted to be there. She couldn't hide forever. And most of all, she wanted to be with Gwen.

"Ready?" Gwen asked as she reached for the door.

Andi nodded. She felt Gwen's hand brush lightly against her back as she followed her inside. The touch was comforting, almost possessive, and Andi realized she liked it. She had never felt so attuned to another woman before, and she wanted to feel more of Gwen's touch. Gwen was attentive and sweet and, despite being overly assertive at times, compassionate. Andi had seen the glimmer of concern in her eyes and how easily she could be hurt despite her attempts to appear in control and charming. The more she learned about Gwen, the more captivating she became.

Andi looked around, taking in her surroundings. The room was bathed in the glow of dim light emanating from hanging lights positioned just above the pool tables that lined the main floor area as they entered the bar. The felt on the pool tables was red, not the usual green Andi was used to. The place was more like a restaurant than a bar, and Andi relaxed a little.

A young blond woman who looked to be in her early twenties came to the table they had chosen at the end of the room closest to the last pool table.

"Hey. What can I get you to drink?"

They each ordered a light beer and watched the young woman bounce around to the bar to get their drinks. Andi glanced around the room nervously.

"Would you like to tell me what's bothering you?" Gwen asked placing a hand on Andi's wrist.

Andi jumped at the touch. She was wound so tight she could snap. As much as she wanted to have a good time with Gwen, she was exposed and reflexively defensive in the unfamiliar surroundings. She hated that Gwen was feeling that. "What do you mean?"

"I mean, you don't seem very comfortable. You don't seem to like it here."

"I'm sorry. It isn't that. I'm not used to going out."

"You mean with a woman?"

"No. Well, yes. What I mean is that I don't usually go out at all. I guess I'm a little out of practice." The admission made her feel lacking, and she wondered what Gwen would think when she found out just how restricted her life really was.

"You mean you just spend all your time in Norris?"

"Pretty much," Andi answered sheepishly. She knew the reasons for her solitude were valid, but the idea of explaining herself now made her feel like a coward. She knew she was allowing fear to stifle her life, and being with Gwen made her realize what she had been missing.

"Why?"

"I have my work. Everything I need is close by. I guess there isn't much need for me to go anywhere else. It's hard to explain."

"That's okay. I have the time. Try me."

Andi saw the sincerity in Gwen's eyes and thought for a moment that she could drown in the twin pools of blue. But this was not a topic she wanted to explore, not now. Right now all she wanted was to enjoy the woman she was with and have a good time. How did she explain something so terrible it belonged in a horror film?

How did she tell Gwen that she could never have a normal life? "No. I really don't want to get into it tonight."

Gwen studied the pleading look in Andi's eyes, longing to reach across the table and brush her fingers across the soft skin of her cheek. Watching the passage of emotions play across Andi's face as she spoke had gotten to Gwen, and she found herself leaning in, wanting to be closer to Andi, wanting to touch her. Right now she wanted to soothe the lost and vulnerable look she saw in Andi's eyes.

"Okay then, let's try to relax and enjoy the special occasion. I guess I should feel honored you came out with me. Maybe you just needed the right friend to come along and shake up your routine a little. You know, since this isn't a date and all."

Andi smiled faintly.

Gwen decided to lighten the mood. "Let's play pool." She got up and fished quarters from her pocket.

Three games later, the competition was rising. Andi'd had a rough start but quickly began to show some skill. Gwen watched as Andi leaned into her shot, her focus steady as she scoped out the path of the ball. She moved behind Andi, appreciating the view. Andi's long legs looked good in jeans and boots. For the next shot, Andi moved around the table, and Gwen noticed the way her shirt parted when she leaned over the table, revealing her tantalizing cleavage and the line of soft lace that caressed her breasts.

Gwen kept imagining her lips pressed against the supple flesh. She bit her tongue when she realized she had unconsciously licked her lips. She looked up to find Andi watching her. Gwen smirked, raising her eyebrows, confidently acknowledging what she had been thinking. They might have agreed to be friends, but that didn't mean she could just turn off her attraction to Andi. There was no harm in looking.

Andi looked away, walked back to the table, and retrieved her beer.

Gwen continued to circle the table, checking out the options for her next shot. She knew Andi was watching her. A few shots later she strolled up to Andi who sat on her stool, waiting for her turn. Gwen allowed her hand to brush ever so gently against Andi's thigh as she handed her the pool cue. She was enjoying Andi's new playfulness. Every brush of Andi's hand, every teasing smile, every unguarded glance gave Gwen a rush of pleasure building into the steady thrum of desire. She wanted to play her fingers through Andi's hair where the subtle curls graced the edge of her face. She wanted to kiss the tender flesh below her ear and smell the tantalizing fragrance that was uniquely Andi. Andi was close enough to touch, and Gwen found herself leaning forward until her lips were only inches away. She could feel the heat of Andi's breath, and Andi's eyes grew dark and stormy.

"You win. I scratched on the eight ball. I guess I lost my concentration there at the end. If you want to play again, it's your break." Gwen tried to sound nonchalant, but inside her heart was racing.

Andi reached for the pool cue and Gwen made sure their fingers brushed. When she caught Andi's gaze, saw a glint of attraction flicker across Andi's face, and Andi didn't look away, Gwen had to take the chance. She let her hand slide down the pool stick and placed her palm lightly on Andi's knee.

Andi drew in a sharp breath, surprised by her own response to Gwen's touch. She was sure she had caught Gwen looking at her breasts earlier, and Gwen hadn't even flinched when she knew she was caught. Andi found the confidence dangerously attractive and wasn't able to even feign irritation. She liked knowing Gwen was looking at her. Her face warmed as physical need began to resonate through her with each pulse of her heart. She wanted to believe she could just be friends with Gwen, but obviously being in the same room with her was enough to send her hormones into overdrive.

Gwen smiled, making Andi's pulse jolt to a pounding rhythm that she didn't even experience when running. When Gwen handed her the pool cue, and their fingers brushed, Andi thought she had been shocked, the sensation was so electric. Now she could feel Gwen's fingers tighten on her knee with just enough pressure to send a jolt straight to her groin.

"What are you doing?" Andi asked, trying to sound unaffected. Gwen's smile only broadened. "Just being friendly."

"Ha!" Andi scoffed. "I don't know about where you come from, but the friends I know don't touch like that."

"Hmm. Okay, you got me there. But was it so bad?"

Andi took a deep breath, the muscles in her stomach tightened, and her heart pulsed a rhythm against her skin. "No. It wasn't bad," she admitted. Honestly, the touch had seemed so natural she had felt it all the way to her core. In that instant the past, all her fear, the people around them, all receded. Gwen was her only focus.

"Hello, ladies," a rough, deep male voice rumbled from behind Andi. Her whole body tensed as she whipped around to confront the source.

He was a large man, tall and broad shouldered. His head and face were clean-shaven except for a bush of hair growing in a point from his chin, too wild to be a goatee. He wore faded jeans and a black T-shirt with heavy motorcycle boots. His eyes were the cold gray of steel.

Panic rose in Andi's chest like a vise, threatening to squeeze the life from her body. Suddenly she couldn't force air into her lungs and she felt all the blood drain from her face. The room was closing in on her.

"Sorry, I didn't mean to startle you. I just wanted to see if you wanted to play my partner and me in a friendly game of pool."

At that, a second man appeared. His hand snaked possessively around the big man's waist and rubbed his stomach.

"Hey, girls," he said playfully, his voice softer and higher in pitch than the first man's.

Gwen stepped closer to Andi, putting herself between Andi and the men.

"Hey, fellas. You go ahead, I think we're sitting this one out, but we'd love to watch you play."

"Oh, girl, I don't think that is anything a lady should watch," the smaller man said with a playful harmonic laugh. "And don't mind Bear," he said as he pinched his partner's nipple through his shirt. "He's harmless. I'm David and this is Mark. Most people call me Boo, and Mark is Bear."

"Pleasure to meet you," Gwen said as she shook both men's hands.

Andi felt Gwen's hand press against her hip where Gwen had planted it the moment the tension had whipped through her like a shot.

"I'm Gwen and this is Andi."

"Hmm," David said as he stepped back, running his eyes up and down both women. "You're cute." He grinned mischievously and bounced over to the pool table where he slapped Mark on the ass.

Gwen moved Andi back onto her stool and stood in front of her so her hips pressed against Andi's thighs. She placed her palm against Andi's face.

"Andi?" Gwen asked softly, lifting Andi's face to look at her. Andi's eyes shifted, still unfocused. She felt Gwen's fingers brush across her cheek and gently cup her face.

"Andi, are you all right?"

Andi blinked, confused about what was happening.

"Andi?"

Andi licked her lips and tried to back away, but she was already pressed against the corner. "Sorry. I'm okay. I was just a little startled. I'm fine now."

Andi moved her head to pull away from Gwen's hands. Gwen's fingers brushed lightly across her skin leaving trails of heat that lingered long after the contact was lost. She looked around the room, expecting to see anger, contempt, resentment, and hatred on the faces of the men around her. She felt confused as she watched the big man run his hand along the other's backside. The scene was a stark contrast to what she had expected. She furrowed her brow, confused.

"They're gay?" she asked, astounded, looking back at Gwen for confirmation.

Gwen stood close, watching her, her hand holding possessively to Andi's hip. Andi knew Gwen had seen her fear.

Gwen nodded.

Andi tried to smile. She was embarrassed that Gwen had seen her weakness. She moved her hand to cover Gwen's. Despite her self-consciousness, she was comforted by Gwen's gentleness and her unhesitant protectiveness.

"I'm so sorry."

"You don't have to be sorry. How about telling me what happened just then. I get it that you don't like to talk about personal stuff, but I want you to feel safe with me."

Andi pressed her hand lightly against Gwen's, allowing her fingers to curl around and take Gwen's hand in her own, pulling it away from her body, not wanting to lose complete contact. Gwen did make her feel safe and she needed to explain. "I was hurt once, a long time ago. I almost died. It still bothers me sometimes. It's hard for me to trust people because of what happened to me." She squeezed Gwen's hand. "But I do feel safe with you, Gwen." Andi smiled uncomfortably. "See, I told you my life was complicated." She knew she had given Gwen the CliffsNotes version of her past, and she hoped Gwen would accept that as enough for now.

"Thank you for telling me." Gwen smiled and squeezed Andi's hand back. "This feels nice."

Andi's face warmed, but she didn't move her hand away. She kept her eyes locked on Gwen's, mesmerized by the intensity of her gaze as she watched her pupils dilate until there was only the faintest ring of blue. She felt the heat rise into her cheeks and knew she was blushing. God, what was she doing? She pulled her hand away, reaching for her drink. She needed to put some distance between them.

Gwen took a step back and pulled her stool closer to Andi. "Do you feel like staying for a while, or do you want to go?"

Thoughts swirled around in Andi's mind, making her dizzy. If she stayed, she had to face her fear and engage in social contact with the two men. If she chose to leave, she would be alone with Gwen, and she would most likely want to know more about what had happened in her past. Not only that, she would have to face her ever-growing need to be closer to Gwen. There was no denying the sexual energy between them. Andi wasn't sure she was ready to face any of these things.

"It's still early. I'm okay staying a while longer if you want."

Gwen smiled mischievously. "You wouldn't be afraid of going home with me, now would you?"

Andi returned the smile. "Maybe a little," she stated shyly, dropping her gaze.

Gwen leaned in to Andi until her lips were almost touching Andi's ear. "You never have to be afraid of me, Andi. Nothing will ever happen between us that you don't want."

Chapter Ten

G wen's breath brushed Andi's skin, trailing ripples of electricity down her neck and arms as if she had been touched. Gwen pulled away but lingered. They were so close, all Andi had to do was sway, and their lips would touch. Andi's eyes drifted to Gwen's mouth and Gwen's tongue slipped across her lips.

Andi shifted on her barstool, afraid she might lean in and kiss Gwen. The desire to taste her was almost more than she could resist. She closed her eyes and pulled back, just as David came back to their table. He was singing Elton John's "Tiny Dancer."

"Oh, girls, you are too hot. I can feel the heat all the way across the room. How about we buy you two a beer to cool you off a little?"

Andi smiled at the young man for the first time, hiding her relief at having been interrupted and her disappointment that she hadn't tasted Gwen's lips. "You just want to get us tipsy so we don't school you in pool."

David laughed. "True, but we also wanted to make up for scaring you earlier. Bear doesn't realize how intimidating he can be. He's really sorry."

Andi looked across the room at the big man. He was definitely intimidating, but she understood he wasn't the man in her nightmares, and she couldn't punish him for someone else's crime. She waved him over.

"Thanks for the beer," she said as he came up to her.

He smiled and shifted uncomfortably.

Andi saw his hesitation and discomfort. "So, I can only guess where the name Bear comes from."

He chuckled, the ice broken. "Yeah, well, I guess I fit the description pretty well."

"Yes," Andi said warmly, "first impression grizzly, second impression teddy."

Everyone laughed.

They shook hands and the tension eased.

To Andi's surprise, she and Mark, otherwise known as Bear, got along beautifully. Once she let herself relax, she found him entertaining and playful. They teamed up against Gwen and David and won three of the four games they played. David pouted when he lost, and Mark petted and cajoled him until he relented and wrapped his gangly arms around Mark's large frame and smacked him on the behind.

Andi kissed David lightly on the cheek as they were leaving. She realized how much she missed having friends. She'd had a good time and nothing bad had happened. It felt good to play and laugh again.

"Thanks for letting us win," she said and winked.

David rolled his eyes. "I know my man. He loves to win, and I love to have him make it up to me."

Andi laughed. Gwen and Mark met them at the door and they all walked out together.

At the car, Mark put his thick arms around Andi and gave her a giant hug, picking her up until her feet dangled in the air as he swung her from side to side until she laughed out loud, before setting her down again. Andi relaxed into the passenger seat, still laughing to herself.

Gwen smiled, looking over at her. "That was fun."

Andi turned and studied Gwen, pleasantly aware of how much she had enjoyed being with her. Gwen had been patient and understanding. She had been playful, yet protective. She had made Andi laugh and forget all the hang-ups that usually got in the way of her life.

"Yes, thank you. I can't remember the last time I had that much fun."

"Good." Gwen put the car in drive and headed home. As she pulled out of the parking lot she reached across and took Andi's hand in hers.

Andi didn't pull away. She closed her eyes and let her head relax against the headrest, sinking into the soft leather, accepting the warmth of Gwen's fingers entwined with her own. It was dark and she knew Gwen couldn't see her, but she could feel Gwen's attention to her. She wondered if Gwen could sense the loosening of the tension in her muscles, the cadence of her breathing, and perhaps the pulse of her heartbeat as it thrummed through her skin.

Perhaps it was the beer or maybe the high from the laughter, but for the first time in years, Andi wasn't afraid. All she wanted was the feel of Gwen's hand holding hers.

Gwen pulled the SUV into the drive. "It's still early. Do you want me to drive you home, or can I ask you to come inside for a while?"

Andi thought for a moment, considering the possibilities if she decided to stay. A thrill surged through her body as she imagined Gwen's lips on hers and then imagined the feel, the taste of Gwen's tongue in her mouth. She was glad Gwen couldn't see her blushing and even more relieved she couldn't read her thoughts.

"I'm in no hurry. We can hang out at your place for a while. I'm not ready to go home yet."

Gwen tightened her grip on Andi's hand. "Good," she said, sliding the pad of her thumb across the back of Andi's hand in a caress.

Andi knew she should move away but couldn't bring herself to break the contact between them. Gwen just felt too good, and she was tired of fighting her own need for closeness.

"So tell me, what's up with you and Bear?" Gwen said teasingly.

"What do you mean?"

"Well, you went from all-out fear at the sound of his voice to swinging full-body hugs by the end of the night. Not to mention, Miss Don't-laugh-at-me-playing-pool—you two schooled us!"

Andi laughed. "Okay, so he was a little scary at first, but then I realized how adorable he is. He's sweet."

Gwen cocked her head to the side and cut her eyes to Andi. "I loved the names, Boo and Bear. That's so Yogi."

They got out of the car laughing. Zeek's deep resonant voice could be heard eagerly announcing their welcome home.

Gwen fumbled with the keys, her hands shaking slightly. She was nervous, and that made her laugh at herself. When she managed to get the door open, Zeek bounced back in a frenzied dance, her big head pushing and bumping into Gwen and then Andi. Gwen finally managed to get her to go out into the backyard, where she eagerly sniffed and explored her territory.

Gwen pulled the door closed and turned back to Andi. "I swear, since we moved here, she's been like a puppy again."

"It's good to see her play. She seems really happy here," Andi added, watching the dog through the glass.

Gwen opened the refrigerator and retrieved two beers, handing one to Andi.

"Thanks."

Gwen took a long drink from her beer as she watched Andi. She rubbed her fingers together, missing the feel of Andi's hand in hers. The touch had felt right. This was the most relaxed she had seen Andi, and she wanted to hold on to that closeness.

"Come on. Let me show you how the house is coming," Gwen said, and she reached out and took Andi's hand again. She led them through the living room that was still unfinished, one corner cluttered with paint cans and drop cloths. She brought Andi to the bathroom first, where she showed off her handiwork.

"It's beautiful," Andi exclaimed. "I love the way you've been able to blend the modern and traditional styles. It seems like everything you've brought into the house has always belonged here."

"I'm glad you like it. Now, check this out." She led Andi to her office. The room was a rich gray, and two walls were floor-to-ceiling built-in bookshelves with a sliding ladder.

Andi gasped and stepped inside. "I've always loved these old library ladders," she said, running her fingers along the rich polished wood.

Gwen stood leaning against the door frame, watching Andi, pleased by her reaction.

"I love this room," Andi said as she looked around at the artwork and diplomas that hung on the walls. "So this is where you do that serious work you were talking about."

"Some of it," Gwen said, stepping into the room and close to Andi, who continued to look around, pulling books from the shelves and looking at photographs of Zeek as a puppy.

Gwen felt the heat of Andi's body close to hers before she actually touched her. Gwen placed a hand on Andi's waist and leaned over her, pointing to a black-and-white photo.

"That's me and Zeek when she was only six weeks old. I can't believe she was ever that small."

Andi leaned back against her, their bodies lightly touching. Gwen's heart raced, beating a pattern in her ears and in much more intimate places. She relished the feel of Andi pressed against her breasts. Andi turned her face so her lips were only a breath away from Gwen's. Gwen wet her lips with the tip of her tongue as she moved her hand gently up Andi's back. She raised her hand and brushed her thumb slowly against the tender skin of Andi's lower lip. She was mesmerized by the feel of Andi's skin against her fingertips and wanted to caress those lips with her own.

Andi's lips parted and Gwen heard her faint intake of breath. She watched Andi's eyes trail across her face and watched her mouth as she moved closer. Time seemed to move in slow motion as she anticipated Andi's lips claiming her mouth.

Andi leaned into Gwen. She felt like she was falling. The desire to touch Gwen was so strong she couldn't stop herself. She turned her head until only breath separated her lips from Gwen's. Gwen's fingers brushed her lips, and she heard herself gasp. She thought she might explode if Gwen didn't kiss her. She closed the distance between them.

Just before their lips met, a loud bellowing howl cut through the silence. Gwen's head shot back, breaking their connection, fear and concern replaced the desire that had been in her eyes only a moment before. The withdrawal ricocheted through Andi like the snap of a whip.

"Zeek!" Gwen turned and ran from the room.

Andi was suddenly in full defense mode at the sound of fear in Gwen's voice. She followed Gwen through the house as she raced to get to Zeek. As soon as they reached the kitchen, a foul smell began to permeate Andi's senses. She grabbed Gwen's arm as she reached for the door, stopping her from going outside.

"Wait, Gwen. It's a skunk. You can't let Zeek into the house!"

"What do I do?" Gwen croaked in a desperate plea. Gwen flinched at the sound of Zeek's cries that had turned to the hurt whines of the wounded.

Andi could see Zeek running around the yard with her face pressed into the ground, trying to rub the offensive chemical from her eyes.

"Give me your keys," Andi said urgently. "I have everything we need at the shop. I can be back here in five minutes. I'll help you get her cleaned up, but you can't go out there yet, and you can't let her into the house."

Gwen nodded, grabbed her keys off the counter, and thrust them into Andi's waiting hand.

Andi sat in the kitchen. It had been a very long night, and Zeek was not a happy dog. She'd been scrubbed repeatedly and her nose and lips were blistered from the skunk spray. She lay on the kitchen floor on the cool tile, looking up at Gwen and Andi as if they'd caused all her trouble. Her big brown eyes shifted from one to the other, and her giant eyebrows danced up and down, emphasizing her dejection. She refused to eat and had to be put on a leash and taken out the front door for bathroom breaks. The backyard still smelled strongly of skunk. The sun was coming up and Andi was exhausted. She needed to get home and shower before opening the store.

Gwen sat across the table, her hands wrapped loosely around her coffee mug. Her hair was mussed and her T-shirt was inside out.

She'd changed in a rush after wrestling Zeek's wet body with the water hose.

Andi smiled as she looked at Gwen in her state of fray. She was beautiful, and she had worried all night over her dog. Briefly Andi's thoughts drew up the memory of how Gwen's thumb had felt on her lips and the desire smoldering in Gwen's eyes as they'd almost kissed. She couldn't believe how close she had come to allowing Gwen to kiss her. Even more unsettling was how desperately she had wanted Gwen to kiss her. She licked her lips, feeling the warmth spill into her, flowing through her like a current. The memory sent a shiver through her and a pulse of pleasure throbbed through her middle. Andi shifted in her seat.

The movement drew Gwen's attention and she looked up.

"I have to go," Andi said. "I'll need to open the store in a couple of hours."

Gwen's eyes softened. "Thank you for staying and helping with Zeek. I wouldn't have known what to do."

"It's okay. I'm glad I was here." And not just because of Zeek. Andi placed her hand over Gwen's, still cradling the coffee cup. "She'll be okay. But unfortunately you'll find when she gets wet over the next few months, it'll bring out the odor again, but only faintly."

"Great," Gwen moaned.

Andi stood to go. She didn't know what else to say or do.

Gwen rose with her and closed the distance between them. "I'm sorry things got a little crazy last night."

"Oh?" Andi flinched.

"I mean, I'm sorry about what happened with Zeek. I'm not sorry about my time with you." Gwen brought her hand to Andi's face as she had done the night before.

Andi thought of running out the door but found her feet wouldn't move. She took Gwen's hand and drew it away from her face. She couldn't trust herself to be this close to Gwen right now, not with the desire surging through her like a tidal wave. She was afraid if Gwen kissed her right now, she would wilt under her need to be touched.

"I have to go."

Gwen sighed. "At least let me drive you home."

"Thank you, but no. I'm just going to the shop. I'll get things opened up, and when my part-time help comes in at twelve, I'll go home and rest."

"Let me take you to the store then."

"You don't have to do that. It's just a couple of blocks from here. I'll be fine. The fresh air will do me good," she said with a laugh.

"I know, but I'm not ready to let you go," Gwen said.

Andi looked at Gwen, surprised by the vulnerability of her admission, and she felt her resolve slip again. She didn't have the energy to argue any longer, and if she was honest, she didn't want to leave Gwen.

Could Gwen be more perfect? Andi sighed. "Okay, to the shop it is."

Chapter Eleven

A ndi jumped at the sound of the bell above the door. She had fallen asleep at her desk, trying to sort through her delivery orders. It had been an exhausting morning as she tried to get a grip on the feelings that had been stirred up by Gwen's touch. No matter how she tried to distract her thoughts, her body wouldn't cooperate. She had been aroused when Gwen had held her, and the recollection of Gwen's thumbs skimming her lips had been enough to stoke her desire for the rest of the night and still lingered, a craving she couldn't sate. Luckily it had been a quiet morning, and she hadn't had to be too focused on work. She heard Morgan's familiar humming and realized it must be time for her to come in for work. Andi was relieved. She couldn't wait to get home, shower, and go to bed.

Morgan tapped on the open door. "Hey, Andi—" Morgan looked at her in alarm. "You look like shit. Are you all right?"

Andi chuckled. "Yes. I'm fine. I just didn't get any sleep last night, that's all. I was up all night helping a friend get rid of fresh skunk spray."

"Ugh, that's nasty," Morgan said with a grimace. "You need to get out of here and go home."

"That's exactly what I intend to do. Will you be okay here by yourself?"

"Of course. I close up the store all the time. I'll be fine. Go."

Andi rubbed her eyes with the palms of her hands. She was exhausted and looked forward to sleep. She was so tired she didn't think even her worst nightmares from the past could keep her awake. She had a lot to think about. She had let her guard down and now had to admit her growing interest in Gwen, but would it be selfish of her to get involved with Gwen, knowing she might never truly be free of her past?

When she walked out the door of her shop, squinting in the bright midday sun, she was surprised to find Gwen standing in the parking lot, leaning against her Land Rover. She had her arms folded across her chest and her legs crossed at the ankles. Andi gasped— Gwen looked so sexy standing there, in all her bravado. It was all very James Dean. Andi's apprehension vanished at the sight.

Andi's body stirred and she shook herself, trying to control her racing heartbeat. She walked up to Gwen, smiling. "What are you doing here?"

"I'm waiting for you."

"And why are you waiting for me?"

"Well, for one, I wanted to see if you would really leave work like you said you would, and second, I wanted to drive you home."

Andi studied Gwen, trying to figure her out. "Why is it so important to you to drive me home?" She recalled Gwen's persistence earlier that she drive her home or to the shop.

"I wouldn't be a very good date if I didn't make sure you made it home safely."

Andi smiled. "I thought we agreed it wasn't a date?"

"Yes, we did, but I'd like it to be a date. And I'd like to see how soon I can see you again."

Andi laughed and dropped her head, looking at the ground. She nervously shoved her hands into her pockets to hide their trembling.

"Don't tell me," Gwen said, pushing away from the truck. "I'm not your type."

Andi shook her head, grinning.

"Boring then?"

Andi shook her head again.

"Hmm…unattractive?" Gwen said, returning the grin.

Andi laughed again. "That's definitely not it." God, could this woman be any sexier?

"Okay, so when can I see you again?"

"You don't give up, do you?"

Gwen peered at Andi, her gaze warm and resolute. "Not when it's important," Gwen said, her voice growing serious.

Andi rocked back and forth on her heels, studying Gwen. If Gwen didn't stop looking at her like that, she might melt right there on the spot. "All right, I'll accept a ride home."

Gwen smiled, moved to the passenger side of the SUV, and opened the door for Andi. Once Andi was securely inside, she jogged around the vehicle with a satisfied smile.

It was a short distance and they pulled into Andi's driveway only minutes later. Andi watched Gwen examine her home. She watched her eyes play over the pale mint-green Hardie Board siding, the stone accents wrapping the foundation and the porch columns, and the flower gardens blanketing the front entrance. Andi knew the moment Gwen discovered the dark wood door accented by a waist-high statue of a black panther.

Gwen studied the cat quizzically but didn't comment. She simply got out of the SUV and came to open the door for Andi.

When they walked onto the porch, Gwen was still eyeing the cat. Andi wondered how long Gwen would hold out before asking about it. She unlocked the door and invited Gwen inside. As they entered the house, Andi reached over and stroked the cat's head.

"Good job, Theo."

When she removed her hand the cat's head bobbed gently.

Gwen laughed. "Is that a bobblehead panther?"

"Yes, it is. That's Theo. He watches the house for me." Andi grinned to herself as she walked into the living room, amused.

"That is so cool."

Andi turned to see Gwen still standing in the door, looking at the cat.

"I'm glad you like him, but be careful not to let Goliath out."

Gwen quickly pulled the door shut and looked around the room nervously as if expecting a real panther to come stalking into the room.

"And Goliath would be?"

"He's my real cat. Don't worry, he may think he's a panther, but he's just a sweet house cat."

Gwen's sigh was slightly exaggerated and the playfulness made Andi smile.

"You didn't think I had a real panther, did you?"

"Well, I do live with Zeek. I guess there must be a cat equivalent somewhere."

Andi laughed. "Can I get you something to drink? Tea?"

"Sure."

"Come on. Let me show you my favorite space and I'll bring us some drinks." Andi led Gwen through the living room into the kitchen and out the back door to a covered porch that looked out over a modest in-ground pool. "Have a seat. I'll be right back."

Gwen sat on the porch, looking out over the glistening water. Gardens filled with vibrant colors surrounded the backyard, making her feel she was in some hidden world only read about in books. She could see why this was Andi's favorite place. It was an oasis. From the front of the house no one could ever have guessed there was such an elaborate garden hidden within.

Andi came out carrying a pitcher of ice tea and two glasses. She took a seat in the chair next to Gwen and placed the tea on the table. She filled both glasses and handed one to Gwen.

"You have an amazing place," Gwen said skimming her fingers across Andi's as she took her glass.

"Thank you."

"Did you do all this yourself?" Gwen waved her hand in the direction of the gardens.

"Yes." Andi looked sheepishly over her glass as she took a drink of her tea.

Gwen watched Andi's lips caress the rim of the glass as she sipped the amber liquid. Gwen's body tingled as she watched Andi's tongue dart out to catch the last drops of moisture. Her stomach tightened as arousal coiled in her middle. She imagined her own tongue rimming the edges of Andi's lips, tasting the sweetness lingering on her mouth.

"How is Zeek?" Andi asked, breaking Gwen's trance.

"She's good. I don't think she'll be as eager to chase a skunk the next time. Thank you again for your help."

"You're welcome." Andi sat back in her chair, closed her eyes, and sighed.

Gwen watched Andi, trying to memorize the contours of her face, the subtle curve of her jaw, the slight tilt at the tip of her nose, the way her long eyelashes curled against her cheek. There was something about Andi that captivated her. Andi was strikingly beautiful, but there seemed to be something more about this unusual woman that drew Gwen like a moth to a flame. She struggled to control the urge to reach out and touch Andi. She wanted to feel her fingers in her hair, and her lips on her skin.

Gwen set her glass down on the table, trying not to wake Andi, but Andi's eyes flickered open at the slight clink of glass on glass.

Andi grinned. "I wasn't asleep."

"But you should be. I need to go, so you can rest."

Andi sighed. "Thank you for the ride home. I'm sorry I'm not being more social."

"Not a problem. It wasn't exactly how I would have preferred to keep you up all night, but I did enjoy your company." Gwen's face grew hot at her own forwardness. "Sorry, I didn't mean that the way it sounded."

Andi thought it sounded perfect. She held out her hand when Gwen stood. Gwen took her hand and pulled her up and out of her chair, sliding her left arm around Andi's waist as she held her hand in her right. Andi felt Gwen's breasts pressed against her own and the feel of Gwen's body warmed her.

Their lips were so close, Andi could feel Gwen's breath.

"Gwen…" Andi reflexively began to protest. Her words implied no, but the subtle shift of her body against Gwen and her imploring gaze said yes.

"Is it too much to ask for a good night kiss?"

Andi's eyes drifted to Gwen's lips and she breathed a barely audible sigh. She nodded a welcome, and before she could say a word, Gwen kissed her.

Gwen's lips were unbelievably soft. Andi savored the taste of sweet tea lingering on Gwen's mouth, making her want to taste more. As Gwen's tongue brushed her lips, she opened and invited Gwen inside. Gwen's tongue met hers with tender strokes that brought her desire roaring to life as pleasure pulsed through her blood, making her middle grow tense and her legs grow weak.

Andi surrendered to the feel of Gwen's lips as if she were brushing against a delicate flower, tasting its nectar. She pulled Gwen inside her, tasting the succulent essence of her mouth. She accepted Gwen into her, her own tongue meeting Gwen's with heartbreaking tenderness, urging her deeper into her mouth. It had been so long since she had kissed a woman, so long since she had experienced the floating, soaring sensation brought on by a woman's touch. Andi's body cried out for Gwen, reawakened after the long absence of touch.

Gwen drew away and breathed deeply, inhaling Andi's scent into herself.

"Now that was worth waiting for."

Andi let her head drop lightly against Gwen's shoulder. Her legs were weak. She tried to steady her breathing as her heart threatened to pound out of her chest. She hadn't meant for this to happen. But now that Gwen had kissed her, she couldn't stop herself from wanting more. And if one kiss could do this to her, she knew she would be in real trouble if she allowed anything more to happen between them.

"You need to go home and rest," Andi said pushing lightly against Gwen's shoulders and taking a step back. She could feel Gwen's hands slide down her back and around her sides, further igniting the ache low in her center.

Gwen groaned. "Yeah, I guess I should go. You must be exhausted." She took Andi's hand and squeezed. "I'll see you soon."

Andi only nodded. She had no idea what she was doing. But she knew she would be seeing Gwen again, and she couldn't wait.

❖

Andi fell asleep almost at the instant her head hit the pillow. She was warm, and her body felt light from the lingering feel of Gwen holding her in her arms, her soft lips claiming her mouth. The light in the room was dim when she woke. She brushed the back of her hand across her face and turned to see the clock.

She stared at the glowing numbers in disbelief. It was six o'clock in the morning. She turned to study the light growing faintly through her windows. It couldn't be morning. She couldn't remember the last time she had slept so long, or so soundly. She smiled, pushing back into her pillow. There had been no haunting dreams, no paralyzing fear. She had simply slept, content and peaceful.

Thoughts of Gwen drifted lazily into her mind. The sudden rush of heat between her thighs made her moan. She pressed her hand between her legs and rolled over, laughing. *I can't believe what this woman does to me.* Reluctantly, she threw back the covers and headed for the shower.

She hardly noticed her surroundings on her bike ride to work. The air that brushed against her face was refreshing and she found a persistent smile pressing at the corners of her mouth. Her steps felt light as she walked across the wooden floor into the shop and tossed her bag on her desk in her office.

The sound of the bell above the door made her look up.

Mrs. Peterson was ambling through the door, pulling a not-so-willing basset hound behind her. "Come on, Churchill, you stubborn old cuss."

Reluctantly the dog followed her inside.

"Hello, Mrs. Peterson. What can I do for you and Churchill today?"

"We just stopped by to see if you had a fresh batch of those banana treats Churchill likes so much. He ran out yesterday, and he's been refusing to do anything but chew my garden shoes all morning."

Andi laughed as she looked down to see the hole that had been chewed in the side of Mrs. Peterson's shoe. Two of her toes were sticking out the side, showing chipped red nail polish.

"You're in luck, Churchill. I just baked a batch yesterday. I'll just go back and scoop out a bag."

As Andi turned to go to the back room, she could hear Mrs. Peterson scuttling along behind her.

"You know," Mrs. Peterson started, "I noticed a strange car at your place yesterday. I thought about calling the police, but before I could get back to the house, it left. Was everything all right?"

Andi knew Mrs. Peterson was just snooping for information. Norris was a small town and everyone knew everyone's business, usually because of Mrs. Peterson's keen observation and determination to be the first to ferret out the news. But Andi knew her intentions were harmless and she was amused by the old woman's antics. "Yes, everything is fine. That was just a new friend of mine stopping by for a visit."

"Hmm. Haven't seen that car around here before, looked like out of town plates to me."

"That's right," Andi replied vaguely. She was enjoying making Mrs. Peterson work for the information.

"Awful short visit for someone to come all that way."

"Not really. Her name is Gwen Palmer—she moved to Norris a few weeks ago."

"Oh, I thought I heard the boys at the diner saying something about a stranger in town. Guess that's her. Didn't she buy the old Harman place?"

"Yep. That would be her."

Andi finished tying up the bag of treats and offered one to Churchill. "Here you go, Churchill, one peanut-butter-banana biscotti."

He snuffled her hand for a moment before taking the crunchy biscuit into his mouth. His big droopy eyes peered up at her thankfully as he smacked his floppy jowls and chewed.

"Looks like that did the trick. Good as new," Andi said, smiling to Mrs. Peterson.

"Can't say the same about my shoe," grumbled Mrs. Peterson, wiggling her toes.

Andi laughed.

"Where'd you say this new girl's from?"

Andi could see Mrs. Peterson wasn't quite satisfied with her fishing expedition just yet. "I'm not sure, but I bet you'll find out soon enough."

"Fine, you don't want to talk about it."

"I'm sure you'll have plenty of opportunity to talk to her yourself, or maybe the boys at the diner already have the scoop."

Mrs. Peterson eyed her for a moment before responding. "Well, the church usually sends out a welcoming committee to visit new residents. Perhaps I'll volunteer. I don't see why you don't want to talk about her though."

Mrs. Peterson brought one of the treats up to her nose and sniffed it before giving it to the dog. "It's about time you had a visitor. You'd think you were as old as me, the way you stay shut up in that house all the time."

Mrs. Peterson changed the direction of the conversation so quickly Andi was caught off guard. Andi put her hands on her hips and cocked her head to the side. "If I didn't know better, Mrs. Peterson, I'd think you're worried about me."

"Well, I suppose I am. And I'm not the only one, you know. We all love the way you look after everyone and take care of things in town. But you're still young. You need to be with people your own age from time to time. It would be good for you."

Andi was shocked by the caring and warmth. She hadn't expected this from Mrs. Peterson.

"Thank you." Andi laid a hand gently on Mrs. Peterson's arm. She was touched by the sincerity and caring and knew it was a rare showing for the usually gruff old woman. Andi realized in that moment that she hadn't been living as isolated a life as she'd thought. She cared about the people of this town, and they were showing her they cared for her too. Perhaps the only walls she had built had been in her own mind. She smiled, realizing Gwen wasn't the only one who had found a way into her heart.

The old gray eyes peered at her as if looking into her soul. "All right then, let's go, Churchill." Mrs. Peterson tugged on the leash, encouraging the stubborn old dog to cooperate. He lumbered out the door ahead of her, his tail swaying contentedly.

Andi smiled as she watched the old pair amble down the sidewalk. She thought about what Mrs. Peterson had said about Gwen, about Andi spending time with people her own age. How about that? If she didn't know better, she'd say Mrs. Peterson was trying to fix her up.

Chapter Twelve

Gwen sat in her office, mindlessly petting Zeek's head as she stared at her computer blankly, the data she was supposed to be entering almost forgotten. Every time she tried to work on the boring numbers, her mind would drift to visions of Andi. It was as if she could feel Andi's lips against her mouth. She squirmed in her chair and shook her head, trying to focus on her work. A forceful knock at the door aroused Zeek from her slumber, and she went bounding down the hall, her booming voice echoing around the house.

Gwen made her way down the hall, her excitement growing. She hoped it was Andi stopping by for another visit. To her surprise and mild disappointment, three women with silver-gray hair stood at her door.

"Hello," Gwen said, "can I help you?"

"Hello, we're the welcoming committee from the Baptist church. We just wanted to stop by and welcome you to Norris and of course invite you to join us for services this Sunday."

Gwen cringed inwardly. She wasn't much of a church person and wasn't really sure how she should handle the situation. She knew she had moved into the Bible Belt and hadn't failed to notice that there were at least five churches in the small town of only 1300 residents. But she hadn't expected a personal visit. It wasn't that she wasn't a spiritual person in her own way, but she wasn't much into organized religion. Gwen studied the three women curiously. They seemed harmless enough. Gwen smiled to herself, amused by her caution regarding three little old ladies. She would just wing it and see what happened.

"Well, thank you, ladies. Would you like to come in for some tea?"

"Oh no, dear, that's not necessary. We're just happy to have you with us. We won't keep you." The shortest of the women was obviously acting as the spokesperson for the group. "Here is a small welcoming gift from the church."

Gwen took the basket, pleased by the warm welcome. "Thank you." Perhaps her trepidation was unfounded.

The woman pointed to the basket. "It isn't much really, just some local honey, blueberries from the local farm, a map of the watershed, a list of our church services, some cookies—and I think Iva put in a few dog treats."

Gwen smiled. "This is wonderful."

The tallest of the group peered past Gwen into the house and finally spoke. "I see you've been hard at work with the house. Have you been able to meet any of the neighbors yet?"

"A few. I've ventured to the diner and the grocery. Everyone's been very kind."

"That's quite a dog you have there. I hope you've had a chance to visit the Pet Guardian, our local pet-supply store. Andi is just wonderful. She can get you anything you need and she bakes the most wonderful dog treats. My dog can't live without 'em."

Gwen smiled at the mention of Andi. "Oh yes. I've had the pleasure of meeting Andi. She has a wonderful place. She's rescued Zeek here already. We had our first run-in with a skunk, night before last. I don't know what we would have done without her help."

Gwen couldn't help but feel the woman was looking for something as she seemed to scrutinize her from head to toe. Gwen wasn't used to neighbors dropping by the house, but she was growing used to the guys at the diner checking up on her and being in everybody's business.

"Wonderful," the old woman said with a wry smile.

"Well," the smallest of the women said, "I'm Margaret Gleeson, this is Evelyn Mathers"—she pointed to the silent woman on her right, who smiled shyly—"and this is Iva Peterson." She gestured to the tall woman. "If you need anything, please let us know. We do hope you'll join us at the church sometime."

"Thank you. It was very sweet of you to drop by like this. I'm Gwen Palmer and this is Zeek."

Gwen shook hands with each of the women, smiling broadly. She noticed that Mrs. Peterson gripped her hand firmly, holding on to her hand a moment longer than was customary. She met the steel-gray eyes that seemed to look into her soul. She thought she saw something pass behind the woman's gaze. Was it a question? A judgment? No. It seemed more like she had recognized something and was almost pleased with the revelation.

"Are you sure you won't come inside?" Gwen said, drawing her hand away.

"Thank you, dear," Margaret answered for the group. "We'll be on our way. We still have to prepare the decorations for the single-senior dance this weekend. It was good meeting you, Gwen."

The three ladies turned and made their way down the walk where they waved good-bye. Gwen couldn't believe what had happened. She had never lived anywhere like this before. It was just one more thing to love about the town.

She went back to her office and sat down at her computer, determined to get her work done this time. She didn't want projects piling up and getting in the way of her plans for the weekend. She didn't want anything stopping her from seeing Andi. It had only been a day since she had seen Andi and it felt like an eternity. All she could think about was their kiss. The idea of having an entire day with Andi was a dream. She felt like she was finally seeing the real Andi, the person she had glimpsed on that first day in Norris. Gwen smiled. She couldn't wait to know more about Andi. Based on what she had tasted so far, she knew she wanted to know everything.

She glanced at the welcome basket sitting on her desk. She would have to ask Andi about the church group too. Maybe she could shed some light on this mystery.

Still smiling, she pulled the pile of papers closer and went to work.

❖

It had been a long week. Andi had stuck to her routine and hadn't contacted Gwen since the day of the kiss. But the closer it came to Sunday, she found herself growing more anxious. She had questioned everything that had happened between her and Gwen. She hoped the distance of the past couple of days would have helped her get a grip on her feelings, but she'd been wrong. With each passing hour she grew more restless. She found herself thinking about Gwen at the most unusual times, which had resulted in more than one error in her work. Just this morning she realized she had put peanut-butter dog-training treats in Goliath's food bowl instead of cat food. He hadn't been amused.

Andi had never taken anyone on the lake with her before, and the thought of going with Gwen made her feel both excited and nervous. She liked wanting to spend time with someone, and being attracted to Gwen made her all the more restless. Despite the nagging feeling that she should limit her time with Gwen and her fear of getting close to someone again, Andi couldn't help but feel excited. She was tired of feeling lonely. She was tired of pretending she didn't need anyone. And honestly, Gwen was just so damn irresistible.

She decided she would load the boats on the Jeep when she got home, so she wouldn't have to worry about it in the morning. She had already planned where they would put the boats in and where she wanted to take Gwen.

Andi jumped, startled by the ringing of the phone. "The Pet Guardian, how can I help you?"

"Hi, Andi, this is Gwen."

Andi's heart stopped. This was it. Gwen had come to her senses and was canceling.

"I thought I'd check in and make sure we're still on for tomorrow."

"Of course," Andi answered, trying to hide the tremor in her voice, the flood of relief making her light-headed. "How do you feel about going early, maybe around eight?"

"Sounds great to me. Do you want me to meet you at your place?"

"No. I'll pick you up. Be dressed to get wet. We'll be using the sit-on-top kayaks, and water will splash all over you. It also makes it easier if you want to go for a swim." Andi shivered as she imagined Gwen's skin wet and glistening in the sun.

"I can't wait. What do I need to bring?"

"Nothing really, your ID is all you might need. I'll take care of the rest."

"Wow, you're really making this easy for me. Is there *anything* I can do?"

Andi thought about the question, images of Gwen's arms around her making her skin tingle. "Nope, I think I've got it covered."

"Then there is no way I can convince you to see me tonight?"

Andi smiled. She liked knowing Gwen wanted to see her. "I'd like to, but I have a lot of work to do at the store tonight, and I want to make sure I'm ready for tomorrow."

"Okay, I give. I'll see you tomorrow then."

"Tomorrow it is." Andi hung up the phone. She knew she would be taking Gwen to some of her most treasured places on the lake and was sure to expose things about herself in the process. She sighed. She was nervous, but not afraid. She couldn't wait. Andi felt more alive knowing she would be sharing something she loved with Gwen. She'd been safe in Norris for three years now. Safe and alone. Surely one day on the lake with Gwen wasn't too great a risk for them both.

CHAPTER THIRTEEN

Gwen was standing on the porch clutching a cup of coffee when Andi pulled into her drive at exactly eight o'clock. She had been driving herself crazy, thinking Andi would change her mind. She was beginning to feel Andi could be someone really important in her life, and she feared Andi might not be looking for the same things she was. Andi's reluctance to spend time with her had further fueled her insecurities. But as soon as she saw Andi, she couldn't hold back the smile that burst across her face. Relief washed over her, instantly followed by joy, and she bounded down the steps to join Andi.

"Good morning," Gwen said as she climbed into the Jeep.

"Good morning."

Andi was quiet and let the Jeep idle as Gwen settled into her seat and buckled her seatbelt.

"Ready," Gwen said, eager to start their adventure.

Andi put the Jeep in reverse, resting her arm lightly on the back of Gwen's seat while she backed out of the drive. Gwen watched Andi's every move. Her excitement was beginning to get the best of her, and she leaned over and placed a kiss on Andi's cheek. She hadn't thought about what she was doing—she just had to kiss her.

Andi met Gwen's gaze for the first time that morning, her green eyes as vibrant as fresh summer grass after a rain. Gwen smiled mischievously.

"Stop it," Andi said with a laugh.

"Stop what? Gwen said, feigning innocence. "I'm just looking."

"Uh-huh."

It was a beautiful clear morning. Faint wisps of fog played along the surface of the water as they put the kayaks into the lake at the marina by the dam. Gwen marveled at the beauty of the scenery surrounding her. Everywhere she looked there was beauty. The mountains seemed to spring up out of the silent misty waters, the sky was a perfect cloudless blue, and the air was clean and crisp. It was perfect.

The water was warm and the air was cool, and Gwen's skin broke into goose bumps as she waded into the water to get close to a family of ducks playing along the dock, looking for handouts.

"Hey, daydreamer, do you plan on getting in that boat sometime today?"

Gwen pulled her attention from the ducks back to Andi. Her mouth fell open slightly at the sight of Andi in her boat. Long, lean legs extended, their toned muscles tanned by the sun. Her bare arms rippled with her movements as she worked the paddle. A pale blue-and-white tie-dyed scarf covered her head, pulling her hair back from her face. Her PFD covered her chest but left the taut muscles of her stomach exposed.

Gwen was stunned by the picture of Andi, relaxed and beautiful, surrounded by water, rocks, and mountains. The sun seemed to sparkle in her eyes like the glowing embers of a slow-burning fire. Warmth spread through Gwen's body with a dizzying effect that made her feel intoxicated.

She took a step to climb into her boat and lost her footing. She stumbled, grasping desperately for her boat to catch herself, but fell back into the water as the boat slipped from her fingers. She came to the surface of the water sputtering, still trying to gain her balance. Water dripped from her soaking hair down her face. She finally stopped fighting and allowed herself to float freely in the water as she brushed strands of wet hair back from her face.

The sound of laughter cut through her confusion, and she opened her eyes to see Andi holding her boat, covering her mouth with her free hand, trying not to laugh.

Gwen smiled, and then broke into laughter herself.

"Okay. Not my most graceful moment."

"Don't worry. Consider yourself christened," Andi said. "Now if you're finished with your swim, would you like to try the kayak?"

"Very funny," Gwen grumbled and skimmed the palm of her hand across the surface of the lake, spraying Andi with cool drops of water.

Andi squealed as the shower hit her. But before Gwen could get the upper hand, Andi angled her paddle and gave the water a swipe, effectively silencing Gwen's laughter with a much more significant wave.

"Okay, okay. You win," Gwen called, her hands held in the air in surrender. She made her way unsteadily to her kayak. Andi held the craft steady as Gwen climbed inside. Her reassuring smile warmed Gwen and she found herself staring—Andi was beautiful, but when she smiled it was as if a bank of clouds had parted, letting the sun shine through, lighting Andi's eyes with electrifying radiance. Andi wasn't like anyone Gwen had ever known, and in that moment she felt overwhelmingly grateful for the changes in her life that had led her to this quiet little town.

What?" Andi asked, interrupting Gwen's reverie.

Gwen grinned and shrugged as she shifted in her boat. "Just really glad to be here."

Andi quirked an eyebrow at Gwen. "Okay then, let's see what else we can get into."

Andi set a slow pace at first. She gave Gwen pointers on how to hold the paddle, techniques for her stroke, and how to use her core muscles so her arms didn't tire too easily. Gwen was a quick study.

Andi looked at Gwen suspiciously. "Hey, are you sure you haven't done this before?"

"Well, I didn't exactly say I hadn't done it before," Gwen admitted.

"Okay, smarty-pants, let's see what you've got. I'll race you to that fallen tree on the other side of the cove."

Before Gwen could answer, Andi surged forward.

"Hey, no fair," Gwen called out, then gripped the paddle and made a swift stroke, accepting the challenge. She leaned forward, putting more strength into her stoke. The boat surged forward with each pass of the paddle through the water's surface, gliding across the water as if skating across ice. She was close enough that she could see the muscles in Andi's shoulders ripple with each movement of her arms alternately lifting the paddle from the water and pulling through her stroke. Despite her efforts, Gwen couldn't catch Andi, but as she watched the movements of Andi's body, she wasn't disappointed.

Andi's boat glided beneath the fallen tree and emerged on the other side, just as Gwen coasted up to her. Gwen was having a good time and loved this playful side of Andi.

"About time you showed up, slowpoke."

Gwen laughed. "You cheated."

Andi shrugged. "Whatever you need to tell yourself," she teased, exhilarated by the challenge and enamored with the weightlessness of her heart. She couldn't remember the last time she had felt so happy. Andi marveled at the joy permeating her usually impermeable defenses.

The morning passed quickly, and much too soon the sound of motor boats intruded upon their solitude.

"Come on," Andi said, "the traffic is starting to pick up. Let go somewhere a little less hectic."

Gwen followed Andi to a secluded cove that the motor boats couldn't enter due to the narrow, shallow passage. Andi put up her hand, signaling to Gwen to stop. When Gwen's boat glided up to hers, Andi reached out and grasped the shell. With her paddle nestled in her lap, she lifted her other hand and pointed to an area just inside the foliage.

Gwen gasped, and Andi realized she'd spotted the small fawn. Andi watched Gwen's face as her eyes widened as the young deer made its way to the water's edge. Gwen glanced at Andi, the awe at what they were seeing plain in her face, and caught Andi watching her. Gwen jerked her attention back to the deer but gasped and grabbed Andi's hand when the fawn waded into the water and swam across to the other side. Andi had never seen anything so pure, so innocent, and so wonderful as Gwen's expression in that moment.

"That was so beautiful," Gwen whispered.

"Yes, beautiful," Andi said reverently.

They beached the kayaks on a sandy bank and watched the sun glisten across the water. Andi pulled two water bottles out of the dry pack. She had frozen the water the night before, and it was still cold. She handed a bottle to Gwen, who quickly twisted the cap free and lifted the bottle to her lips, taking a long drink.

Gwen couldn't draw her eyes way from Andi's lips as the translucent liquid spilled into her mouth. She remembered how soft Andi's lips were, and she stifled the urge to reach out and brush a drop of water from the corner of Andi's mouth. She felt something inside her shift, lifting another barrier in her heart, and she opened a little more to Andi. She tried to shake the sensation by busying herself with her own water bottle, but she could feel an invisible link growing between them. She tried to temper her feelings, reminding herself how easily she could get hurt if Andi sent her away again. But it was well past the time for caution. She wanted Andi. She wanted her in her life. She wanted to love her.

When she was with Andi, the sun seemed brighter and the air fresher than she had remembered, and she felt changed as a result. Her skin tingled with the warmth of the sun as a breeze brushed across her body making her shiver. Maybe the reason she had never mattered to anyone was because she was looking in the wrong places. More than anything, she wanted to be someone who deserved Andi.

Gwen reached out and took Andi's hand.

"Thank you for bringing me here."

Andi's smile was earnest and she glanced away.

"I was really nervous about asking you to come with me. I've never brought anyone out on the lake before."

"Really, why not?"

Andi looked thoughtful as she gazed out over the water.

"This has always been mine. Something that takes me away from everything that goes on in the world. Out here I'm free."

Gwen waited, feeling there was more that Andi hadn't said. She watched Andi's gaze roam from one point to another, and she wished she could read her thoughts. She thought she understood what it had meant for Andi to bring her here, and her heart filled to bursting as she grew more and more enamored by the beauty and complexity of her.

After a few moments of silence, Andi dropped her head and laughed softly. She squeezed Gwen's hand and glanced up at her. "Besides, I never had anyone I wanted to ask," she said in a quiet voice.

Gwen smiled. "That's hard to believe. I imagine there are lots of women who would love to be here with you."

Andi's eyes dulled and grew distant. "No. Not for a very long time."

Gwen could hear the hurt in Andi's voice and saw the flicker of pain that stole the smile from her lips. Gwen felt the pain, dull in her chest, as if it were her own when she saw Andi's smile fade as if stolen by a memory. She wanted nothing more than to bring that smile back. Her heart longed for it.

She moved closer and placed her arm around Andi's waist, pulling her next to her.

"There is no where I would rather be at this moment than here with you."

Andi turned her face to Gwen, the corner of her mouth curving into a faint smile. "Me too," she said, pressing her lips to Gwen's, a gentle brush of soft skin.

Gwen smiled as Andi pulled away. She wanted to pull Andi into her and kiss her back, but she was frozen in place, the sound of her racing heart pulsing in her ears. Instead, Gwen leaned closer, relishing the soft feel of Andi's skin against her shoulder as she turned her gaze out over the water.

The day was really beginning to heat up, and Gwen reached up and brushed a bead of sweat from Andi's temple.

Andi smiled at Gwen. "I'm ready for a swim," she said as she stood and stripped off her PFD, revealing a lean torso with a gentle curve of muscle that ran along her side, framing her flat stomach.

Gwen was breathless at the sight of Andi's body. She stared wordlessly, watching Andi walk into the water until only her head bobbed above the surface. Gwen's stomach tensed and her insides tingled when Andi leaned back and allowed the water to rush across her head, pulling her bandanna from her hair. Andi captured the wayward fabric in her hand and brushed the water from her face.

Gwen swept her hand across her mouth, her fingers over her lips, wanting the touch to be Andi's. She watched Andi swim for a long time. It was like watching an angel. She had to make herself sit still so she wouldn't follow Andi into the water. She wanted to feel Andi's slick wet skin glide against her own. She wanted to run her fingers through Andi's hair and kiss the tender exposed skin of her neck.

"You should come in—the water is wonderful," Andi called out, grinning.

Gwen shuddered, trying to control the urge to go to Andi. Things were going so well. She didn't want to risk doing anything that might push Andi away again.

"I took my swim this morning, remember?" She hoped Andi couldn't hear the desire that she knew was thick in her voice.

"I remember," Andi said with a chuckle. "But the water is much more inviting now that the sun is fully up."

Gwen hesitated, warring with herself. But Andi had made the invitation, and that was all Gwen needed to rationalize her decision. She stood up and pulled her shirt over her head. She wasn't about to pass up an invitation to be close to Andi, although she was sure what she was thinking was not what Andi had in mind.

Gwen stretched out her arms in front of her as she walked into the water and pushed herself under in a swift lunge. "This feels wonderful," she said as her head broke the surface only a few feet away from Andi. "How do you get up and go to work every day when you could be doing this?"

A broad smile broke across Andi's face and she laughed. "I schedule my days so I can get out here several times a week if I want. It's one of the perks of being self-employed."

"No kidding. This is heaven." Gwen swam a little closer, testing Andi's limits, wanting to see if Andi would move away. She smiled when Andi didn't move. Maybe things with Andi could be different. She didn't want to think that Andi was like all the other women who had seen her as a temporary amusement. And she wanted there to be more between them. She decided to be content with letting things reveal themselves slowly, and she tilted her head back and allowed her body to float to the surface. She closed her eyes and drank in the warmth of the sun on her face and the gentle lap of the water against her skin.

Andi watched Gwen float in the water, mesmerized by the peacefulness she felt. She wondered about her first impression of Gwen as a pushy overconfident player. That image seemed wildly incongruent with the picture of the woman in front of her now. She was beginning to realize there was much more to Gwen Palmer. She had shown kindness and gentleness with a hint of the protectiveness that Andi craved. She sighed deeply and lifted her feet to join Gwen in her worship of the sun.

A warm pleasing feeling filled Andi as she allowed her hand to drift until her fingers brushed Gwen's hand. She was glad she had decided to ask Gwen to come to the lake with her. She was happy to have a new memory of her favorite place to keep with her forever. She knew she wasn't keeping her promise to put distance between herself and Gwen, but the more she was around Gwen, the more she wanted to believe she could have a different life, that she was safe and Gwen was safe and maybe, just maybe, she could be happy. A warning pricked at the back of her mind telling her that wasn't possible, but she pushed it away. She wanted to pretend things were different. Just for one day, she wanted to be happy.

She felt Gwen's hand slide into hers and smiled when their fingers laced together. Andi took a deep soothing breath. She had this one perfect day and she was very happy.

Chapter Fourteen

The day had been remarkable so far, and Andi couldn't remember the last time she'd felt so…normal. For the past four years she had believed her chance at happiness had passed. Meeting Gwen had opened a world of possibilities that she prayed were real but dared not hope for.

Andi put on some music and began to do the prep work for dinner. She embraced the music, letting her body sway to the rhythm until she was dancing around the kitchen, singing along with the lyrics. She hadn't danced in years, but she was having the best day she could remember and dancing felt good. She jumped at the sound of the knock at the door. She turned to see Gwen standing at the door grinning, and she felt her cheeks grow hot with embarrassment.

"How long have you been standing out here?" she said as she opened the door.

"Not very long. Nice song, I like your voice."

Andi buried her face in her hands. "Oh God, you heard me?"

"Just a little," Gwen said. "The dance was cute too."

Andi swatted Gwen lightly on the arm. "Now you're just being mean. I lost track of time and wasn't expecting you so soon. You weren't supposed to see or hear any of that."

"Sorry, but you're busted. Don't stop on my account. I was enjoying the show."

Andi sighed, resigning her dignity. There was nothing she could do about it now. That's what she got for making fun of Gwen earlier.

"Come on in and have a seat. What would you like to drink?"

Gwen held up the bottle of wine she had brought along. "I brought this. I couldn't just show up empty-handed. But I'll have a beer if you have any."

Andi retrieved the beer for Gwen, opening one for herself. She watched the way Gwen settled into her chair, an air of belonging in the way she draped herself, legs outstretched and an arm casually thrown over the back of the chair. Andi found she liked the gesture and was happy Gwen was so relaxed with her. What pleased her even more was how comfortable she was with Gwen. Gwen just seemed to fit into her life.

They grilled steaks and portobello mushrooms paired with a light salad. Night fell all too quickly—time melted away when she was with Gwen. She knew it wouldn't be long now before Gwen would go, and she would be left alone again in her silent home with her silent thoughts. She wasn't ready for the day to end. She had been so lonely before meeting Gwen, and she was tired of that life. Maybe she couldn't have forever, but she had right now. The thought was exhilarating.

She felt Gwen's hand slide across her arm with a smooth caress that was so faint it could have been a breeze. The touch drew her out of her thoughts, and when she looked up, she met Gwen's inquisitive gaze.

"What were you thinking just now?"

Andi looked at her, blinking away her loneliness. "Nothing really, just how quickly the day has gone by. I've had a really good day and I hate to see it end."

Gwen looked at her watch. "Are you tired? Should I go?"

The suggestion startled Andi, and she was surprised by her reaction. She was afraid that if she let Gwen go, the spell would be broken and the magic that had surrounded this one perfect day would vanish. "No, please, just the opposite. I've enjoyed being with you so much today I felt a little sad when I thought of you leaving. I'm sorry."

"Don't apologize. I'm having a good time with you too."

Andi met Gwen's eyes, telegraphing her gratitude. She smiled warmly at Gwen and placed her hand on her shoulder and let her fingers glide down the length of her arm.

"How long did you say you've lived here?" Gwen asked curiously.

"Oh, I guess it's coming up on three years now."

"Have you always lived here alone?"

Andi knew what Gwen was asking. She wanted to know more about her, and Andi wondered how much she should share. The truth would mean the end of this fairy tale, and she wasn't quite ready for that.

"Yes, it's always just been me."

"No girlfriends?"

Andi was thoughtful for a moment before answering. "No, I haven't dated anyone since moving here." The familiar hollowness had begun to fill her chest as she tried to answer Gwen's questions. There was a very good reason why she didn't date and here she was, breaking her own rules. She could continue to lie to herself that what they were doing wasn't dating, but her heart knew she already cared too much for Gwen to just be friends.

"Does it bother you that I'm asking you about your personal life?"

Andi looked away, suddenly focused on the flickering candle flame. "I guess it does. It isn't something I'm used to talking about."

"Should I stop?"

It would have been easy for Andi to push Gwen away, to refuse to answer or find a clever way of avoiding the discussion, but she knew the conversation was unavoidable and didn't want to rebuild barriers between them. She wasn't ready to share the whole truth, but she decided on honesty instead.

"No. You can ask. But there may be some things I decide to keep to myself."

"Fair enough. Tell me something about yourself. Tell me about your family."

"Hmm, I'm not sure that's a safe topic. I'm the only child of parents who were only children. They both died when I was young.

I don't really have any family." She wasn't used to talking about her life, but Gwen had been so patient with her, she found sharing some of her past comforting. She wanted to trust Gwen with her story.

Gwen shifted in her chair, and Andi knew her answer had made Gwen uncomfortable.

"That must be really hard," Gwen said, her voice softer than before.

"For a long time it was. But luckily I grew up and built a life of my own. Now it just seems like it's the way things have always been. I don't think about it much anymore."

"Where did you live after your parents died?"

"I was a state custody kid. I moved from group homes to foster homes as they were available. I was lucky and met some really caring people along the way who made a difference."

"I'm sorry, Andi."

"It's okay. It was all a long time ago and, like I said, I built my own life." Andi drew her hand through her hair and sighed, ready to change the subject. She didn't want to bombard Gwen with too much information all at once. "Now it's your turn, tell me about your family."

Gwen laughed softly. "I come from a brood of people. I have two brothers and a sister. My parents are still married and having the time of their lives being grandparents to my nieces and nephews."

"Do you miss them?"

"Oh yeah, I think that's been the hardest part of the move. I'd gotten used to seeing them almost every week. I promised I'd make trips home for the holidays and things like that, and we talk on the phone almost every day. But I still miss them."

It was comforting to hear about the closeness of Gwen's family, and Andi loved the look in Gwen's eyes when she talked about them. Gwen was someone who was used to having a large family, being close to people, sharing her life with those she had known forever. She could see Gwen's love for her family as her expression brightened and light glinted in her eyes while she talked. Andi couldn't imagine that closeness with anyone, and the thought made her melancholy. She remembered her parents, but the memories seemed vague and distant, as if she were remembering scenes from a movie, instead of something she had actually lived.

"Your family sounds wonderful," Andi said reverently.

"They are. I know they don't understand my decision to move away, but they're supportive, and I guess it's their job to give me a hard time."

After some time, Gwen yawned and stretched. "It's getting late. I should be heading home. Thank you for dinner, and the wonderful day." She stood and reached for Andi's hand, pulling her up from her chair the way she had done the day she'd brought Andi home after the ordeal with Zeek.

Andi felt a rush of anticipation quickly followed by fear. Gwen pushed a strand of hair back from Andi's face and brushed her fingers across her cheek. Andi held her breath as Gwen moved closer. She wanted so much to feel the softness of Gwen's lips, but as they had talked she had realized she couldn't be the woman Gwen wanted. She didn't know how to be a part of a family. A family was something she could never have. She thought she had accepted that, but Gwen had made her want things she hadn't dared dream of before. How could she explain the things that had been done to her and the threat that still lingered in the shadows? She couldn't expect Gwen to live a life of uncertainty, anticipating the worst the way she did.

Andi started to pull away. "Gwen, I don't think this is a good idea."

"You think too much," Gwen whispered.

She had felt so close to Andi throughout the day and she couldn't bear to feel her pull away now. She had wanted to reach out to Andi when she talked about growing up without her parents. Gwen had wanted to comfort her and heal her wounds. She couldn't imagine what Andi's life had been like. Every part of her soul wanted to wrap around Andi and soothe her.

Her breath caught and she looked from Andi's eyes to her lips, arousal spreading through her, making her tremble. She could see the desire darkening Andi's eyes despite her hesitation. Andi's lips were moist and parted slightly in invitation, and Gwen couldn't hold back any longer. She thought she would combust if Andi didn't kiss her.

"Please, Andi."

"Yes," Andi whispered, then leaned forward and closed the distance between them.

Andi sighed and dissolved against her. At the touch of Andi's lips, Gwen was soaring. When Andi's hands slid around her shoulders and tightened the embrace, Gwen's lips became more searching, and she clung to Andi, the pressure of the kiss insistent and passionate. She couldn't get enough. Andi was consuming her.

Gwen had never felt such tenderness before and knew she had not been truly alive until that moment, when she joined with Andi. She was floating. Her body disconnected from her mind. All her focus shifted to the feel of Andi's mouth on hers. She was filled with longing and her body tingled from head to toe. Each stroke of Andi's tongue sent waves through her body until she was no longer connected to the earth. The only thing keeping her together was the feel of Andi's body against hers and the pressure of strong arms caressing her.

Andi whimpered, belatedly realizing the sound, a mix of pleasure and need, came from her. She knew she should stop but couldn't. Gwen just felt too good. She had given herself one day of happiness, and there could be no better ending than in Gwen's arms.

Gwen held Andi close to her even as their lips parted. Andi could feel Gwen's gaze and her arousal became an insistent throb in her center.

"You amaze me," Gwen whispered.

Andi dropped her head against Gwen's chest. Her hand slid down from Gwen's shoulders, and she drew small circles with her fingers against the fabric of Gwen's shirt over her collarbones. She drew in a deep breath, gently pushed against Gwen, and took a small step back.

Gwen's hands loosened and trailed light touches down her arms until Gwen was holding both her hands.

"Andi?"

Andi tried to steady her breathing and struggled to regain control of her body. If she didn't put some distance between them, she would be unable to stand much longer. Her thoughts raced. She wanted Gwen. Her want was more than seemed possible. But somehow she had found the strength to stop. She tightened her fingers around Gwen's hand and tugged, leading Gwen out the front door toward her car.

Gwen followed without a word. At the car she turned, and Andi thought she would melt from the desire she saw in Gwen eyes. Gwen's smile was tender and reassuring, and Andi knew Gwen wouldn't push this time. But she suddenly found it difficult to meet Gwen's eyes. She was afraid if she looked at her again, she wouldn't be able to let her go.

Gwen squeezed Andi's hand, lingering a moment. "Good night, Andi." She leaned in and kissed Andi's cheek as she had that morning.

"Good night," Andi said as Gwen got into the car. She could still feel the heat of Gwen's lips on her skin as she watched Gwen drive away. "Thank you for a perfect day," she whispered into the darkness.

CHAPTER FIFTEEN

The store was open on Saturdays but closed on Sundays and Mondays. Andi had found that very few people ever came in the store on Mondays, so she'd adopted them as her official weekend. Despite the reprieve, she was up early, consumed by thoughts of Gwen. When they had said good night, Andi had felt a sense of loss. Her body was so charged with sexual energy she found she couldn't rest. It had taken her forever to fall asleep and she was up by dawn. She had weeded the back garden, watered the flowers, cleaned the kitchen, and was now gathering her things to head out for a long bike ride. But despite how busy she kept herself, she kept wondering what Gwen was doing. The lingering thrill of Gwen's lips sent shivers through her, making her weak in the knees.

She shook her head at her growing infatuation. She knew it wouldn't be fair for her to bring Gwen into her haunted world where she never knew if she was safe. But now that she had held her, tasted her lips, and brushed against her soul, how could she live without her?

Andi focused on the hum of her tires on the smooth pavement and the smell of fresh-cut grass that permeated the air as the lawn service got an early jump on the day. She allowed her energy to flow through her body, and she pushed herself up the many hills along her route until her legs burned, weak from fatigue.

By the time she rode back through town, her skin was hot and her clothes drenched with sweat. Although her body was tired, she felt exhilarated. Riding always gave her a feeling of freedom that she imagined was most like flying. On the bike she was in control. All of her attention had to be on the path ahead of her, the pace and distance of the traffic around her, and the energy pouring out through her limbs pushing her forward.

She couldn't wait to get home and plunge into the pool to cool off. There was nothing like the sensation of cool water surging across her hot skin after a long ride. Although she did feel a little guilty for not completing her weekly Sunday run, she figured that since she spent Sunday with Gwen on the lake, her lapse was justified. The ride had been just what she needed, and she knew if she went for a run today she would have gone by Gwen's house. At the mere thought of seeing Gwen, she felt a twinge of excitement.

Her response to Gwen's kiss the night before had shown her just how weak she was to her physical attraction. She couldn't risk allowing her sexual desires to dictate her behavior. She just needed to stay in control. She didn't have to act on her feelings. She rode on, trying to purge herself of her need for Gwen and get her mind back on track.

Andi looked up as she pushed her way up the final hill leading to her house and almost rode into the ditch when she saw Gwen standing in front of her house talking with Mrs. Peterson. Oh crap! What was Gwen doing here? And what was she doing talking to Mrs. Peterson? *Great, now Mrs. Peterson is going to be poking around in my personal life.*

She brought the bike to a stop beside the two women.

"Hi, Mrs. Peterson, Gwen," she said making brief eye contact with each. "What are you two up to?"

"Well, speak of the summer peach, there you are. I was just talking with Gwen here," Mrs. Peterson said in an unusually cheerful tone. "Seems she was looking for you this morning. I tried to explain that you are a hard one to nail down, always having to be doing something or the other. Just look at you, red as an apple and sweating so much you look like someone turned the hose on you."

Gwen was just standing there watching the exchange, looking very amused by the old woman's demeanor. Andi felt her cheeks grow warm as an entirely different heat spread through her. She hoped her discomfort was masked by the heat of exertion that still burned her face.

"Nice bike," Gwen said. "I've always been a fan of Orbea." Gwen gestured toward the bike, and Andi was grateful to Gwen for moving the attention away from her.

"How was your ride?" Gwen asked a moment later.

Andi smiled warmly at Gwen. "It was great, thanks. Umm, would you two like to come inside for some tea and maybe lunch?"

"How wonderful," Mrs. Peterson answered, surprising Andi. "I would love a good glass of tea. It's hot as a wiener roast in hell out here."

Andi looked at Mrs. Peterson, dumbfounded. In all the years she had been asking her in for tea, Mrs. Peterson had never, not even once, taken her up on the offer. Now here she was, eager to come inside like it was the most common thing in the world.

Gwen grinned. "Sounds good to me."

Andi pushed her bike up to the back entrance and into the house, leaning it gently against the wall. She pulled off her shoes and padded barefoot across the floor. She led the two women into the kitchen where she washed her hands and pulled three tall glasses from the cupboard. She retrieved the carafe of tea from the fridge and brought it to the table. She could see Mrs. Peterson steadily taking in all the changes she had made to the old house in the last three years.

Apparently satisfied with her assessment of the kitchen, Mrs. Peterson turned to Gwen. "So tell me dear, how is the old house coming?"

"Very well, thank you. I think it's habitable at this point. I can actually cook a meal now that doesn't require using the outdoor grill. I'm very pleased with the changes."

"And what do you think of the renovations, Andi?"

Andi stiffened slightly at the question, understanding that Mrs. Peterson was trying to find out how much time Andi and Gwen had been spending together. She was sure Mrs. Peterson had seen Gwen's Land Rover in her drive the previous evening.

"Oh, I think Gwen's doing a wonderful job with the place. She has a good eye for it."

"That's good, that's good. I'm glad to see you've been helping out our new neighbor. It's always so nice to feel welcome in a new place."

Mrs. Peterson turned her attention back to Gwen again. "Are you as crazy about all this running and bike riding and all that madness as Andi is?"

Gwen chuckled. "I guess I am. I haven't been on my bike since I moved here, but I'm happy with the things I've experienced so far."

Andi warmed, hoping Gwen was thinking of their time together.

"Maybe you should get Andi here to show you around a bit. I'm sure she knows all the places to go. Isn't that right, Andi?"

"I guess so." Andi studied Mrs. Peterson over the rim of her glass as she took a drink of her tea. She was perplexed by the questions. What was the old woman up to? It seemed Mrs. Peterson was trying to make sure Andi and Gwen spent time together, something Andi thought was very odd. Come to think of it, the old woman had been acting strange for weeks now.

Andi decided to turn the tables on Mrs. Peterson. "How's Churchill? I'm surprised he isn't with you today." Andi hoped if she got Mrs. Peterson distracted, she could avoid any further inquiries.

"Stubborn as a mule. You know, he wouldn't even come outside this morning. I guess he thought it was just too hot for a walk. He just sat there on his pillow staring at me like he had never seen me before in his life. When I hooked his lead onto his collar, he just lay down and groaned at me. Wouldn't budge an inch."

"He hasn't run out of his banana biscotti has he?"

"I take it Churchill is your dog?" Gwen asked.

Andi chuckled, "He's the sweetest basset hound you have ever met and very strong willed."

"Strong willed my rear end," Mrs. Peterson scoffed. "He's a stubborn ass."

Both Andi and Gwen laughed. Gwen coughed, almost choking on her tea.

"I tell you what, Mrs. Peterson, I'll send Churchill a special batch home so you can butter him up. Maybe he'll be a little more amenable if he thinks he'll get something special. I've been trying out a new flavor." Andi went to the pantry and retrieved two small gift bags of treats. She gave one to Mrs. Peterson and the other to Gwen. "You'll have to tell me how he likes these. Churchill can be my new test market. Gwen, you can take some for Zeek as well."

Mrs. Peterson smiled and took the offering. "You keep spoiling my dog this way, he'll be as big as a house."

"Maybe so," Andi chuckled. "But at least he won't be eating your garden shoes."

"Humph." Mrs. Peterson nodded. "Well, I best be off. Who knows what that troublesome lump of mutt is up to? I better get home. Thank you for the tea. It was good to see you again, Gwen."

"You too, Mrs. Peterson."

Andi walked Mrs. Peterson to the door. "You'll have to come over again sometime."

"I might just do that. You have good tea." She smiled at Andi, patted her on the cheek with a weathered old hand, and ambled out the door.

Andi sighed. So much for keeping some distance, thinking of Gwen sitting in her kitchen.

She found Gwen still sitting at the kitchen table with a sly grin on her face.

"What?" she said, pretending to be annoyed.

"Sweet woman."

Andi glared at her, trying to keep the smile from creeping into the corners of her mouth.

"I take it the neighbors are more than curious about what you've been up to. Does she come over and check out all your visitors?"

Plopping down in the chair, Andi rubbed her face in her hands. "Well, she might if I had visitors. To be honest that's the first time she's ever accepted one of my invitations. She's never even been inside the house."

Gwen looked shocked. "Seriously? Wow, she must really be rankled. You'll have to tone down those late-night dinner parties you've been throwing."

"Ha-ha. It seems to be you she's interested in. She's never behaved that way before. And it sounds like she's already paid you a visit. Maybe she has a crush on you."

"That's it," Gwen said raising her eyebrows. "We're secret lovers. Didn't I tell you I had a weakness for older women?"

Andi laughed. The friendly play was so natural she forgot all her earlier worries.

"Mrs. Peterson and two other women from the church stopped by to visit me at my house a few days ago. As I recall, she was very interested in whether or not I'd been to your store. Maybe she's jealous."

"I doubt that," Andi chuckled. "So, what brings *you* by?"

"Well"—Gwen took a long drink of her tea—"I was hoping I could repay you for your hospitality and offer to cook you dinner tonight. I have the kitchen all ready to go, and I'm dying to try it out—I hate to cook for myself. What do you say?"

This time Andi didn't hesitate before answering. Seeing Gwen's soft smile, her radiant blue eyes, and her scrumptious body made Andi melt. Of course she would say yes.

"I'd like that."

"Great. How about five thirty? I already have everything planned out. You don't even need to bring anything."

A thrill ran through Andi at the thought that she would be seeing Gwen again later. "That'll be great."

"You know, you really should give me your phone number so I can just call you. If I keep showing up here, your neighbors are going to talk." Gwen smiled her heart-stopping smile. "I'm sorry I just showed up out of the blue like this. Am I keeping you from anything?"

Andi couldn't think. Had she been planning to do something? All she could think of now was Gwen's warm mouth on hers. "Umm, no. Nothing really." She looked out the window and saw the crystal blue water glistening in the sun and suddenly she remembered. "I was just going to go for a swim to cool off. Do you want to join me?"

Gwen seemed to consider it for a moment before answering. "Well, it does sound pretty inviting, but I don't have a bathing suit. I'd have to go home and change."

"You could just swim in your shorts and sports bra, or I could lend you a pair of board shorts. They may be a little snug on you, but they should be good enough."

"Okay."

"I'll be right back." Andi went into the bedroom to change and came back with a pair of red board shorts with a blue-and-white stripe at each side.

"These might work," she said handing the shorts to Gwen. "You can change in the bathroom. I'll be outside, come on out when you're ready."

Gwen smiled and took the shorts. She hadn't anticipated getting to spend time with Andi, but she was very happy she had stopped by. The idea of seeing Andi in her bathing suit again made her heart race.

"I'll just be a minute."

"Take your time."

Gwen stepped out onto the back porch a few minutes later to see Andi gliding beneath the crystal blue water. The muscles in her back rippled as she propelled herself through the water with her strong, lean arms. Her body was beautifully toned and held a tantalizing femininity that made Gwen go weak in the knees.

Gwen stepped to the edge of the pool just as Andi surfaced and threw her head back to push the wet hair and water away from her face.

"Hey, they fit," she said, peering up at Gwen.

Gwen smiled. "Yeah, as long as I don't do any serious squats. They're a little snug in the butt."

She turned to model the shorts and pointed out the slight tension in the fabric. She was pleased to see Andi's eyes roam the length of her body.

"Looks good to me. Come on in, the water is fantastic." Andi pushed off from the side of the pool and did a backstroke away from Gwen, never taking her eyes off her.

Gwen dipped a toe into the water before she stretched her long arms over her head and dove in, immediately curving her back so the momentum pushed her toward the surface. The water was perfect, the coolness just enough to be refreshing without the shock of cold.

"Wow. This is great," she said as she turned to find Andi.

They swam and talked until the grumbling sounds of Andi's stomach warned that it was long past time to eat.

"I'm going to grab a snack," Andi said. "Would you like something?"

"No. I can wait until dinner. I had a light lunch before heading over here."

"Suit yourself. I'll be right back."

Gwen watched Andi walk out of the pool, the water streaming off her body. The sun glistened off her golden tan, and Gwen felt the urge to suck the water from her skin and brush her fingers along the delicate curves. She was still lost in her fantasy when Andi returned, holding two more glasses of tea and a tray of cheese and crackers.

Gwen climbed out of the pool and accepted the towel Andi offered her. Although cool from the water, her body flushed with heat when her hand brushed Andi's fingers. Andi had quickly pulled away and was busying herself with the cheese and crackers.

Taking a chair across from Andi, Gwen watched her with growing hunger. The small movements of her hands, the way the corners of her mouth curved into a faint smile as she savored the tasty morsel of cheese. Gwen tried to keep her expression neutral as she imagined her tongue skirting the edges of Andi's lips.

The sound of Andi's voice drew her eyes upward where she felt she would drown in the soft eyes that studied her.

Andi held out a small yellow piece of paper. "Here's my number—it'll save you the trouble of having to track me down the next time, although I like how this has turned out."

Gwen felt the tension in her middle grow, coiling into a tight fist of desire. She was incredibly attracted to Andi and she was pleased to find how easy it was to be with her. Andi was one of those rare people who instantly made Gwen feel at home, and she hadn't been able to stop thinking about the way she felt when she kissed Andi.

She knew she was dangerously close to giving in to her impulses and was afraid if she pushed too hard, Andi would pull away again. Although things were progressing between them, Gwen wanted to guard herself. She didn't want to be hurt again. She hoped Andi would give her a chance.

"Me too." Gwen smiled. "But I guess I better get going. I have a few things to take care of before dinner. Thanks for the swim."

"Anytime. Are you sure there isn't anything I can bring for dinner tonight?"

"No. I want this to be my treat. You've been doing so many wonderful things for me, the least I can do is dinner. I'll see you in a few hours."

Andi agreed with a warm smile that made Gwen twitch with the urge to taste her. She swallowed and turned to go. She imagined she could feel Andi watching her as the left. It had turned out to be a day full of surprises and the hope for more. Only a few short hours separated her from seeing Andi again. She could hardly wait. Andi had really warmed up to her over the past few days, but she could tell Andi was holding back. She had to get this right. If there was even the slightest chance that Andi would let her in, she was going to take it.

Chapter Sixteen

Andi knocked on the door at precisely five thirty. She waited for Zeek to sound the alarm but was surprised when Gwen appeared at the door alone.

"Hey there."

"Hi." Andi's heart stuttered at the sight of Gwen. Even though it had only been mere hours since she had seen her, each one was an eternity. She smiled to hide her nervousness. "Where's Zeek?" Andi asked as she stepped inside the door.

"She's outside. I needed her to stay busy while I was cooking." Gwen opened the door wide and motioned for Andi to come inside. Gwen closed the door and stepped in front of Andi, blocking the way to the kitchen.

"What?" Andi asked feeling self-conscious.

"Nothing. I just wanted to look at you. You're beautiful."

Andi shifted uncomfortably back on her heels and looked away. She was pleased by Gwen's attention but wasn't sure what to say.

"I'm glad you're here."

"Thank you," Andi said as Gwen stepped closer and placed her right hand on Andi's cheek.

Gwen leaned in and kissed Andi lightly on the lips, a tender kiss that said *I missed you.*

Andi felt her head spin and her knees go weak. She brushed her fingers along Gwen's arm, not wanting the slight contact to end.

When Gwen pulled away, her eyes were closed as if savoring the taste of something exquisite. A moment later her eyes opened and she smiled warmly at Andi. "I promised you dinner," she said as she took Andi's hand and led her to the kitchen.

Gwen served clams in a lemon caper sauce with fresh baked bread and mushrooms stuffed with crab and spinach. They drank a very nice white wine that brought out the flavor of the clams.

Andi was very impressed. Taking her last bite, she wiped her mouth and sat back in her chair. "That was amazing."

"Thank you. I'm glad you liked it."

"Where did you learn to cook like that?"

Gwen smiled. "I've made it a hobby over the years. At first I was too poor to eat out, and then I was too busy. Then I met a French woman a few years ago who introduced me to real cuisine and the art of cooking."

Andi raised an eyebrow. "French, huh?"

Gwen grinned sheepishly. "Yes."

"I'm afraid to ask what else she taught you."

Blushing profusely, Gwen took a sip of her wine. "A girl doesn't kiss and tell."

Andi didn't know what made her do it, but all her doubts and inhibitions had abandoned her. She placed her napkin on the table and slowly pushed back her chair. She stood and strode purposefully around the table, closing the distance between them in two determined strides. She stepped into Gwen so she was straddling Gwen's legs and sat in Gwen's lap, facing her. She could feel the heat surge from Gwen's body as Gwen's hands came up to grasp her waist, and she leaned in and claimed Gwen's mouth with her own.

Andi's body tingled as every inch of her skin came alive with energy as Gwen's lips pressed hungrily into hers. She savored the warmth of the tender flesh against her mouth, the acidic taste of lemon and wine, and the subtle taste that was uniquely Gwen. There was no hesitation in the kiss. Andi was tired of holding back, tired of being alone, and Gwen was everything she wanted.

Andi deepened the kiss, brushing her tongue into Gwen's mouth. Gwen moaned and Andi felt the vibrations resonate throughout her body, reverberating in her clitoris, making her ache with want. She was completely consumed by her need for Gwen.

She sought connection with Gwen along every inch of her skin. She wanted her so much, she wondered if it was possible to die from too much pleasure. As she absorbed the tenderness of Gwen's flesh she felt another barrier crumble. Her need for Gwen was greater than her fear, and it filled her with determination. She was done hiding. In that moment all that mattered was Gwen. "Gwen." Andi broke the kiss with a gasp. Her pulse resonated throughout her body. No thoughts managed to find their way through her consciousness. All her attention was focused on the feel of her body, the feel of Gwen's body, and her desire for more.

The moment she broke away, Gwen's mouth found her neck and expertly played her tongue along the tender spaces around her ear and along her throat.

"God, I've wanted to do this forever."

"Mmm." Andi's head dipped and she let her lips find Gwen again as she pressed her center into Gwen's pelvis. Her hands had moved to Gwen's chest and she cupped her breasts, her thumbs rubbing the pebbled nipples.

Gwen moaned. "Oh yeah, that feels good."

Gwen's hand slid beneath Andi's shirt and brushed her bare back, sparking tiny trails of electricity across Andi's skin, igniting a desire that tore through her like lightning on a summer night. She had never wanted anything more in her life, had never in her wildest imaginings experienced anything so exquisite. Gwen's touch was heaven and Andi never wanted this feeling to end.

Andi drew back and peered into Gwen's eyes, seeing the raw tenuous need as the blue of Gwen's eyes darkened and a low growl rumbled in her throat. Andi was lost in the feel of Gwen's touch. She reached places Andi believed were closed forever. Places she had been afraid to accept were still a part of her. Gwen was bending her need into glorious pleasure, and God, it felt good.

Nimble fingers found their way to the buttons of Andi's shirt, and she could feel the fabric being slowly removed from her shoulders. She moved her hands away from Gwen's breasts long enough to allow the offensive barrier to be stripped from her arms and tossed carelessly to the floor.

"Is this okay?" Gwen asked as she traced tender circles against Andi's back and across her shoulders.

"Yes," Andi whispered breathlessly.

Andi sat back against Gwen's legs and quickly tugged Gwen's T-shirt over her head. She gazed down at the perfect bare chest. Small round breasts, soft and supple, were a perfect contrast against her otherwise lean, muscular body. The dark, perfect nipples hardened under Andi's gaze, making her ache to taste them.

A faint growl escaped her throat as she played her fingers across one of the hard nubs and flicked her tongue teasingly across Gwen's lips.

"You're perfect."

"More," Gwen gasped and pressed her fingers into Andi's hips. Andi's body pulsed, and the ache of desire throbbed within her as she felt herself grow hard. It had been too long since she had allowed anyone to touch her, and her body was screaming for release. A strong hand ran along Andi's side to the waistband of her shorts and pulled the button open with a tug. She heard the zipper slide open. Andi hesitated only briefly, but before she could register the thought, Gwen's hand was cupping her, moving against her with the most delicate touches. Andi moaned and rocked against Gwen. Nothing else mattered now. She needed Gwen's touch. She needed to feel her, taste her, and lose herself in the joy of her touch.

Gwen arched her back and groaned in pleasure as Andi's lips closed around her breast. She brushed her hand lightly along the thin layer of lace that separated her from Andi's delicate folds. She couldn't believe this was happening. Andi felt so wonderful she couldn't think. For a moment she wondered if she should slow things down. She wanted her first time with Andi to be special. She wanted to be special to Andi.

Andi pushed her weight into Gwen's hand and Gwen felt the wetness seep through the thin layer. She couldn't think anymore. The needs of her body overrode the warnings of her heart. She wanted to feel Andi. She wanted everything Andi would trust to give. Gwen pulled her hand away from Andi's sex, leaned forward, and slid Andi off her lap as she stood, and then pulled Andi into her arms.

"Oh, Gwen, please."

Gwen took both Andi's hands and placed them on her breasts, squeezing Andi's fingers into her flesh. When she felt Andi's finger and thumb close around her nipple, she moaned in pleasure as she looked down and met Andi's gaze. She could see the desire in Andi's eyes like liquid fire, and it made her clitoris jerk with a jolt of anticipation.

Gwen took Andi's hand and led her down the hallway to the bedroom. She kept her fingers laced firmly around Andi's, not wanting a moment of separation from her touch. As they reached the bed, Gwen reclaimed Andi's mouth with her own as her hands glided over her soft, smooth skin. With a snap of her fingers she released Andi's bra and slid the straps off her shoulders, allowing it to fall to the floor. She cupped one breast in her hand as she gently explored Andi's mouth with her tongue. She felt Andi tremble in her arms.

Gwen brushed her lips against Andi's ear, caressing the tender lobe between her teeth with a gentle tug. "Do you have any idea what you're doing to me?" she whispered hoarsely.

Andi shuddered. "Mmm. I know if you don't touch me soon, something in me is going to break."

Andi's fingers slid through Gwen's hair, pulling her against her, the kiss deepening into a ravenous frenzy of need. Gwen gasped breathlessly as Andi pulled her mouth from her only to lean down and take her breast into her mouth. The feel of Andi's wet, hot mouth on her made her legs go weak, and she clung to Andi as she moved her hips against her, seeking more contact.

Gently pulling away, Gwen slid her hands down Andi's chest, stroked her abdomen, and hooked her fingers in the waistband of Andi's shorts. She kneeled in front of Andi as she tugged the shorts over Andi's hips to the floor and pressed a kiss to Andi's stomach. She felt the muscles ripple beneath her touch as Andi's hands pulled at her hair and drew her face up. Gwen stood and kissed Andi before she stepped back and removed her own shorts and underwear in one stroke. She led Andi onto the bed and looked down at her near-naked body lying stretched out before her. She felt her heart would burst at the sight of such beauty. She ran her fingers along the band of lace that hugged Andi's waist and gently began to slide it over her hips until Andi was fully revealed to her.

"You are so incredibly beautiful," she whispered as she gazed reverently at the woman before her. "I want to look at you, touch you, know you everywhere."

"I want to feel you," Andi whispered in return.

Gwen lowered herself, sliding her thigh between Andi's legs, allowing their hips to join. When their breasts touched, Gwen was overwhelmed with the pleasure of the supple softness against her own. Andi's leg slid around her and pulled her closer.

In moments they were a tangle of arms and legs as their bodies became one.

Gwen was lost in the glorious pleasure of Andi's mouth on her body as Andi kissed and tasted every inch of her. Gwen relished the way Andi's body quivered against her. She was mesmerized by the feel of Andi, by the way she moved, by the subtle sounds of pleasure emanating from her as she devoured her. Gwen moaned when Andi's tongue stroked across her breast and slipped farther down her body. She ached to feel Andi's mouth on her. Her pleasure was building and surged through her like the tide, gently pushing and pulling against her, bringing her closer and closer to the edge. Gwen slipped her hand between Andi's legs and slid her fingers through the folds of her flesh, seeking the special place that would bring her to ecstasy. Andi answered by sliding her own hand between Gwen's legs, gently stroking her.

"Oh God, Andi, you feel so wonderful."

Gwen rocked against Andi's hand and she gasped as Andi entered her. Gwen was totally lost now. Gwen slid deeper into Andi until she felt the world melt away and all that mattered was the feel of her fingers swathed in Andi's succulent velvet flesh.

"I never thought I could feel this. I feel you in places inside me I had lost. Oh, Gwen," Andi whispered as she shifted her hips, allowing Gwen's fingers to slide deeper into her.

Gwen felt Andi shudder as she filled her. Pleasure surged through her with each stroke as she felt Andi close around her fingers. She heard the vulnerability in Andi's voice and was swept away by the tenderness in her touch. Gwen felt so alive, so connected and she didn't want the sensation to end. Andi began to tremble, and Gwen marveled at the delicate muscles tightening around her fingers.

"Oh, Gwen. God, oh yes. You feel so good." Andi's voice rasped against her ear, the heat of her breath intensifying the ecstasy until Gwen was pushed to the edge of her own pleasure, spilling out in wave after wave of orgasm.

Gwen cried out, "Oh God. Yes!"

Before Gwen could recover, Andi's mouth claimed her again. Her body still pulsed with the aftershocks of her orgasm. She never stilled her hands, and despite the release, she felt her hunger grow. She wanted to feel Andi melt in her hands, she wanted to taste her, hold her, and touch her everywhere and in every way.

She levered her arm around Andi's waist and lifted her shoulder, rolling them until Andi lay nestled beneath her. She grinned down at Andi. She dropped a kiss on her chin and slowly made her way down Andi's body, slowing sucking each breast, playing her hands along Andi's sides as she brushed kisses across her abdomen. She left wet trails as she nipped and kissed until she finally buried her face between Andi's legs, taking her into her mouth.

Andi gasped and her legs tensed as Gwen played her tongue along Andi's engorged clitoris. The sound urged Gwen to take more, to give more.

Gwen moaned in pleasure when her lips closed around Andi's clitoris. Andi feathered her hands in Gwen's hair, guiding her, holding her to her with desperate need. Gwen felt Andi begin to quiver as her orgasm built and the pleasure spilled out through her veins.

"Yes, oh please, yes," Andi whimpered. Gwen felt the first ripples of Andi's orgasm flow though her as her muscles tensed. Gwen relished each wave as Andi's body quivered and her hips thrust against her. Gwen waited until Andi's body quieted and the last ripples of pleasure subsided before drawing her head away and pressing soft kisses against Andi's belly.

Gwen rested her head against Andi's stomach. When the trembling stopped, Gwen slowly kissed her way back up Andi's body. She brushed her hand against Andi's face and trailed kisses from her ear across her cheek until she once again found her mouth.

Andi's fingers were like a cool breeze in July as they brushed across Gwen's chest, and a shiver ran through her. She pulled Andi close. The feel of Andi pressed against the length of her was the closest thing to heaven she could imagine.

"I don't think I have ever experienced anything so beautiful," Gwen murmured.

Andi nuzzled against Gwen, rubbing small circles along her abdomen with the tips of her fingers.

Gwen lay with Andi's head on her chest. She could feel the brush of Andi's breath skim across her skin. She cradled Andi in her arms, her fingers pressed lightly against her skin, feeling her heartbeat return to a more normal rhythm until her breathing deepened and she felt Andi drift into sleep.

Gwen lifted her hand and toyed with strands of Andi's hair. Andi's sudden aggression had taken her by surprise. As they'd made love Gwen felt something shift between them. It was like seeing another delicate layer of Andi for the first time, only this time Gwen thought Andi had dropped some of her defenses and allowed her inside. Andi had been so vulnerable to her, allowing Gwen to see her need, her want, and her tenderness. She had allowed Gwen to see her pleasure. Even now Andi seemed delicate in her arms, and Gwen felt a sense of protectiveness wash over her. This was so much more than a one-night stand, and she hoped Andi felt the same. She pressed a kiss to Andi's head, closed her eyes, and drifted off to sleep.

Chapter Seventeen

Bright shafts of sunlight streamed in through the window, beckoning Andi to wake. The birds singing joyously outside sounded like raucous laughter. A snuffling sound next to Andi's ear was the final signal to her brain that roused her from sleep.

Andi slowly opened her eyes to find a cold, wet nose only inches from her face. Big brown eyes looked back at her imploringly. Andi slowly took in the information being telegraphed to her brain by her body. There was a giant dog staring at her. She felt warm and glowingly satisfied. And Gwen's body was stretched out behind her, cradling her like a second skin. Gwen's arm draped lovingly across her waist, her hand cupped her breast, and the warm breath against her back told her that Gwen's face was nuzzled against her neck. The knowledge that she had just woken up in Gwen's arms made her smile.

She had rested well and was grateful for the tenderness that had lulled her to a peaceful sleep. She let her mind draw up the images of the night before, and her body tingled with the memory of Gwen's breast in her mouth, Gwen's lips on her, the exquisite sounds Gwen had made at the moment of her orgasm.

The faintest movement and a light kiss on her shoulder told her Gwen was awake.

"Good morning," Gwen said between kisses.

Andi rolled over to face her and cupped Gwen's face in her hand. She kissed her lightly on the lips. "Good morning."

"Umm…" Gwen murmured, rubbing her hand along Andi's waist and down her thigh.

Andi pressed closer, sliding her leg between Gwen's thighs and trailing her fingers down her bare chest. She lifted her face and kissed Gwen again. Now that she had made love to Gwen, the dam had been broken and she wanted more.

"I thought I dreamed you."

Gwen brushed Andi's hair away from her face and trailed her fingers down Andi's jaw in a touch so gentle it was as if Gwen were reaching into her soul.

"This is very real, Andi."

A whining noise began at the side of the bed and grew more insistent as they lay together, exploring each other. The sudden thump of two giant paws next to Gwen's head finally got their attention.

Gwen moaned. "She needs to go out. I'll be right back." Gwen pulled away from Andi and got up.

Andi watched Gwen move across the room and studied her still-naked body. The sight of Gwen's soft round breasts, flat stomach, and toned muscles sent a rush of arousal through her middle and a new surge of wetness slicked her thighs. After Gwen left the room, Andi got up and made her way to the bathroom. She had been swept up into a whirlwind. Being with Gwen was amazing and to her surprise the world hadn't ended. Andi smiled to herself. She knew things were not that simple, but in that moment nothing could subjugate her happiness. She wouldn't think of tomorrow. All she wanted was this perfect moment. Now that she was here, she wanted to savor each moment with Gwen.

When she returned, Gwen was waiting for her. She had put on a T-shirt and shorts and was holding a steaming hot cup of coffee, which she offered to Andi.

Andi took the mug and sat down on the edge of the bed, pulling the sheet up around herself.

Gwen tugged at the sheet. "Hmm…I liked you better without the covers."

Andi laughed. "No fair. You got dressed."

"That can easily be rectified."

Gwen stood on her knees in the middle of the bed and grabbed the T-shirt in both hands, pulling it up over her stomach. She moved slowly, watching Andi's response. She lifted it higher until her breasts were bare, then stretched her arms and pulled the shirt over her head.

Andi watched in rapt amazement as she studied Gwen's body. She could see the firm muscles in Gwen's stomach roll beneath the skin as Gwen's ribcage thrust outward when her arms extended above her head. Andi gasped, unable to hold back her awe.

"God, you're sexy."

Gwen flashed a predatory smile at the sound and quickly slid out of her shorts. Fully naked, she fell to her hands and knees and crawled across the bed like a tiger stalking her prey and playfully pulled at the sheet. Andi watched Gwen's breasts sway slightly with the movement. Every cell in her body craved Gwen.

Andi sat frozen, unable to move, barely able to breathe. The sight of Gwen captivated her. Her own body cried out to touch her, to feel the silky smoothness of her skin. Andi was suddenly ravenous in the deepest reaches of her being. She pulled her eyes away from Gwen long enough to put the mug down on the table next to the bed. With one movement of her hand, she let the sheet fall away as she reached for Gwen. As if released from a spell, she pressed her hands against Gwen's chest, pushing her back onto the bed. She threw her left leg over Gwen's hips and sat on top of her with her sex pressing into Gwen until she could feel the heat pouring from Gwen's body like a warm breath.

She ran her hands up the length of Gwen's torso and caressed her breasts as she rubbed herself rhythmically against Gwen.

"You are amazing," Gwen murmured. "And God, you feel good."

Gwen shifted beneath Andi, and Andi felt herself glide against Gwen's skin. Gwen began to move her hips and Andi moaned at the building pleasure. Gwen was hot and tense beneath her, and the rhythmic buck of Gwen's hips had her writhing in pleasure.

"Gwen. Oh, Gwen."

Andi pinched Gwen's nipple between her thumb and finger and felt it stiffen. She could feel Gwen's hands on her thighs as Gwen pushed and pulled against her to increase the pressure between their bodies.

Gwen moaned. The deep throaty sound inspired Andi's growing arousal making her swell with pleasure. Things were moving a little too fast. She wanted to slow this down and bask in the sounds, the feel, the taste of Gwen. Andi lifted and slid down Gwen's thighs until her mouth pressed gently into the soft triangle of hair. She could smell the sweet fragrance of Gwen's juices mingled with her own, and she knew how wet Gwen would be. She parted Gwen's lips with her tongue and was met with a flood of sweet nectar. She moaned her pleasure into Gwen, felt her tremble at the vibration of sound. Gwen's body seemed to echo with each stroke as Andi continued to lick and tease her with her tongue.

Andi pressed her hands against Gwen's thighs opening her farther as she engulfed her clitoris with her mouth and thrust her tongue into her. Gwen's hips began to move against her mouth. Andi wanted to devour Gwen. She wanted to discover all Gwen's secrets and tease and tame them until Gwen cried out in surrender.

Gwen's hand snaked down Andi's face, placing gentle strokes of encouragement upon Andi's cheek and into her hair. Andi reached for Gwen's hand, entwining their fingers. She felt the tension building as Gwen's thighs began to tremble, her grip tightened around her fingers, and the sounds of pleasure rose with each stroke of her tongue.

Andi was mesmerized by the joy she felt in pleasuring Gwen. With every stroke and every breath she melted into Gwen as if their very souls were joining. Andi felt Gwen's body stiffen, heard her gasp in pleasure. Andi wanted to hold back, wanted to draw this moment out so it would never end. Gwen shuddered and collapsed against the bed. Andi continued her gentle explorations of Gwen's body, savoring each current of orgasm that rippled through Gwen.

Gwen shifted away. "Please, Andi, let me feel you. I need to feel you inside me."

Only then did Andi take her mouth from Gwen with a moan of pleasure. Andi kissed her way back up Gwen's body, shifting to take Gwen in her arms. She met Gwen's lips as her fingers slipped into the wet folds, and she felt the tender walls engulf her. Gwen thrust her hips in answer. She felt Gwen's fingers cup her, then a finger parted her, gliding into her with eager strokes.

Andi gasped at the sudden fullness within her and sank hard against Gwen's hand. The momentum became feverish until Andi felt Gwen's muscles tighten around her fingers, and her own pleasure began to coil within her belly, filling her until she could feel the pressure behind her eyes, hear the pulse of her pleasure beating within her ears, rushing though her body until her skin tingled. She leaned forward and pressed her lips against the damp skin of Gwen's neck, biting down on the tense muscle. Her breasts rocked gently against Gwen's.

Gwen groaned and called out her name. Andi felt Gwen tremble and knew she was close.

"Come with me," Andi purred against Gwen's ear.

"Oh yes."

The pleasure coiled throughout her body as she felt her own sudden rise to orgasm, the sensation spiraling through her, opening, unfolding like the petals of a flower. The pressure behind her eyes blinded her to anything but the beautiful sensations flooding her body in a kaleidoscope of cascading color.

"Gwen...oh, Gwen."

At the sound of Andi's voice, Gwen stiffened and her orgasm erupted and she exploded into a million little pieces of golden light. She felt the world fade away until there was nothing but the feel of Andi's body against her and the fullness of Andi inside her. As if in answer to the pleasure surging though her, she felt Andi clamp down on her hand, holding her tightly within her, milking her fingers with shuddering jerks of her hips.

Andi cried out and Gwen felt Andi thrust deeper inside her, pushing her even higher. Gwen clutched at Andi's back, pulling her tighter against her, sharing the last shudders of her orgasm. In that moment Gwen felt completely connected to Andi and wanted to hold on to the moment forever. Being with Andi was beyond anything she had imagined.

A sheen of sweat coated Andi's back and tears ran from the corners of her eyes as she collapsed on top of Gwen.

"You are the most amazing woman," Gwen whispered through ragged breaths. "I don't think I have ever felt anything so wonderful in my life."

"Shhh…" Andi whispered almost inaudibly. "Just hold me. I want to listen to the beat of your heart so I can believe this is real."

"It is very real, Andi."

"I just didn't think I would ever feel this…"

Gwen held very still, not wanting to miss a single breath as she listened to Andi.

"You've made me feel things I've spent years pretending I didn't need. Thank you."

Gwen stroked Andi's arm and closed her eyes. She knew so little about Andi's past, but in this moment she didn't want anything more than to hold her in her arms.

"You are quite possibly the most beautiful woman I have ever met. After what you just did, I should be thanking you."

Gwen tightened her arms firmly around Andi and held her. Every moment she was with Andi she felt their connection grow. Could anything really be this perfect? Did she dare hope? She couldn't shake the gnawing fear that her night with Andi would be just that—one night—and she hated her insecurity. But Andi's admission went a long way in diminishing her fear that Andi saw their relationship as a superficial fling. Gwen felt like she and Andi were at a beginning of something powerful, something enduring. She closed her eyes and breathed in the scent of Andi's hair, wanting to memorize every detail of her. She was falling for Andi and nothing had ever felt so right. And Andi obviously felt the same.

❖

Andi smiled to herself. The night with Gwen had been amazing. It had been a long time since she had made love and she'd missed the soft feel of another woman's body against hers. Had it really been almost four years?

She hadn't expected Gwen to come along like a tropical storm that stirs the sand, rattles the rafters, and then quiets into a fresh new day. From the moment she had looked into those deep blue eyes, she had been captivated, no matter how she might have tried to convince herself otherwise. She found Gwen more than attractive—Gwen stirred something deep within her. Gwen was confident and strong willed, yet giving and tender. God, she was so tender. Andi laughed at herself. Just the thought of Gwen resulted in an immediate flash of heat that started at her core and spread like fire through her body.

Gwen rose and propped her elbow on the bed, her head resting in the palm of her hand. "What's so funny?"

Andi looked up at Gwen, wondering how much she should reveal. "I was just thinking about you and how wonderful you are." *How I could fall in love with you.* Andi knew she was standing on the edge of an emotional cliff and all she had to do was jump and her life would be transformed. She would have to tell Gwen the truth. It wouldn't be fair to bring her into her life not knowing the risks. She wanted to believe she could have love, that she could share her life with someone. Maybe it was time to stop living in the past. Maybe her future would be different if she would allow it to be.

"Tell me something about yourself that I don't know."

Andi laughed. "Like what? What do you want to know?"

"I don't know, anything. I want to know everything about you." Gwen thought for a moment, absently stroking her fingers through Andi's hair. "Tell me about your first love."

Andi grimaced. "You don't pick the easy stuff, do you?" This wasn't exactly her favorite story, but it was cute that Gwen was asking, and Andi was touched that it was something Gwen would want to know.

"Okay. Her name was Sharon Aldi. She was a girl in my high school who had been out since middle school. She was on the debate team and the student council and I thought she was a goddess. I even wanted to take her to prom."

"Why didn't you?" Gwen asked, grinning.

"My foster mother made me go with the neighbor boy, David Guinness. He was a year older than me and had had a crush on me since moving in to the neighborhood when he was thirteen. My foster mom wouldn't even hear of me going to prom with another girl."

"That sucks. What did you do?"

Andi pulled Gwen's hand between them, toying with her fingers as they talked.

"I went with David." She grimaced. "It was a complete disaster. By the time we reached the community center where the prom was being held, I had already removed his hand from my knee, pushed him away when he tried to kiss me, and had to drape my wrap backward across my chest to cover my cleavage. He wasn't able to keep his eyes off my breasts, and I was afraid he would drive the car off the road."

Gwen stopped smiling. "Sounds like a real jerk."

Andi laughed. "Yes, but Sharon got the better of him."

Gwen raised her eyebrows in an inquiring gesture.

"She confronted him during a dance and demanded that he remove his hand from my ass. When he refused, she removed it for him by punching him in the face." Andi smiled at the memory. "I think at that point, it was the highlight of my life."

Gwen laughed with Andi. "Good for her. What did you do?"

"We left together. She took me to a rented campsite at one of the parks where she had a pop-up camper. We drank wine coolers, kissed, and engaged in some heavy petting. I had never done anything with anyone and I was terrified of course."

"And did you two…"

Andi grinned. "Yes." She looked at their hands entwined and thought of how far away that time in her life seemed. "We had sex. It was awkward at first, but we quickly discovered the secrets we were seeking. It was the first time for both of us. It was our first time for everything."

"Sounds very romantic"

Andi giggled. "It was."

She thought back on the memory fondly. Over the years there had been other women of course, some she had loved, and some she had not. She had been hurt more times than she cared to remember. At thirty-five, she was surprised to find herself infatuated with another woman. But thinking of her feelings for Gwen, Andi knew this was much more than simple infatuation. She was on the verge of falling in love with Gwen, and that thought stirred her fear.

She promised herself not to have expectations, not to get too carried away. She promised she would just let things happen with Gwen. She would enjoy this time while she could, until Gwen discovered her secrets. Andi shuddered and tried to push the thought aside. She didn't want to think of the past. Right now, all she wanted to think about was Gwen in her arms. Right now, she wanted to believe she could have more.

CHAPTER EIGHTEEN

A ndi pushed Gwen away playfully and made her way to her post office box. The past few weeks had been amazing. Gwen had given her reason to hope, a reason to trust, a reason to surrender. The days and nights of exuberantly exploring Gwen's body, mind, and soul had quieted the demons from her past. She had never known such happiness and had slipped into a state of euphoria. Gwen was unlike any lover she had ever known, always attentive to her needs, so alert to her that it was as if Gwen could sometimes read her mind. Andi's earlier promises of taking things slow and protecting her heart were quickly discarded as she found herself unable to imagine her life without Gwen securely in her arms.

She gathered her mail and met Gwen at one of the large tables next to a recycle bin set up to discard unwanted junk mail. Halfway through her sorting, Andi froze. The address glared up at her with menacing force. The words Tennessee Department of Corrections were stamped boldly in the upper left hand corner of the envelope. Andi's blood went cold.

"What is it?" Gwen asked.

Andi felt the color drain from her face and felt the earth fall away from beneath her feet. She grasped the edge of the table for support, trying to keep her world from flying apart.

She took a steadying breath when she felt Gwen's hand close around her arm and felt Gwen's palm press against her back. She saw Gwen's gaze shift to the envelope in her hand and she quickly shuffled the letter in with the rest of the mail. She didn't want anything about that part of her life touching Gwen, as if ignoring her past could keep Gwen safe. Andi ground her teeth, steeling herself against the knot of fear that was gathering in her gut. She tried to convince herself that the letter was one of the routine correspondences she received once or twice a year. Surely it was nothing. Her heart ached, fearing that wasn't true. She didn't want to lose Gwen and the happiness they had found with each other, but there was nothing she wouldn't do to keep Gwen safe.

Gwen put a hand on Andi's shoulder. "Andi, are you all right? Is something wrong?"

"No, nothing. Nothing's wrong," Andi said, not meeting Gwen's eyes. "I just got a little dizzy for a minute. It's nothing."

"Andi?"

"I'll be all right,"Andi said, now meeting Gwen's eyes with the most reassuring gaze she could muster. "I just need to check on a few things. I'm going to get back to the shop. I'll talk to you later."

Andi brushed her hand along Gwen's forearm and gently entwined their fingers, but her hand was cold and sweaty, and when Gwen tried to tighten the embrace, Andi pulled away.

"I'll call you," Andi said and made her way hastily out the door.

When she arrived at the shop, Andi shut the door forcefully, the bell above the door clanging against the frame with a harsh clatter. She went to her office and threw the stack of mail into a pile at the corner of her desk. She stared at it. She didn't know what to do. As long as the envelope remained closed she could pretend everything was okay, that her life could go on as it was, that she and Gwen were safe.

No. Not now. She hadn't even told Gwen about her past. There was still so much she needed to do, so much she wasn't ready to give up. She closed the door to the office. She needed time to think.

To her relief, the day was hectic. She spent the afternoon sorting through the deliveries and restocking the shelves. She felt troubled and distracted, and she jumped every time the bell above the door rang when someone walked into the store. She was relieved when it came time to close up and go home for the evening.

Andi turned out the lights and closed and locked the door behind her. When she turned she was surprised to find Gwen waiting for her.

"Hi." Gwen's voice was calm and soothing, and Andi wanted to run to her and throw herself into her arms. She wanted to go back to believing they could be together. But fear and reality made her stand her ground. She had no idea what to do.

"I grabbed takeout and a bottle of wine. How about that relaxing evening we talked about earlier?"

Andi hesitated. She brushed her fingers to her lips, trying to fight back the sob that knotted in her throat. "I don't think I'm really up for company tonight. Can I take a rain check?"

Gwen's shoulders rose and fell as she pushed out a sigh. "Let me take you home then."

Andi couldn't bear the thought of sending Gwen away. "Okay."

Gwen stepped forward and took Andi's hand and led her to the SUV. Gwen was unusually quiet, and Andi waited for the questions she knew Gwen wanted to ask. But Gwen didn't ask. She just drove Andi home and walked her to the door.

When Andi opened the door, Gwen followed her inside. Andi stowed her bag and her papers on the table next to the door and turned to face Gwen.

"I'm sorry it isn't a good night for me. It's been a long day and I just need to be alone for a little while."

Andi glanced up and was shocked to find Gwen's gaze boring into her as if she were looking into her soul. Andi shivered.

Gwen took a step closer and framed her hands around Andi's face. "The last thing you need right now is to be alone."

The words caught Andi off guard, and she drew in a sharp breath before Gwen's mouth was on hers, claiming her. Andi was completely distracted by the consuming feel of Gwen's lips. Gwen felt so right. All Andi wanted to do in that moment was lose herself in the safety of Gwen's arms. How was she ever going to explain? How could she go back to a life without Gwen? That was a thought she couldn't bear to accept.

Gwen broke the connection and starred at Andi as if reading her mind.

"I know something's wrong. If you don't want to talk right now, that's okay. But I don't want you to run away from me every time something is bothering you. I need to know you trust me. I'm here, Andi. Whatever you need, I'm right here." Gwen pinched Andi's chin between her finger and thumb and pulled Andi close. "I can't bear it if you push me away."

Andi heard the insecurity in Gwen's voice and felt a stab of pain knowing she had put it there. She wanted to believe Gwen. She wanted to curl up beside her and tell her everything. But she couldn't bear the thought of Gwen pitying her.

"I do trust you, Gwen—"

Before Andi could protest, Gwen kissed her again. Gwen's mouth was possessive and consuming and Andi melted under the touch, all thoughts of the past pushed from her mind. Andi felt as if her body was being systematically disassembled and remolded in Gwen's hands. In that moment with Gwen, the world couldn't touch her. She melted into Gwen, needing one last touch, one last kiss, one last night to hold Gwen before facing the truth of her life.

Gwen was up early, unable to sleep. She made coffee and sat at the island in the kitchen, trying to make sense of the sudden change in Andi. She could feel Andi's withdrawal from her as clearly as she could feel her own heartbeat. She knew something was bothering Andi, and the fact that she wasn't talking wasn't a good sign. Even when they made love the night before, she could feel Andi pull away. It was as if an invisible wall was being erected between them. Maybe she was imagining things. Maybe there was some other explanation, but in her heart she feared she was losing Andi.

Gwen heard the shower come on and knew Andi was up. She opened the fridge and gathered the makings for breakfast. She wouldn't give up. Andi was too important.

Andi's hair was still wet from the shower when she entered the kitchen. Gwen studied her as she moved through the room. Her eyes seemed distant and tired, and some of the glow had gone from her face as if the joy was being drained from her.

"Good morning, beautiful." Gwen wrapped her arms around Andi's shoulders and held her against her. Andi felt fragile in her arms and Gwen's fear grew. "I thought I'd make you breakfast before I have to go to work."

"Thank you. You're an angel."

Gwen settled Andi onto a stool at the island and set a steaming cup of coffee in front of her before returning to the french toast.

She cocked her head and looked at Andi with a sheepish grin, trying to keep her tone light and playful. "We didn't talk much last night. Do you want to tell me what had you so upset yesterday?"

Andi stiffened and Gwen could see her trying to close off her emotions.

Gwen sat a plate of french toast in front of Andi.

When she spoke, Andi's voice was restrained, as if she was trying not to fall apart. "It's nothing really. I just have a few things I've been putting off that caught up with me."

Gwen took a sip of her coffee, trying to appear unaffected. "Anything I can do to help?"

Andi brushed her fingers across the back of Gwen's hand and smiled. "You already have."

Gwen felt only slightly reassured. She wanted to ask if they were okay but feared the answer. She forced a grin, leaned across the island, and planted a kiss on Andi's forehead. "Okay. I can see you aren't ready yet. I can wait." Gwen glanced at her watch. "Unfortunately I have to run. I'll only be gone a couple of days. I'll call you from the road if that's okay."

"You better."

❖

Andi reluctantly finished her breakfast and cleared away the dishes. She had seen the hurt and insecurity in Gwen's eyes, heard it in her voice. It had even been there in her touch. But there was nothing she could do to stop Gwen's pain, and it was tearing her apart. She was hurting the person most precious in her world.

When she ran out of ways to distract herself, Andi decided it was time to open the letter. She was glad she had put it away. She hadn't wanted Gwen to see it. She had wanted to pretend her life was normal for a little while longer, but her time was up now.

With trembling hands she riffled through the stack until she found what she was looking for. The letter bore the unmistakable seal of the State of Tennessee. Andi felt a little sick as she stared at the envelope. Biting her lower lip, she slid a finger beneath the seal and opened the letter. She held her breath as she read. Her heart raced as the words sank in. She had to read it several times over before she could believe the words.

Tears leaked from Andi's eyes onto the paper, the words made harsher by her pain. The illusions Andi had about her life shattered as the past caught up with her. In that instant she knew her life was over.

Chapter Nineteen

G wen called The Gourmet Pet when she couldn't reach Andi's private line. She hoped Andi would be there, but it was Morgan who answered the phone. Andi had left town for a few days and had left her to run the store. Morgan didn't know when Andi was coming back.

Gwen paced the small area around her tent. None of this made any sense. Andi hadn't said anything about out-of-town plans. But according to Morgan, Andi had left on the same day she had. What the hell was going on? Why hadn't Andi said anything? Was this Andi's way of telling her to get lost, or was something wrong? Hurt and dread warred in her mind.

Gwen fought back the nausea that had been threatening for the past two days. Something was wrong. She had felt it. She had wanted to push Andi to talk about it but was too afraid she would push Andi away. "Damn it." Gwen slammed her palm into the side of the work truck. She loaded her gear, then made sure the campsite was clean and the embers from her fire were fully extinguished. Gwen got in the truck and headed for home, hoping Andi would be there when she arrived.

❖

Gwen dropped Zeek at home and got her settled before going to Andi's. The house was dark and quiet, and as far as Gwen could tell through the window of the garage, the Jeep was gone. When she came back around to the front of the house, Mrs. Peterson was standing by her SUV.

"She's gone you know." Mrs. Peterson peered at Gwen through squinted eyes. "Left day before yesterday."

Gwen's voice was pleading when she spoke. "Did she say where she was going?"

"Nah. Just loaded up a bag and that cat and left." Mrs. Peterson eyed Gwen suspiciously for a moment. "You two have a fight or something?"

Gwen jerked, shocked by the question. "No. What made you think that?"

"I see the way that girl looks at you. Before you came here, she didn't let anyone around. Seemed lonely. Someone comes along and changes your life that much, must be pretty important. I thought maybe if you two had a fight, she might need some time to get her head straight."

Gwen was surprised by the frank assessment of her relationship with Andi. "We didn't have a fight. She just...disappeared."

Mrs. Peterson appeared thoughtful for a while as if she was considering whether or not to say something. "That girl's troubled. Seemed like she was always runnin' from something if you ask me. Whatever wounds she carries run deep. Reminds me of these feral cats around. They stay where they think they're safe enough but never let anyone close enough to touch."

Gwen's mind was racing. This was crazy. What the hell was going on? She leaned heavily against the side of the Land Rover. She didn't know what to do. Maybe Mrs. Peterson was right, maybe Andi was running. But what if Andi was running from her?

"Damn it. I've been over things in my head a million times. I can't think of anything I could have done wrong to make her run like this." Gwen ran her hand through her hair, desperate to grasp onto something that would help her understand what was happening. She thought of their last night together. Maybe Andi was trying to tell her it was over. She had pushed Andi into letting her stay even though she'd felt the distance Andi was trying to put between them.

Gwen rubbed her face with both hands. She was frustrated, worried, and scared and she had no idea what to do.

"Give her some time, Gwen. If something's spooked her, it may take her a while. But she'll be back." The old woman placed a rough, weathered hand on Gwen's arm and squeezed before ambling off down the drive.

Gwen went by Andi's house every day for the next week. Finally, she stopped by the police station to see if there had been any accident reports or any news they could tell her about Andi.

The young officer shrugged and shook his head. "Nothing here. Do you want to file a missing person's report?"

"No." Gwen felt her insides shaking at the thought that Andi might be missing, but everything said that Andi had planned this, and despite her growing unease, she was trying to respect Andi's space. But why didn't she say anything? Why just leave without a word? Maybe Andi didn't think it was any of her business. If that was the case, she didn't mean anything to Andi. That just couldn't be right. She could feel Andi in her heart.

Defeated, Gwen left the station and went by Andi's house again. She walked the property, peering into windows, but nothing had changed. As she came around the house to her car, a police cruiser pulled in behind her.

A young woman got out of the car and walked toward her with a stiff, confident air of authority. Gwen eyed the officer with hope and dread. Her uniform was unfamiliar. She was about five foot six with auburn hair and an athletic build. Her pretty face was marred by a scar that ran across her left cheekbone, and her golden brown eyes seemed to take in everything around her without ever breaking Gwen's gaze.

"Hello, can I help you?" Gwen asked.

The woman studied Gwen for a moment before answering in a curt professional manner. "I'm looking for Andrea Massey. Is this her residence?"

"Yes, this is her house. What's this about?" Gwen said with growing unease.

"I'm Officer Melissa Stuart. I need to speak with Andi. I know this must seem a little unsettling, but I'm an old friend."

Gwen tried to relax at the explanation, but something in her gut told her that—friend or not—this was not a social visit.

"And you would be…?"

"Gwen Palmer. I'm…" Gwen hesitated. What was she to Andi? Was she her girlfriend, her lover, or just someone Andi slept with? "I'm a friend."

Officer Stuart tilted her head to the side and raised an eyebrow knowingly.

Gwen shifted uncomfortably. "Andi isn't here right now."

The officer eyed Gwen, unasked questions on her face. Gwen didn't get the feeling the appraisal was suspicious. She seemed more curious than anything else.

"Do you know when she'll be back?"

The officer seemed to be taking in Gwen's fearful expression, and her hand crept up to rest on the heavy belt at her side.

Gwen let her eyes drift to the gun holstered on that belt.

"No. She left sometime last week. She didn't tell anyone where she was going." Gwen swallowed hard before asking the question that was needling her brain. "Is Andi in some kind of trouble?"

Officer Stuart shook her head. "No. I wouldn't say that. I just need to speak with her on a private matter."

Gwen decided to push a little harder to see what the officer would tell her. She needed some answers. Andi's disappearance and the officer's visit couldn't be a coincidence. Andi didn't have friends and she never had visitors. "You say you're a friend of Andi's, but I haven't seen you around here before. How do you know Andi?"

To her dismay the officer didn't take the bait. She just turned and looked around the house and gardens as if analyzing something.

Gwen felt like her head would burst if she didn't get some information soon. "Look, I know something's wrong. It isn't like Andi to just disappear like this. If she's in some kind of trouble, I want to help."

"Thank you," the officer replied as she stepped aside. "But like I said, I just need to talk to Andi about a personal matter."

Gwen was frustrated. Things just kept getting weirder and weirder, and she needed some answers.

The officer turned back and faced Gwen, her gaze curious, as if she were studying pieces of a puzzle. "You say Andi took off last week? Did she say where she was going?"

Gwen shrugged. "No. That's just it. She left without a word to anyone, except covering the shifts at the store. Look, I'm worried sick here. What the hell is going on?"

"I appreciate your concern and your help, but there really isn't anything I can tell you. I'm sure Andi's fine." The officer handed Gwen a card. "Here's my number. If…when Andi comes around, have her call me." The officer nodded her head, turned, and went back to her cruiser.

Gwen stared after the officer with a new pain growing in the pit of her stomach. She pulled out her cell phone and dialed Andi's number. The same as every day for the past week, the call went to voice mail. Gwen left a message, pleading with Andi to give her a call. She mentioned the officer and prayed it would be enough to get Andi to call her back. That new fact gave Gwen hope, but it also stung. Why wouldn't Andi at least return her calls? She had gone so far as to plead with Andi to let her know she was okay. But there had been nothing. At this point, she would feel better if Andi just called to tell her to get lost. Anything would be better than this not-knowing questioning limbo she was stuck in.

❖

Andi sat alone in the old rustic cabin only a few miles from her home. When she'd gathered her things, and she and Goliath had set off, she had no real idea where she was going. She needed time to think, and isolation was the only thing that made her feel safe. She stared at the phone as it vibrated on the small hand-hewn table. Gwen's number was vividly displayed on the screen. She reached for the phone, wanting to answer, needing to hear Gwen's voice, but afraid of not knowing what to say. How could she explain to Gwen that they were over?

A single buzz of the phone told her Gwen had left another message. Andi sighed and pushed the button to check the message.

Her heart ached at the anguish in Gwen's voice. She missed Gwen and hated that she was the cause of Gwen's pain.

Andi's hands clenched into fists and her stomach threatened to be sick when Gwen mentioned that an officer had been to her house. Oh, God, they'd found her already.

She said her name was Melissa Stewart and her card says she's with the Hamilton County Sheriff's Department. She said she was a friend of yours and needed to talk to you.

Andi's hands began to shake. Melissa was here? Of course she would come. She would have received the same letter. Christ, would any of this ever be over? Melissa would need her help getting through this, but Andi wasn't sure if she could do what she needed to do.

She paced the cabin. Gwen had met Melissa. What had Melissa told her? Gwen's voice sounded so desperate, so hurt. Andi sighed. Gwen was already drawn into this whether Andi liked it or not, and she was angry with herself for putting Gwen in harm's way. She stopped her pacing and looked out the cabin window into the woods, resigned to what she needed to do. Ignoring the problem wasn't going to make things any better. And it wasn't fair to keep hurting Gwen this way. It was time to go home.

The next evening Andi pulled her Jeep into the garage and gathered her assortment of things. She tucked Goliath under her arm and walked down the steps onto the back patio. She was shocked to find Gwen asleep on the lounge chair by the door. Her heart stopped at the sight of her. Andi didn't want to move. She just wanted to stop time and watch Gwen sleep. As long as she didn't wake Gwen, she wouldn't have to say the words that she knew would hurt her.

Goliath shifted uncomfortably and Andi moved to open the door and set him inside. When she did Gwen jerked awake.

"Andi?"

Andi slipped the cat inside and shut the door. She walked over to the lounge chair and sat next to Gwen. There were dark circles under her eyes, and her skin looked a little pale.

"What are you doing out here?" Andi asked.

Gwen frowned and reached for Andi's hand. "Waiting for you. I've been so worried about you."

"I'm sorry, Gwen." Tears began to cloud her eyes and she blinked rapidly trying to hold back the wave of emotion that threatened her resolve.

"What's going on? Where have you been?" Gwen's words were not accusing, simply hurt and filled with concern.

"I needed some time to clear my head. I'm sorry I worried you. I should have called."

"Why didn't you?" Gwen sat up, wincing at the stiffness in her shoulders. Something in Andi's expression told her that she wasn't going to like what Andi had to say.

When Andi didn't answer right away, Gwen put her hand on Andi's knee. "Talk to me. Please."

Andi swallowed and shifted away from Gwen. She drew in a trembling breath. "I can't do this anymore."

"Do what?"

"We can't go on seeing each other."

"What?" Gwen choked. "What the hell are you talking about?"

"Please, Gwen. I don't know how to explain. I just need some time to work some things out, and I need to be alone. I don't want to hurt you, but there is no other way."

"This is insane. You can't mean this." The thoughts swirling around in Gwen's head made her dizzy, and she desperately searched for some reasoning that would make sense of what was happening. "Does this have anything to do with that cop that was here? Is she your ex or something?"

A memory flashed in Gwen's mind and she flinched. Instantly she was back in a hotel room. Miranda striding to the door, her purse clenched in her hand, her hair perfect. The only sign of the sexual encounter that had taken place only minutes before was the rosy pink hue flushing her cheeks. Otherwise she was as poised and cold as a statue. *Really, Gwen, you couldn't possibly think this could go anywhere. What could you possibly offer me other than a good roll between the sheets?*

A car door slammed, sounding like it came from the drive. Andi and Gwen both jumped at the sound. A few moments later there was a persistent pounding on the front door. Andi moved to go inside and Gwen followed her, uninvited.

Andi peered out the glass. Her hand shook as she opened the door.

"Hello, Andi," the officer said in a low, sad voice. "Sorry to just drop in on you." She hesitated. "Can I come in?"

Andi still hadn't spoken, but she stepped aside and allowed the officer to enter her home.

Andi placed a hand on the arm of her chair as if to steady herself. "Melissa, what are you doing here?"

"I'm really sorry, Andi. I wanted to talk to you before…" The officer's—Melissa's—words broke off.

Gwen watched the exchange between her lover and this stranger, and the tension in the room was palpable. At first she'd thought they were friends, old lovers perhaps, but as she watched Andi struggle to maintain control, she realized something was very wrong.

"We received word—you'll probably be notified too." Melissa glanced at Gwen. "We need to talk. It can't wait."

"What's going on?" Gwen couldn't stand the suspense any longer, and her voice was hard with concern.

Andi looked at Gwen, uncertain what to say or do. Her new, perfect world had just been turned upside down, and she wasn't ready. She had wanted to believe the past was behind her and that she was safe and could be happy again. But as she took in Melissa's defeated look, she knew it had all been an illusion. She had been wrong to allow Gwen into her life. She had been wrong to bring another person into her dangerous, painful world.

Andi turned to Gwen. "Let's go outside."

Gwen nodded.

"Excuse us for a moment, Mel. I promise I'll be right back."

Andi led Gwen out onto the back porch, leaving Melissa alone in the house. Gwen followed without question.

"I know you don't understand any of this, and I'm sorry, but I can't explain everything right now. I need to ask you to give me some time. I have some things I need to talk to Melissa about. Some things I need to work through."

"You keep saying that. What *things*? Why can't you just tell me?"

Andi shook her head. There was too much to explain and she had run out of time.

"Gwen, please."

"You want me to leave," Gwen said, making it sound like a statement, not a question.

"Yes, for now. I'm sorry. Once I have a better idea what's going on, I'll explain everything."

"Please, Andi, just tell me what all this is about."

"I can't right now. It isn't easy to explain and it's a long story. Please don't make me do this now."

Gwen could see the pain clouding Andi's eyes, and she was desperate to understand. Andi was tying her hands, shutting her out. When Andi lifted a trembling hand to her face, Gwen felt her heart breaking. She wanted to put her arms around Andi and keep her safe, but that wasn't what Andi was asking of her.

"I don't want to leave you." She kissed Andi's lips and squeezed her trembling hand. "Whatever this is, I want to be here with you."

Gwen placed her hands on the sides of Andi's face and kissed her again. She felt as if a wall had suddenly been flung up between them, and she wanted to pound her fist against the surface, to scream for someone to tell her what was happening. She wanted Andi to let her in.

Andi's fingers wrapped around Gwen's wrists and pulled her hands away from her face. "I need you to go." Andi's eyes were filled with pain, and Gwen could see her resolve when she looked away, severing their connection. Gwen stood frozen, unable to believe what was happening. She felt Andi's hand slip away, and without another word, Andi turned and went back inside, leaving Gwen standing alone, peering after her.

Chapter Twenty

A ndi stepped back into her living room after walking Gwen out. She felt like something inside her was dying, and she had to push her way back into the room, her body heavy with fear and loss and regret.

Melissa looked up at her, meeting her gaze. "I'm so sorry, Andi. I just didn't want you to be alone when you found out. I didn't know what else to do."

"You're here about Kevin James. I got the letter last week."

Melissa nodded. "Yes. A parole hearing has been scheduled. They're considering letting him out."

It had only been four years since she had sat in a courtroom and told her horrific story of how Kevin James and Curtis Boyd had abducted her and Melissa. How she had been raped, Melissa beaten, and how Kevin James had tried to kill her. "How is that possible? It's too soon."

"I know. I thought the same thing. Nothing makes any sense to me. I've felt so confused since I got the letter." Melissa's voice was pained and her eyes were hollow and shadowed with haunted memories.

Hearing the pain in Melissa's voice, Andi felt her barriers break. She crossed the room to where Melissa sat. "I'm sorry," Andi whispered as she wrapped her arms around her.

Melissa let her head fall against Andi's shoulder. Andi vacillated between fear and relief to finally have contact with the one person who understood her pain. The one person who knew what the nightmares were about.

They sat together for a long time, just holding each other. Finally Andi broke the silence.

"He wasn't supposed to be eligible for parole for another ten years. Why do they want to let him out now?"

Melissa shrugged noncommittally. "Overcrowding, financial problems, who knows." Melissa's tone was flat and tired. "I've been trying to figure out an answer myself since receiving the notification of the hearing. But no matter how hard I try, nothing makes any sense."

Tears flooded Andi's vision, and she felt the familiar tightness in her throat as the memories of that terrible ordeal came flooding back. She felt Melissa's arms tighten around her, rocking her gently back and forth, trying to soothe her. Andi placed a shaky hand against Melissa's chest and pushed her away.

"Does Jimmy know?" Andi asked, looking into Melissa's eyes.

Melissa gave a slight nod, looking away from Andi for the first time.

Andi noticed the change in Melissa's posture and wondered again what else she was missing, what she didn't know. She felt impotent and helpless as she watched Melissa struggle.

"She wanted to come with me, but I needed to see you first. I needed to tell you that Jimmy and I are…"

"Oh," Andi whispered in understanding. Something settled inside her and some of her guilt was replaced with gratitude. "How long?"

Melissa looked up at Andi again, a new hope beginning to glow in her eyes.

"Two years."

Andi smiled faintly. "That's good."

"Really?"

Andi smiled, genuinely happy for Melissa. "I saw how she was with you through the trial. I guess I just assumed you would…"

Melissa stared at her.

Andi had refused to see Melissa or anyone else that had been a part of the ordeal surrounding Curtis Boyd and Kevin James and the attacks. It had been over three years since she had last seen her friend. Andi had tried to shut out the past and in doing so had left Melissa to deal with her demons alone.

"I'm glad she was there for you." Andi dropped her gaze and pulled away. "And I'm sorry I wasn't."

Andi tucked her hands securely under her thighs to hide the trembling.

"What can we do, Mel? I can't go through this again. Not this soon. I'm just starting to get my life back together. I can't let him destroy it all over again."

Melissa stood and placed both hands on Andi's shoulders and peered into her eyes. "Hey, slow down. We need to talk to Jimmy. She'll have some ideas about what to do."

Andi sighed in exasperation. "Okay. That sounds good."

"In the meantime, I'll do some digging and find out what's going on. Just don't panic. Just because they have a hearing, doesn't mean he'll get out. Just hang in there. We'll figure this out."

Andi still felt overwhelmed, but knowing she had Melissa's and Jimmy's help gave her hope. "Oh, Mel, I've missed you so much. I'm so sorry. I know this is hard for you too."

Melissa shrugged and wiped tears off her cheek. "I'm okay. It helps to see you." She dropped her head and looked at her shoes. "Most of the time, I just need to know you're okay."

"I understand. I really am so sorry, Mel. I just wasn't strong enough to face it. I had to have some time."

"I know."

Andi's head was spinning, and she felt like her life had been hijacked. She picked at her fingernails nervously and had worried a sore spot on the inside of her lip from biting it. When the silence seemed too much to handle, she clapped her hands on her knees and said with more strength than she felt, "Let's call Jimmy. We need a plan."

❖

By eight o'clock that evening, Gwen was worried sick. She kept telling herself to give Andi some time and space, that she would talk when she was ready, but she couldn't shake the feeling that something was terribly wrong.

The look on Andi's face when she had seen Melissa Stuart at her door had been one of shocked terror. Whatever had happened in the past, Gwen knew Andi was scared, and she felt helpless and shut out.

She thought about what she knew about Andi. She knew she didn't have any family, she owned her own business, stayed close to home, had few friends, and didn't like to talk about herself. She had grown up in the care of the state as an orphan and had no sustained relationships from her childhood.

They had talked vaguely about growing up gay, their past relationships, and college days. But even those discussions had been guarded, and Andi had often changed the subject when Gwen's questions became too personal. Andi's vague responses and avoidance hadn't seemed like a big deal at the time, but now took on new meaning.

Frustrated and worried, Gwen shook herself and decided it wouldn't help to speculate about what was going on. She knew her imagination would likely be worse than the truth. She had no choice but to wait for Andi. She had called three times and gotten no answer. What else was left for her to do besides wait?

Her heart ached. Andi's words came back to her over and over again, telling her it was over. Had Andi meant what she said? Did she really want to end their relationship?

Gwen cradled her head in her hands and rubbed her temples, trying to message the tension away before the headache could set in. She felt sick to her stomach and couldn't sit still. She didn't know how she could ever let Andi go. But how could she convince Andi to stay?

❖

A persistent knocking roused Andi from sleep. She had been up most of the night, trying to get a grip on what was happening. When she had finally gone to bed at four in the morning, she had slept fitfully. The dreams were back with a vengeance.

The knocking continued. She climbed out of bed, pulled on a pair of shorts and a T-shirt. She shuffled down the hall to the door.

"Who is it?" she asked cautiously.

She heard Gwen's voice answer from the other side of the door. "Your secret admirer, of course."

Andi closed her eyes and sighed, letting her head slump forward and rest on the cool wood of the door. She wasn't ready to see Gwen, but she knew it wasn't fair to avoid her either. Andi took a deep breath and let it out forcefully. Before she could change her mind, she opened the door.

Gwen swept past her into the room as soon as the door opened. "I brought brunch." Gwen carried a small cooler and a small grocery bag into the kitchen.

Andi didn't know what else to do, so she closed the door and followed Gwen. She took her usual seat at the island and watched Gwen unpack her treasures.

Gwen cheerfully put a plate in front of Andi and poured two mimosas. She piled fresh fruit and a sweet dipping sauce onto a plate and placed bagels into the toaster.

Despite her fear and anxiety, Andi thought the food looked and smelled good. There was something comforting about having Gwen here with her.

When the food was ready, Gwen sat down on the stool across from Andi and said in a sweet voice, "I missed you last night." Before Andi could think to respond, Gwen continued, "Not that I can't spend the night by myself. I'm a big girl, but the problem was that Zeek sat by the door most of the night whining. I think she was waiting for you. She wanted to come with me this morning, but I reminded her that Goliath didn't like to share, and she decided to stay home and have me tell you she said hello."

Andi smiled. She didn't know what she had done to deserve such a wonderful woman in her life. Then her smile fell as she realized she had to let Gwen go. She couldn't pretend the fairy tale was real any longer.

"That was smart of her, and very sweet," Andi said in a small voice.

Gwen studied Andi. The corners of her mouth curled in a playful grin as she took a bite of bagel. "You look like shit."

Andi scoffed. "Gee, thanks."

"You look like you haven't slept."

"You're right. I haven't slept much."

Gwen waited, but Andi didn't elaborate.

Gwen let out her breath and her shoulders slumped forward. "If you won't tell me what's going on, tell me one thing. Did you ever see us going anywhere, or was this all just a game? Was I just someone to pass the time with?"

Andi was shocked by the question. She knew she had been sending mixed signals and she had told Gwen it was over, but she'd never wanted Gwen to feel unimportant to her.

"What? No, Gwen. It isn't anything like that."

"Really? It feels that way to me right now. I've been here before. That's *my* story. I'm never good enough for the long run. I'm just a plaything that gets tossed aside when the new wears off."

Andi couldn't believe what she was hearing. Gwen was always so confident, so self-assured and gentle and kind and amazing. She couldn't imagine anyone treating her this way. But hadn't that been exactly what she had done? She'd brought Gwen into her life, and then abandoned her without trusting her with the truth. How did she expect Gwen to feel?

"Gwen, I've never felt that way about you. I tried to tell you from the beginning that my life was complicated. But this time with you has been more important to me than anything in my life. I wanted to believe it could last forever."

Gwen looked up, and Andi could see the pain as if it were a physical wound. "I'm sorry I was weird yesterday, and for disappearing last week, and for hurting you the way I have. Some things have come up and I didn't handle them very well. I wasn't expecting Melissa to show up like that yesterday either. I needed some time to process a few things."

"Are you in some kind of trouble, Andi? Is that why a police officer—"

"No, it isn't anything like that. Melissa really is a friend."

"I think it's time you tell me what's going on. I think I deserve that much."

Andi closed her eyes for a moment and drew in a long deep breath. Gwen was right. Gwen had trusted her enough to expose her fears. It was time for her to do the same.

"Let me make us a drink and I'll tell you everything."

Andi led Gwen into the living room. She sat with her back against one corner of the couch, a pillow clutched in her arms and her knees drawn to her chest. A glass of white wine sat on the table untouched.

Gwen took the seat next to Andi and folded one knee up on the couch. Facing Andi, she wrapped her fingers around Andi's hand. "Talk to me, Andi. What is it?"

Andi tried to find the right place to begin. It was important that Gwen understand how important she was to her. "We've only known each other for a couple of months, but I"—Andi's voice broke off—"I feel things for you that I've never really felt for anyone before. This week I realized just how important you are to me. I never wanted to hurt you, Gwen. That's part of the problem."

Gwen pulled Andi's hand from the pillow and laced their fingers together. She studied Andi intently.

"That's why I have to tell you these things now. But I'm afraid you'll…"

When Andi's voice broke off, Gwen stroked her thumb across the back of her hand. "I'm here, Andi. You can tell me anything."

"This won't be easy for me, but I want you to hear me out before you say anything."

Gwen nodded. "Okay."

"Before moving here I had a completely different life. I used to work as an in-home therapist in a rural community about two or three hours from here. I used to see kids at school, juvenile detention, court, and I sometimes worked with the families in the home. A few years ago a case went terribly wrong. I uncovered severe physical and sexual abuse of two teenage children, and they were removed from the home. The father, who was the perpetrator, ran from the police. He became fixated on me because he blamed me for taking his kids. That's how I met Melissa. She was a police officer in the town where I lived and she tried to protect me."

Andi paused, trying to gather the strength to tell her story, thankful for Gwen's patience. "When this man finally got to me, he went after Melissa as well. We didn't know at the time that he was working with one of the police officers in the town where the abuse happened. They had some kind of child pornography ring going on, and with the ties to the police department, they had intimate knowledge of my location. They came after us one night while we were on our way to Melissa's house. I had been going stir crazy and needed a break from the confines of my apartment. They managed to stage a car accident that pushed us off the road."

Andi felt like a weight had settled on her chest making it difficult to breathe. "It was really bad. The cop, Kevin James, had it in for both of us—in a small town, you cross paths with everyone eventually. He hated Melissa because she'd once filed a harassment claim against him. And he had it in for me because I had rebuffed his advances and because I was a lesbian. Kevin James beat Melissa and then made her watch when it was my turn. The father of the two children, Cutis Boyd, had me. He beat me and then forced me…" Andi's voice quavered and she could hardly form the words she needed to describe that horrible night. She squeezed her eyes shut and tried to focus on pulling air into her lungs.

Gwen hadn't moved. Andi was vaguely aware of her sitting next to her, and she tried to focus on the feel of Gwen's fingers laced around her own. Centering her. "I kept fighting him, trying to get free. They had taken us into the woods and Boyd had me on the ground. I could hear Melissa fighting, trying to get to me. Somehow, I managed to dislodge a rock from the dirt and I hit Boyd in the head with it. It was a lucky blow, catching him in the temple. His body went limp and he collapsed on top of me. At first I didn't know what had happened, I thought I'd knocked him out. I managed to push him off me. It wasn't until I saw the cold stare of his blank, dead eyes that I knew I'd killed him."

Andi couldn't control the shaking in her hands. Her voice sounded cold and distant to her own ears. She felt disconnected from her body, and she forced herself into a place within where she could numb herself from the pain. She pushed herself to continue. "Kevin James lost it when he saw what I'd done. In his rage he lost his focus on Melissa, and he came at me. Melissa managed to hit him and knock him down. While they struggled I managed to grab the gun Curtis Boyd had been holding on me. I wanted to shoot him. I wanted him to die for what he had done. But I couldn't pull the trigger."

Andi shuddered. "There was a long trial and Kevin James went to prison. I sued the police department. A settlement was reached, and then I ran. I couldn't deal with the memories of that place."

Andi paused as her guilt swelled. "I ran and left Melissa to deal with things on her own. I didn't even explain. I just left her. Eventually I ended up in Norris and started the store. It was easier to be here where no one knew me."

Andi felt Gwen's arms slide around her shoulders, pulling her tightly against her chest. Andi was relieved by the comfort and allowed herself to cry.

"Shhh," Gwen said. "You're safe now."

Andi pulled away. "No. I'm not safe. I'll never be safe again. They want to let him out." Her words were rushed and desperate. "He's coming up for early parole. He's promised to kill me when he gets out. As long as there's a possibility that he can get out, I'll never be safe."

Gwen clasped Andi's hand. "You don't have to be alone anymore, Andi. We'll make sure he doesn't get to you again."

Andi shook her head. "No one can promise that. He got to me before. He can do it again. The last time, he almost killed Melissa. I don't want anyone else to get hurt. I don't want *you* to get hurt. I'm sorry I didn't tell you. It wasn't fair for me to get close to you like this."

Realization slowly dawned on Gwen's face.

"Don't say that." Gwen squeezed Andi's hands. "Being with you is the most wonderful thing in my life. It doesn't matter about your past. I'm so terribly sorry you've had to endure this pain, Andi.

But even if I had known, it wouldn't have changed the way I feel about you. It wouldn't have changed us."

Andi wanted to believe Gwen. She sat with her legs stretched across Gwen's lap, an arm around her shoulder and her hand holding Gwen's. It felt good to tell her everything. She made everything feel different.

"For years now," Andi continued, "I shut everyone out of my life. I was so afraid. Then I met you and everything changed. You made me feel alive again, happy. I started to believe I could have the fairy tale. Then the letter came and Melissa showed up."

Gwen's grip on Andi's hand tightened again. "So you believe this man will try to hurt you again?"

"Yes." Andi looked into Gwen's eyes. She needed Gwen to understand the risks. "He's made threats while in prison." Andi sighed. "I don't know if this will ever be over. That's why I had to tell you. You need to know that being with me isn't safe. These things that have happened, the things I did, live in my skin like a virus."

"Andi, sweetheart, it drives me crazy to think of what you've been through. But what kind of person would I be if I let something like that keep you from me? Do you have any idea how many women are assaulted by men every year? It's a threat we all live with, all the time. There is nothing you could tell me that could change the way I feel about you."

Andi stared at Gwen in disbelief. She didn't know how she should feel. She vacillated between joy, disbelief, and fear. "But, Gwen, I killed a man."

Gwen nodded and pulled Andi closer. "Yes, you did. You did what you had to do to survive. You protected yourself and someone you loved. You only did what he made you do."

Andi rubbed her tear-streaked cheeks with the palms of her hands, growing more confident as Gwen's reassurances sank in. Somehow hearing this from someone who wasn't involved in the trauma made her feel less blame, less shame, and less guilt.

"What happens if he gets out? Don't you see? I can't live with the thought of him hurting you. I won't let him hurt you."

"Then we'll deal with it."

"You don't know what you're saying, Gwen."

"Yes, I do, Andi. I understand that I've fallen in love with you. I want more than anything to have you in my life, always. I won't let that crazy beast take you away from me. Not now, not ever."

Andi's heart ached with the love she had for Gwen. She had waited her entire life to hear those words, but now they were bittersweet. Tears welled in her eyes and her body trembled from holding back so much. She pushed forward and wrapped her arms around Gwen. For the first time in her life, she wasn't alone.

"I love you, Andi. I love you," Gwen said over and over again as she rocked Andi in her arms. "I can't live without you. Please promise me you won't shut me out."

Andi shook her head. "No. I can't."

Suddenly remembering her talk with Melissa, Andi pulled her head back and peered down at Gwen. "There's one more thing."

Gwen's hands twisted in Andi's shirt along her back. "Anything."

"I need to go out of town this weekend to meet with Melissa and my attorney. We're going to figure out a plan to try to block the parole." Andi studied Gwen closely, to read her reaction. "Will you come with me?"

Gwen's eyes lit up with relief. "Of course I will." She buried herself in Andi's neck.

Relief washed over Andi and she cradled Gwen's head against her.

"Come on, you need some rest," Gwen whispered.

Andi nodded, too tired to argue. She let Gwen lead her to the bedroom.

Gwen pulled back the covers as Andi slid beneath the cool sheets. Then Gwen slid into bed beside Andi, pressing their bodies together.

Andi curled into Gwen's embrace, resting her head on Gwen's chest, one hand clinging to her waist. Nothing had turned out the way she expected. She still wanted to keep Gwen safe, but she realized for the first time that she could only keep her safe by holding her close. She had to protect Gwen's life, but she would also protect her heart.

CHAPTER TWENTY-ONE

The sun was just coming up as Andi gathered the last of her things and set her bag by the door. Gwen would be arriving any minute. Everything was so quiet and peaceful in the still of the morning, and Andi was thankful for the moment of peace. She wished she could just stop time and never have to face the demons that were uprooting her life.

When she'd first received the letter about the parole hearing, she'd wanted to run, but Gwen had shown her she had too many reasons to stay. It was time to face her past so she could have a future.

But she had to admit she was anxious about going back to where it had all started. Andi looked up to see Gwen pulling into the drive, and some of her worry lifted. As much as she wanted to protect Gwen from the problems before her, she was glad to have her by her side. She would face hell itself if she had to, if it would keep Gwen safe.

Andi opened the door for Gwen as she bounded up the steps.

Gwen smiled. "Hey. That didn't take too long did it?"

Andi threaded her arms around Gwen's neck and planted a light kiss on her lips. "Not too long at all. Is everything okay with Zeek?"

"She's all set. Morgan will have her spoiled rotten by the time we get back."

"Good. The best dog is a spoiled dog."

Gwen laughed. "If you say so. Are you ready?"

Andi sighed. "As ready as I'll ever be. How about you? Are you sure you want to do this?" She was anxious and needed reassurance that Gwen would really go through this with her.

Gwen brushed her thumb across Andi's cheek. "Definitely."

Gwen put the Land Rover into gear and backed out of the drive. "So, tell me about this meeting were going to. Who'll be there, what's the goal, that sort of thing."

Andi turned sideways in her seat so she could face Gwen. "Well, you already met Melissa, sort of. She'll be there of course. I'm looking forward to seeing her and Jimmy together. They're a couple now."

"And Jimmy is your attorney?"

"Yes. I don't know how Melissa or I could have gotten through the trial without her. I'm glad she's been there for Mel." Andi looked away. She felt guilty for not being a better friend, for not being there to help Melissa deal with what they had been through.

"So in a way this is a social visit too. You guys get to catch up a little and regroup."

"Yeah, something like that." Andi smiled and looked back at Gwen. "Hopefully they'll have some news for us, and Jimmy will have a plan." She prayed there was something, some way to keep Kevin James from reaching her again.

The two-hour drive passed quickly as they talked, and Andi was surprised to see the city emerging from the mountains far sooner than she had expected. It seemed strange to be revisiting this chapter of her life, and she wondered what price she would have to pay this time, what sacrifices she would have to make.

Andi smiled when Melissa answered the door. Despite the memories and the pain, it would be good to see her and Jimmy again, and she was excited for Gwen to get to know her friends.

"Hey, you made it." Melissa pulled Andi through the door by her hand and hugged her. She turned to Gwen with a smile. "Hello, Gwen. It's good to see you again. I'm glad you were able to make it." She shot a grin at Andi before shaking Gwen's hand.

"Come on inside, Jimmy's out on the back deck."

Andi reached for Gwen's hand and laced their fingers together. Gwen looked into her eyes and smiled reassuringly before following

Melissa through the house. The space was open and very modern, and Andi wondered whose taste the house reflected most. If she had to guess, this was mostly Jimmy. Melissa was a bit more reserved and somewhat understated. Jimmy was the all out there, show your cards kind of girl.

As soon as they stepped through the open glass doors to the deck, Jimmy stood, her six-foot-four frame towering over them all. Despite her imposing presence, her smile was warm and disarming. She leaned down and kissed Andi's cheek.

"Damn, it's good to see you, Andi."

Andi placed her hand on Jimmy's arm and smiled. "You too."

Jimmy looked past Andi to Gwen. "And who do we have here?" she said, offering her hand in welcome.

Andi felt the warmth spread through her cheeks as she tried to find the word to describe Gwen's place in her life. "This is Gwen," she offered, the pride evident in her voice. "Gwen, this is Jimmy."

Gwen took Jimmy's hand, and Andi was pleased by Gwen's relaxed, open posture and Jimmy's genuine welcome. Some part of Andi unwound as she felt her two worlds connect for the first time. These were the three women she cared for most in the world, and it was important to her that they all got along. She laughed to herself for ever questioning that they would all be anything but friends.

They talked most of the day and got caught up on the changes in their lives since Andi had left. She could see the shimmers of pain in Melissa's eyes as they talked, and she recognized the hollow stares that often made Melissa seem aloof and distant. Only Andi knew the demons that Melissa wrestled with in her thoughts and memories.

Mustering all her courage, Andi finally dared to bring up the reason for their reunion.

"So, what do we know about this parole hearing, and what do we need to do about it?"

Jimmy met Andi's eyes and squared her shoulders as if readying for a fight, a posture Andi recognized from endless days sitting next to Jimmy in the courtroom.

"Well, it's part formality but does present a real risk. We all have to decide what we're willing to do. The best thing would be for everyone to appear at the hearing and testify as to why Kevin James is still dangerous and should be considered a threat to society. We already have documentation that he has continued to make threats against you, Andi, while he's been in prison and has shown no remorse for what he did."

Melissa spoke up at this point, her voice cold and bitter. "The state is trying to tighten the belt on the budget, and this is one way to do it. They're trying to early release as many people as they can without negligent risk to the community. We have to convince them that Kevin James is still dangerous and that releasing him goes beyond negligent. I don't even know how the bastard made the list."

"Do you really think he could get out?" Andi asked, the fear thick on her tongue.

"It's possible," Jimmy said, "but not likely. These are special circumstances, and I can't see the state wanting the responsibility for any future crimes that could result from his release. But like I said, that depends on everyone being ready to fight. We can ask for letters from people involved in the case, victims of course, authority figures in the community, psychologists working with James, and so on. We have to protest his release. The district attorney believes we can stop the parole."

Jimmy studied Andi, her dark eyes soft with empathy. "I'm sorry, Andi. I know this is difficult for you."

Andi stared at her hands, clasped tightly in front of her on the table. A long silence stretched between them. She was angry and scared and she hated all of it. Then she felt Gwen's hand slide onto her thigh with a reassuring squeeze. She was grateful for the contact and the love she felt in the simple gesture. She looked to Gwen, and there was no hint of pity in her gaze, only comfort and concern.

Andi smiled and took Gwen's hand, giving it a return squeeze.

Melissa was the first to break the silence. "I'll be there with you if you want to testify, Andi. I know we can get through this together."

Andi looked up into Melissa's sad eyes, hearing the plea in her voice. She knew Melissa had never forgiven herself. She still carried the guilt that wasn't hers to shoulder.

"I don't know if I can face him again. All this time I've been trying to purge the image of his face from my mind. I can't let him back inside my head."

Andi's voice started to tremble and her insides were shaking. When Jimmy reached out for her hand, Andi flinched away from the contact, afraid that even the simplest touch would make her shatter like an already-fractured piece of glass.

"Okay," Jimmy said, leaning back in her chair to offer Andi some space. "I'll get the ball rolling on the letters for the hearing. That means you two will need to write out statements as well. We have to put a stop to all of this." She clasped her hands in front of her with an air of finality. She grinned. "For now, what's for dinner?"

Andi and Melissa both looked at Jimmy as if she were suddenly speaking a foreign language. Andi blinked a few times, trying to clear the torrent of thoughts from her mind, not able to process the sudden change in subject.

"Steak," Gwen said with a dramatic rub of her stomach.

"Lasagna," Melissa answered, "or sushi."

Andi smiled in understanding. It was time to change the subject.

There was no further discussion about Kevin James over dinner. The business at hand was handled, and now it was time to fill in the blanks of three years of their lives. Andi was oddly relaxed as she studied the two women who had been such an integral part of her life, but that she now knew very little about. She was unprepared when the conversation turned to her.

"So, Andi, what's new in your life?"

Andi didn't answer for a moment, feeling her tongue swell within her mouth, making it difficult to form words. A loud ringing in her ears permeated her thoughts so that she forgot what had just been said. "I'm sorry, what was your question?"

Jimmy put her elbows on the table and leaned in so she held Andi's full attention. "I asked, what's new in your life? You said you were finally getting your life back on track when we spoke on the phone."

Andi felt the heat spread from her chest, up her neck, and into her face. She cleared her throat and took a long drink of water.

She glanced at Gwen and was embarrassed by the heat spreading through her.

"Well I opened my own business. I spent the last three years just trying to act normal and start over."

"Yeah. So, how did you and Gwen meet? Have you known each other long?"

To Andi's surprise, Gwen answered the question. "Andi and I just met this summer, after Andi had a run-in with my dog. I pretty much followed her around for a few weeks after that, trying to convince her to go out with me."

Andi couldn't repress her smile. The memory of meeting Gwen still made her shake her head at the strangeness of the whole event. As Gwen continued to talk, Andi began to realize once again how important Gwen had become in her life. She couldn't imagine her life without her. It had become hard to remember what her life had been like before meeting Gwen. The life she had once found peaceful and safe, now just seemed empty. Gwen had filled her life with hope, laughter, excitement, adventure, unimaginable good sex, and unexpected love.

Andi felt herself blush at the thought.

"Are you in love with her?" Melissa asked Gwen, her voice gentle.

Gwen looked pointedly at Melissa. "Yes. I am totally and completely in love with her." She turned to Andi. "She's everything to me."

Andi was still gazing at Gwen, in awe of her openness and the certainty in her declaration. Her heart swelled with happiness.

"And what about you, Andi? Has Gwen here managed to steal your heart as well?"

"Mel," Jimmy said with a warning tone.

Andi thought about it for a moment and smiled. She hadn't told Gwen she loved her and wouldn't make her first declaration in public, even in front of friends. But she knew she couldn't deny it. She fell a little deeper in love with Gwen every day. "Hmm...she's definitely very special to me." She took another sip of her water, watching Gwen's reactions.

Gwen smiled, lifted Andi's hand to her lips, and kissed the backs of her fingers. Andi suddenly wanted to be alone with Gwen. These were feelings she wasn't ready to explore with anyone but Gwen. But she waited for Melissa to volley the next round of questions.

At last Jimmy interrupted the conversation, stretching out her long arms over her head. "I think I'll see if I can convince Gwen here to go for a walk with me so you two can catch up. What do you say, Gwen?"

Gwen nodded. "Sounds perfect."

Jimmy got up from her chair and leaned down to kiss Andi on the cheek. "It's really good to see you, Andi. We've missed you."

Andi stood and kissed her back, wrapping her arms lightly around her shoulders. "Thank you—for everything."

Jimmy grinned and winked at her before turning her attention to Melissa. "I'll see you in a bit. Take your time." She leaned down and kissed Melissa tenderly on the lips.

Andi could see the love vibrate between them, and she was happy they had each other. She was glad someone had been there for Melissa when she hadn't had the strength to be there herself.

Gwen brushed her fingers along Andi's back as she passed, pausing only a moment to drop a kiss on top of her head. "See you in a bit."

Andi smiled as Gwen and Jimmy left the room together. She was happy at how well they were getting along. There was no telling what trouble those two could get into together. They were like two peas in a pod.

It amazed her how much peace she felt at that moment when there was so much danger looming ahead of her.

Chapter Twenty-two

Melissa and Andi made their way to the back deck where they sipped beer and gazed up at the stars.

"So," Melissa started after a long silence, "you've been a little quiet this evening. Are you doing okay?"

Andi realized Melissa had waited until they were alone to ask the serious questions. She knew Andi wouldn't have wanted to talk openly in front of Jimmy. She saw the worry in Melissa's eyes.

"I'm as okay as I can be." She paused. "I think I had started to believe I could put all this behind me. I just wanted to live a normal life."

"You still can, Andi, nothing has changed."

"Hasn't it? For the rest of my life I'll be looking over my shoulder. I'll never be certain he won't come after me. Even if he doesn't get out this time, it'll happen eventually."

"No one has any guarantee that something bad won't happen, Andi. But you can't stop living. You can't just sit around and wait for something that may never come."

Andi picked at the label on her beer bottle. "It's all so crazy. We weren't even supposed to have to think about this for years."

"I know. But we're going to put a stop to it. He won't get out."

"I hope you're right." Andi sighed and took a drink of her beer.

Melissa regarded her for a long while, and the attention made Andi self-conscious.

"What?"

Melissa pursed her lips as if trying to decide if she should say something. "You and Gwen look really good together. I can tell she's crazy about you. God, could she be any more gorgeous?"

Andi smiled. "She is, isn't she?"

"She seems to be taking this pretty well. Does she know everything?"

"Most of it. She knows about Boyd and James."

Melissa was studying her and it made Andi uneasy.

"What about the other stuff?"

Andi didn't answer. She looked off into the darkness, not wanting to admit her cowardice.

Melissa sat up in her chair and looked hard at Andi. "You haven't told her, have you?"

Andi met Melissa's gaze. "No."

"Andi, you have to tell her. Let her be there for you," Melissa said, sounding incredulous.

Andi closed her eyes tight and thought of Gwen. She liked having someone in her life who didn't know about her past. She felt more normal not having Gwen look at her and see everything. By telling Gwen her story, she would allow the evil to soil the purity of their relationship and the innocence would be lost.

She tried to explain the inexplicable. "Maybe if all this had happened when we thought it would, I would have had time to build a life with Gwen I couldn't let go of, but not now. I can't let anyone else get hurt because of me. We're just getting started, Mel. This isn't something I can just tell her."

"You're afraid she'll leave you the way J.C. did."

Andi's hands clenched at the mention of J.C.'s name. Gwen was nothing like J.C. She was so much more.

"She's different, but yes. I know she would never walk out on me the way J.C. did, but yes, I'm afraid I'll lose her. I'm afraid all this will be too much to handle or, worse, that James will get to her. I couldn't live with myself if anything happened to her."

Melissa reached out and placed a hand on Andi's arm. "Oh, sweetheart, Gwen will understand. But you have to tell her. I saw the way she looked at you. She loves you, Andi."

Andi shook her head. "I just don't know."

"Do you trust her?"

Andi sighed. "Yes."

"Okay then, tell her. Wouldn't you want to know how to help her if things were turned around?"

Andi knew Melissa was right, but she had no idea how to tell Gwen the truth. The whole truth.

"You say you want a normal life. Well, that means letting people into your life, letting people love you, and letting them help."

Andi dropped her head back onto the seat with a thump. "I let you in and look what happened."

"You were not responsible for what happened to me, Andi. I can't tell you how much I wish things had been different."

Melissa dropped her gaze. Andi could see the muscle in Melissa's jaw jerk as her teeth clenched.

"Hey, we can't go back there," Andi said, getting up to go sit next to Melissa. She put her arm around her shoulder.

"I know," Melissa said, her voice weak as she glanced up and met Andi's eyes. "But I've missed you."

"I know," Andi said with a sad smile. "I'm sorry I ran away."

They were silent for a while as they drank their beer and watched the stars.

Andi was the first to break the silence this time. "How do you get through it, Mel? How do you make the nightmares stop?"

Melissa's gaze burned into Andi, all the emotions of the past four years pouring out like a tsunami. "I don't know. Sometimes I spend hours talking to Jimmy. Sometimes I don't sleep at all. I don't know that the nightmares will ever stop. There are times when the memories are so vivid it's like it's happening all over again."

"Yeah. I know."

"When I saw what they did to you, it killed me. What they did to me was nothing compared to seeing you hurt that way."

"Mel."

"Don't worry. I'm okay. Things happened so fast and there was so much going on. You were vulnerable, and I never should have let things get out of hand. If I had done my job and protected you better, you wouldn't have been hurt. I didn't blame you for leaving."

"You're wrong, Mel." Andi took Melissa's hand. "You did everything you could. What happened was not your fault. I ran because I couldn't face you, knowing that every time you looked at me, you would see what he did. I thought it would be best if I wasn't around as a constant reminder of what happened. If it wasn't for me, they never would have hurt you." Andi's last words came out strangled, and she swallowed, trying to hold back her emotions.

Melissa stared at Andi, her expression a mixture of hurt and surprise.

Andi squeezed Melissa's hand. "After everything you had been through because of me, I knew you would never be able to look at me the same way. I would always be a reminder to you of the horror and pain. I thought it would be better for you if I just…disappeared."

Once the words had started, all her feelings poured out. Andi couldn't hold anything back. "I felt so much shame and guilt. Throughout the trial I could hardly look at you because I could still hear your screams in my head. I was reliving every minute of that night, and I didn't want to be that reminder for you."

"Oh, Andi." Tears spilled from Melissa's eyes and ran down her cheeks. She knelt in front of Andi. "I'm so sorry, Andi."

Andi leaned in to Melissa and wrapped her arms around her. "I'm sorry too, Mel. I'm sorry I was a coward."

Melissa's lips brushed Andi's cheek before she buried her face in Andi's shoulder and cried. They held each other, mourning their loss and trying to heal the hurt with a small portion of understanding. When they broke apart, Andi stroked Melissa's cheek with the back of her hand.

Melissa gave her a half-crooked smile and sighed. "I can't believe we never talked about any of this."

Andi shook her head. "So much has changed. You have Jimmy now."

"And you have Gwen," Melissa said with a grin. "What do we do now?"

Andi's eyes burned from the remains of her tears. "We fight back."

"See, this is exactly why you have to tell Gwen everything. Just be honest with her. You're going to need her."

Andi shrugged apologetically. "I just can't."

"Shit!" Melissa pulled away from Andi suddenly as she stood and began to pace.

"Mel?" Andi was confused by Mel's sudden change. Was she having a panic attack? Had Andi somehow triggered it?

"Give me a minute." Melissa waved her hands in the air as if she was fighting to breathe. Her pace was frantic and she wouldn't make eye contact with Andi.

Andi stood and approached Melissa, placing a hand on each of her shoulders. Melissa tried to turn away, but Andi held her tight in her grip.

"Mel." Andi's voice was commanding and it made Melissa stop and look at her. "Talk to me."

Melissa's voice trembled. "When you left, you left me believing I failed you."

Andi's heart sank. "I'm sorry, Mel. I thought I was doing the right thing. I couldn't ask you to forgive me. I was falling apart. You were trying to heal and I couldn't ask you to take on my part in this too."

Melissa pushed Andi away, her eyes hot and glaring, burning into Andi. "Damn it, Andi, that was my decision to make, not yours, and it isn't yours now. Gwen deserves the truth! She needs to choose whether to stay or go, or your *kindness* will haunt her forever. Stop trying to figure out what everyone else thinks, needs, or feels. Just let us in."

Andi stood dumbfounded. She had never considered that Melissa would have made a different choice. Would Gwen?

❖

Gwen watched Andi get ready for bed. She had been distant and distracted since her time alone with Melissa, and Gwen was beginning to worry. She was aching for some way to ease Andi's unrest and somehow make her nightmare end.

"Is something wrong?" Gwen asked as Andi rearranged her clothes in the drawer for the third time.

Andi shook her head without looking up. "No. I just have a lot on my mind."

"Why don't you come to bed and tell me about it?"

Gwen was hopeful when Andi closed the drawer she had been studying and made her way to the bed. She stopped just short of Gwen. She looked down at the bedcovers, avoiding eye contact. When Andi didn't move and didn't say anything, Gwen sat up and took Andi's hand.

"Hey. What's going on with you? Talk to me." She brushed her thumb across the back of Andi's hand. "Did something happen between you and Melissa?"

Andi's eyes flickered with pain as she glanced up at Gwen. "I feel like I keep messing things up for the people I care about."

Gwen gently pulled Andi onto the bed and wrapped her in her arms. "None of this is your fault, sweetie. You're a good person who got hurt by some really bad men. You didn't do anything wrong."

Gwen felt Andi's head shake against her shoulder. "Melissa never would have been hurt if it wasn't for me." Andi went rigid against her.

"Andi…"

"Then I left her to deal with it all on her own. I let her go all this time believing she had let me down. She thinks she failed me."

Gwen closed her eyes against the pain she felt for Andi. She couldn't imagine what she and Melissa had gone through. "You didn't know that. You were doing the best you could to take care of yourself."

"No. I was just running. I wasn't taking care of anything."

Gwen held Andi tighter, brushing her fingers gently though her hair. "Well, you're taking care of things now. Maybe you both needed this time to deal with things on your own before you could be ready to face this one last fight together."

Andi lifted her head and looked at Gwen. Her expression was so sad, so lost that Gwen became afraid. "What?"

"If you had known my story from the beginning, would you still be here?"

Gwen didn't hesitate. "Yes. I believe I would. Our story might have started out differently if you had told me about your past, but

I think I fell in love with you on that very first day, standing in my kitchen. It happened when I was holding your hand under the water and you let me work the rocks and rubble out of the cut on your palm. You were so trusting and patient despite the obvious pain you were in. And you were just so damn beautiful. I think I would have loved you no matter what you told me."

The look in Andi's eyes was so desperate, so wounded, that Gwen realized this was about more than just the issues with Kevin James. "Talk to me, Andi. Tell me what's upsetting you. What happened in your life that makes it so hard for you to believe you can be loved?"

Andi stared at Gwen.

"I don't have a family," Andi started. "From the age of eleven I was an orphan. I grew up as a ward of the state."

Gwen sat holding Andi's hand, listening intently.

"I've told you a little about my time in foster care. It wasn't easy to place a child of my age, so I bounced from home to home and spent a lot of time in group homes as a teenager." Andi's eyes had grown distant as she recalled her childhood.

"Unlike most of the children I met, I threw myself into my schoolwork. I didn't like most of the other kids, who were often in custody because of behavioral issues. I just didn't fit in. Every time I got close to one of the girls, they would be moved to another placement, or I would. When I turned eighteen, I opted to stay in custody for the maximum allotted time so I could attend college and obtain a degree. I learned pretty early on to keep my sexuality a secret for the most part, except for prom."

Gwen smiled, and she was glad Andi had shared what seemed to have been the one happy moment of her teen years with her.

Andi continued her story. "Prom was great, but when my foster mother found out she had the state move me. I came out when I was nineteen. I met a young woman in college who was in my criminal justice class. We were alone in my room one evening when my case worker decided to make a surprise visit. Mae, the girl I was seeing, was sporting a black T-shirt that read *Lipstick Lesbian* on the front, and I had a love bite on my neck."

Gwen chuckled. But Andi didn't even crack a smile.

"Mrs. Anders, my case worker, was not pleased by the situation and placed me on a sort of probation. She kept a painfully close eye on me. I couldn't have visitors in my room and I had a nine o'clock curfew. I even had to check in with the RA every evening. Needless to say, Mae lost interest pretty quickly. After college I threw myself into my work and earned my master's degree. Although I was finally free to live my life, I was distant and guarded and didn't make friends easily. Traits you've pointed out are still an issue."

Andi and Gwen continued to talk for the next two hours, both sharing stories of heartbreak and vanished dreams. Gwen felt like she was getting a rare glimpse into the heart of the woman she loved. She wanted to know everything. The more Andi talked, the more Gwen understood about Andi's emotional distance and reluctance to get close to people. She had been hurt and abandoned throughout her entire life. Gwen realized just what a task it would be to prove to Andi that she loved her and that she would never leave.

When they arrived at the topic of Kevin James, Andi stiffened.

Gwen stroked her hand down Andi's arm and brushed her fingers through her hair to reassure her. "It's okay, sweetheart. Take your time."

"When this whole mess started, I lost everything all over again. I thought I had found a place to belong through my work. I was dating a local police officer in the town where I worked. She wasn't out and was very clear about not wanting anyone to know about us. I convinced myself I could settle for my relationship with J.C. because I knew where she stood, and I had accepted that she would leave me eventually. I had learned to believe that was how my life worked."

Gwen grew still. This was the first time Andi had talked about anyone she had dated, and Gwen knew this was an important part of Andi's story. "So you were seeing her when the thing with Kevin James happened?"

Andi nodded. "She left me. Boyd was already on the run, and I was scared to death."

Gwen tensed. "But she didn't just leave. She left you alone when you needed her. She abandoned you." Gwen knew this had to be true. It explained Andi's reluctance to trust Gwen's feelings for her or her own value in her relationships with those around her.

Andi nodded. "I thought I was ready for it, but I felt betrayed, rejected, shunned. Her leaving said that my life didn't matter. When you came into my life, I never thought you could love me. I was too damaged. My life is too broken, too dangerous, too uncertain for anyone to love me."

Gwen wept, and her tears landed on Andi's hand. "I can see how you might have believed that then, but not anymore. You'll never be alone like that again. You may not believe this, Andi, but I love you and you are everything to me." Gwen knew it wouldn't be her words that would convince Andi of her love, but her actions. It would take time, but she would show Andi she could trust her love.

Gwen pulled Andi closer against her. "Thank you for telling me." She knew it had been hard for Andi to talk about her past and to reveal her insecurities. And despite the pain she felt for everything Andi had been through, a part of her glowed with the understanding of what it meant for Andi to let her in.

Andi was restless. Gwen lay beside her, sleeping. She looked so serene, so peaceful that Andi found herself mesmerized by how beautiful she was. She wished she could join Gwen in her dreamworld where no harm could come to them. Since her reunion with Melissa and Jimmy, the past was no longer locked away in the cell Andi had created in her mind. The memories of that terrible night with Kevin James and Curtis Boyd flashed behind her eyelids as vivid as if she were watching the events play out before her very eyes. She could feel Boyd's hot breath on her neck and smell the stench of sweat from his body as if she were still beneath him. Her hands clenched involuntarily, and she thought she could feel her fingers close around the cold, rough stone.

Lying on her back with an arm cast over her eyes, Andi tried to force the memories from her mind and tried to make sense of her life. Although the memories were painful, she felt a sense of power over them now. She had taken the first step toward healing. She couldn't take back the mistakes she had made. Looking back, she remembered her fear and loneliness, and how she had desperately thought she was doing the right thing by leaving.

Andi sighed. She had been selfish. But the truth was, if she had never let Melissa close to her, Melissa would have been safe. Everything seemed so clear now. She couldn't take back the mistakes that had hurt Melissa so much, but she could make sure she didn't make the same mistakes again.

Gwen shifted in her sleep, and Andi felt her tender fingers brush across her stomach as Gwen's arm came around her. Gwen nuzzled close to her, the heat of her body warming Andi in her deepest recesses.

The thought of losing Gwen was like having her skin peeled away, leaving her exposed and raw.

Andi thought of how wonderful her days had been since Gwen had come into her life. She pictured Gwen in her mind, seeing the graceful movements of her body, her hands, her mouth. She thought of how she'd avoided Gwen after learning of the parole hearing, how Gwen had come to her and held her in her arms, allowing her to rest. Gwen had shown her so much tenderness. She had put up with Andi's distance and silence and still hadn't given up.

Despite her best efforts, Andi had fallen in love with Gwen. She had to stop running. She had told Gwen everything, and Gwen still stayed.

Andi rolled over and brushed her lips against Gwen's forehead, her cheek, her nose. She trailed her fingers lightly along her side until she felt Gwen tremble against her.

Gwen slowly opened her eyes as her lips curved into a smile. "Mmm. Am I dreaming?"

Andi brushed her fingertip across Gwen's breast and smiled when Gwen's eyes darkened with desire and her nipple pebbled against her touch.

"If this is a dream I hope I never wake up," Andi answered.

Gwen's arm tighted around Andi as she pulled her close and kissed her.

Andi was soaring. She wanted Gwen. She needed her. And she wouldn't waste another moment of loving her.

❖

A faint knock at her door drew Andi out of her thoughts. It was their final day with Melissa and Jimmy, and they were supposed to be leaving for brunch soon. Slowly she got up from her bed and went to the door.

"Who is it?"

"It's me. Can I come in?" Melissa's soft voice was faint through the door.

Andi drew in a deep breath and opened the door. Melissa stood there sheepishly, looking very much like a little girl.

"Of course you can come in." Andi stepped aside, holding the door as Melissa stepped into the room. "What is it?" she asked, seeing the anxiety written across Melissa's face.

"Where's Gwen?"

"She just got back from a run." Andi glanced at her watch. "She's in the shower. Is there a problem?"

Melissa shook her head. "I need to know you're okay, Andi. I need to know you aren't going to shut me out again."

Andi breathed a sigh of relief and sat down on the edge of the bed.

"I'm not going anywhere. I'm just sorry it took me so long to let you in. I'm still not totally sure I can face the parole hearing, but I promise to keep in touch—and you promised to visit."

Melissa sat down next to Andi on the bed, her eyes looked tired. "Jimmy and I are happy together. I just hope you'll allow yourself a little happiness too."

Andi glanced at Melissa, "What do you mean?"

"I mean Gwen, of course."

A faint smile edged the corners of Andi's mouth at the mention of Gwen's name.

"Did you tell her?"

"Yes."

"And?"

Andi sighed contentedly. "She was wonderful. *Of course.*"

Melissa smiled. "Well, from everything you've told me about her and seeing you two together, I think she's the real deal. Let her make up her own mind about the rest."

"Part of me knows if I just walk away, she'll be safe. I can't help but think that's the right thing to do. But no part of me wants that. I can't let her go."

Melissa shook her head. "You feel that because you can't see an alternative ending to this story. I get it that you want to protect Gwen. But you'll be hurting her if you leave. Keep talking to her, Andi."

Andi sighed. "Part of me knows you're right, the other part of me says run."

"Look, Jimmy and I are planning to visit you in two weeks. We thought that would give you time to get things worked out, and we could discuss what we need to do next about the parole hearing. You don't have to have any answers before then. In the meantime, trust her. Trust yourself. I know this is going to work out."

Andi was shocked silent.

Melissa smiled at the look on Andi's face. "No more hiding in that quiet little town of yours. We're coming. From what I've seen and read about the place, you've been holding out on us. It's time you shared all that serenity."

Andi nodded. Smiling, she took Melissa's hand, grateful for her friendship. "Okay."

"Okay? Are you serious?" Melissa said, sounding surprised. "No stonewalling? No excuses? You aren't even going to argue?"

Andi laughed. "Doesn't sound like I have much choice in the matter."

Melissa threw her arms around Andi and kissed her cheek. "Thank you, Andi."

Andi hugged her back. "Come on, let's get Gwen and go find that gorgeous girl of yours. You know she's starving by now."

They both laughed, and Andi's heart softened a little. It was nice to have friends.

Chapter Twenty-three

Andi was glad to be home, and even happier to be sitting in her kitchen, drinking tea with Gwen. So much had changed for her over the brief weekend. She had learned so much about herself and her friends and she felt a new sense of belonging that she hadn't experienced before.

She could never undo the mistakes she had made with Melissa, but she was determined not to make the same mistakes with Gwen. She reached across and laid her hand on Gwen's thigh. It didn't matter how close Gwen was, she could never be close enough. Andi needed to touch her. Gwen put her hand over Andi's and laced their fingers together. Andi's heart skipped.

"You okay?" Gwen asked.

Andi nodded. "I'm thinking about the hearing. Things are going to get crazy."

"Maybe," Gwen agreed. "But it's all going to work out. We'll just take things as they come."

Andi studied Gwen's face, trying to memorize every curve, every line. She knew Gwen wasn't going to like what she was going to say. "I don't want you to go to the hearing."

Gwen glanced at Andi and the muscle at her jaw jumped. "What are you talking about? Of course I'll be there."

Andi pulled Gwen's hand into her lap. "It isn't that I don't want you there. I've been thinking about Kevin James. I don't want him to know about you. I don't want to give him any more ammunition. If he doesn't know about you, he won't hurt you."

"Andi, no one's going to hurt me. I don't want to hide from anyone. I want to be there with you."

"I know you do. And I love that you do. But you don't know him. I could never forgive myself if anything happened to you because of me."

Gwen was silent for a long time. Andi didn't want to argue with Gwen, and she was afraid of hurting her.

Gwen sighed. "I get what you're saying. I don't agree, but it's something I'm willing to consider. Let's wait and see if you even have to go to the hearing before we make this decision. Okay?"

Andi nodded. "Sure." She rested her head against Gwen's shoulder. She tried to calm the worry and fear churning within her. She knew Gwen believed wholeheartedly that things would be okay, and her fierce determination made Andi want to believe it too.

As if sensing Andi's unease, Gwen brushed a kiss against Andi's head. "Don't worry. If it will make you feel better, I won't go to the hearing. I'll trust you to tell me what you need. And I hope you'll trust that I won't ever do anything to hurt you."

Andi wrapped her arms around Gwen and raised her head to place a quick kiss on her lips. "Deal." She knew Gwen needed to know that she wasn't going to shut her out. Now that she understood more about Gwen's past, she was more aware of how her decisions could affect Gwen. Keeping Gwen safe wasn't just about keeping her away from Kevin James—it was about protecting her heart.

She had no idea how it was going to be possible to do both.

Andi glanced at the clock as she finished straightening the shelves after putting up the last of the new stock. Goodness, could it really be three in the morning? The floors were already cleaned and everything was ready for opening in the morning, and she was tired. She had gotten into the habit of coming in late at night to do important things in the store when Gwen was out of town with work. She left most of the daily operations to Morgan. Andi kept up with the deliveries and baked the treats, but other than that, she was out of the store as much as possible, letting herself heal.

It had been a long week, and she missed Gwen more than she wanted to admit. When Gwen was away it was like a part of her was missing, and she felt unsettled and off balance. Gwen kept her grounded and gave her a sense of purpose like no one ever had.

She stretched her aching back and let out a tired sigh. It was time to go home. She turned out the lights and locked the door on her way out. Just as she was about to turn down the sidewalk, she heard movement in the shadows. Startled, she peered into the darkness, her heart pounding in her chest as adrenaline flooded her system.

"You're working late," a familiar smooth voice said from the shadows. "Don't you ever sleep?" Gwen stepped out of the darkness, her face illuminated by the silvery light of the moon.

Andi's heart clamored with the excitement of seeing Gwen, then calmed as her world righted itself. The sight of her lover was like having a long cool drink of water after days in the desert. She had the impulse to run to her, wanted to throw her arms around her. "What are you doing here? I thought you weren't supposed to be back in town for another day," she said instead.

Gwen shrugged. "I wrapped up early. I would have called, but I thought you'd be sleeping. I was going to surprise you with breakfast in the morning. I decided to take a walk and saw the light on." Gwen motioned a hand toward the store. "Did you have another skunk emergency?"

Andi laughed at the memory of poor Zeek and their night of trying to get the acrid smell of skunk out of her thick fur. "No, just the usual. How is Zeek? I bet she's glad to be home."

Gwen shrugged noncommittally. "Good, still on squirrel patrol." Gwen paused a moment before adding, "She misses you and wants to know when she can have a sleepover."

Andi smiled. Gwen had only been gone for a few days, but when she traveled for work, Andi didn't sleep. The bed was too empty without Gwen nestled beside her.

"Well, she's pretty special, but I kind of had hopes for some personal time with her mom." Andi stepped closer to Gwen and raked her fingers down Gwen's arm. She felt Gwen shiver beneath her touch. "Hmm, it seems I'm not the only one needing a little personal time."

Gwen placed her hand on Andi's hip. "You mean because every time I see you I want to put my hands on your body, because I want to taste you on my lips." Gwen stepped closer. "Is it because I want to hold you in my arms and keep you safe?"

Heat surged through Andi's body and her knees felt weak. "That's definitely on the list."

"Hmm. What else?"

"I think I'd rather show you than tell you. Maybe after that surprise breakfast tomorrow." Andi turned and began walking away.

Gwen chuckled. She caught up to Andi in a few quick strides. Their arms brushed as Gwen matched Andi's pace.

Andi stopped and faced Gwen. "What are you doing?"

Gwen shrugged. "Since I'm already here and I don't want to wait until tomorrow to see you, I thought now might be a good time for that show-and-tell you mentioned."

Andi laughed. "What if I don't want to play tonight?"

Gwen grasped Andi's hand, pulling them to a stop. "Yes, you do." Gwen cupped Andi's cheek in her palm and brushed her thumb across Andi's lips. "I know that look in your eyes. I know that rasp in your voice. You want me just as much as I want you."

Desire spread through every inch of Andi's body. She liked the playfulness and the teasing, but if she didn't get her hands on Gwen soon, she would explode.

Gwen smiled. "But if you really want to wait, I only ask for one thing."

"What?" Andi whispered. God, was Gwen really going to make her wait?

"Kiss me."

Andi chuckled. "Just a kiss, huh? That's all you want?"

Gwen shrugged. "If you can convince me in one kiss that you don't want me, I'll go home."

Andi knew there was no way she would be able to stop if Gwen kissed her. "You can't be serious. You're out of your—"

Andi's words were cut off as Gwen's mouth closed over hers. She felt herself harden as Gwen's hands gripped tightly around her, pulling their bodies together. The sudden heat of Gwen's tongue pressing into her mouth, scouring her tongue, the pressure bruising her lips, made her head spin. Andi molded herself against Gwen. Her hands snaked around Gwen's back and up into her hair, pulling Gwen deeper into her. She couldn't think of anything but how right Gwen felt in her arms.

Gwen insinuated her thigh between Andi's legs and Andi whimpered.

Andi drew away from the kiss with a gasp of pleasure. Her body was screaming out for Gwen to touch her. Tears pricked at her eyes and she crumpled against Gwen's chest.

Gwen stilled and Andi felt strong arms surrounding her, and all the fear and fatigue she had been carrying overwhelmed her. All playfulness had vanished and she was ready to beg Gwen to come home with her. She needed to feel Gwen's hands on her and feel the safety of her arms around her. She needed to reclaim her lover after the days of absence.

Gwen stroked her hair. She kissed her temple, her cheek, and her eyelids. She ran a trembling hand through Andi's hair and stroked her face with tentative fingers. "It's okay, Andi," Gwen whispered. "I've got you. Hold on to me, baby. I've got you."

Andi pulled away from the warm, tender embrace and looked up into Gwen's angelic face. She searched her eyes in the dim light wanting to see the crystal blue warmth, but her eyes were shadowed by the dark obscuring the thoughts and emotions she sought.

She placed a trembling hand lightly against Gwen's chest. "I missed you."

Gwen's arms tightened around her and she felt soft lips kiss her hair. It felt so good to be in Gwen's arms. She wanted to lose herself in Gwen's touch. She shivered with want.

"Are you cold?" Gwen asked rubbing her hands along Andi's back.

"Not cold, just…it scares me sometimes how much I need you."

"I love that you need me." Gwen pressed their clasped hands against her chest. "Don't think right now, just feel. Feel my heart beating with yours. This is what feels right."

Andi slid her fingers into Gwen's palm. Reassured by Gwen's touch, she wanted to feel more of her. "Let's go home."

"I thought you'd never ask."

This time, Andi didn't protest. She didn't move away as Gwen slid her arm protectively around her waist, Gwen's fingers gripping the waistband of Andi's jeans along her hip. Andi craved the warmth of Gwen's body and the tenderness in her touch. But mostly she needed Gwen's love. Andi snaked her arm around Gwen and leaned her head against her shoulder. At that moment, she didn't care where they were going. She was already home.

CHAPTER TWENTY-FOUR

October—and the parole hearing—came all too quickly. Andi held her breath as she and Melissa were led into the prison. The air was cold inside the institutional gray stone walls. They had walked through the metal detectors and had been physically searched upon entering the facility. The smell of cleaning products mingled with the odors of human sweat and fear, making the air feel toxic.

The heavy metal doors slamming shut behind them sounded hollow and ominous, like the lid to a steel coffin grinding to a close. Andi imagined those doors closing on her, locking her in forever. Her skin felt chill and she wondered if the blood was even making it to her extremities. Her heart pounded against her chest, echoing in her head until she feared something would rupture and blood would pour out her ears.

A steady hand grasped her palm and long fingers laced through hers. She closed her hand, trying to find strength in the strong, unwavering touch. She looked up and met Melissa's gaze. She squeezed her fingers tight against Melissa's touch. She knew the fear that lurked in Melissa's heart, but all she saw now was determination and strength. The solidarity seemed to make the cold and fear of the prison recede. She refused to be touched by the evil that lived there. Gwen wasn't with them. She'd respected Andi's need to keep Kevin James ignorant of their relationship, even though Andi knew Gwen wanted to be with her, holding her hand.

They waited in a small five-by-eight room. There was no window, and the thick metal door housed only a small viewing glass in the center. The hum of the florescent lights seemed deafening in the otherwise silent room. A camera nestled in the corner of the ceiling winked its red light at them, reminding them that, despite the solitude, they were not alone. Although the silence was uncomfortable, neither of them spoke. Everything had been said. Nothing was left but the waiting. Jimmy had gone into the hearing and was presenting their case. She wouldn't call on them unless it was absolutely necessary.

A guard came to the door. It was time. It was happening. They were being summoned to speak before the parole board.

A wave of fear washed over Andi, and she thought she might be sick. She closed her eyes trying to fight back the bile that burned in her throat. She had to face the demon again. Ice once again threaded its way through her veins.

Melissa stood first, squared her shoulders, and moved toward the door. Just as she was about to exit she paused and looked at Andi who had followed her lead. Although she didn't say a word, the message was clear. She wouldn't fail this time. She quirked a faint smile and took Andi's hand.

The tight fingers laced in her own told her she was safe. And no matter what happened in the next few hours, she was loved. Andi tried to focus on her breathing. She wouldn't be any use in the hearing if she passed out before even getting into the room. She thought of Melissa and Jimmy and all they had suffered. She thought of Gwen and her unwavering love and the dreams that hung on today's decision. This was a fight she could not run from. She had to take a stand to protect those she loved.

Andi watched a muscle twitch at the side of Melissa's jaw. Andi could see the tension in her back and wondered if the muscles would snap under the strain. Her anger flared when Melissa brought her hand to her face and ran her fingers over the scar on her cheek. She would bear the reminder of that terrible night for the rest of her life. Andi's hatred for Kevin James boiled, and once again she wished she had pulled the trigger when she'd had the chance. She shook the thought from her mind. She wouldn't allow Kevin James to hurt her anymore. It was time to face the darkness.

Sooner than expected, the guard stopped outside another massive steel door. He spoke into his shoulder mic and instantly the familiar sound of the metal locks sliding open echoed around the hall. The heavy door glided weightlessly on its hinges, and in seconds they were guided into the room.

The room was cold. Bright florescent lights illuminated the room. Wood paneling lined the walls and the seal of the state of Tennessee hung on the wall above a long wooden table where four men and three women sat, reviewing a stack of papers. Jimmy was standing at the front of the room facing the panel.

When Andi's gaze settled on the man in the orange jumpsuit, her heart leaped into her throat. Kevin James looked as calm and reserved as the last time she'd seen him. His hair had grown out a little but was still combed back from his face. He was clean-shaven. The familiar two-day stubble was gone. He had put on weight and his eyes bulged from their sockets like a wounded animal cornered by a predator. Andi knew him better than anyone in that room. He might look calm and reserved, but she knew that was just a cover. Inside he was a beast and she knew he was sizing up his prey.

Sweat gathered at the back of Andi's neck and a tremor ran down her spine. She marveled at the incongruences in the room. She felt like the prisoner being ushered in for trial, just like she had every time she had testified about the horrors Kevin James had brought to her life. Kevin James was no innocent.

When his eyes fell on Andi, he smiled in a menacing sneer showing yellow, stained teeth. His hands tightened into fists, restrained by the shackles on his wrists, secured to the chain around his waist that trailed to the shackles on his ankles. A guard stood behind him, holding a black rod about two feet long. Andi looked at this curiously wondering what it was for. Two more guards stood by each door, the one that Andi and Melissa had come through and another several feet behind Kevin James.

❖

In the visitors' area, observers shifted as Melissa and Andi made their way to the front of the room. Gwen sat back so she was obscured by the movement of the large man beside her as Andi and Melissa passed by her. She didn't want Andi to see her. She didn't want her distracted from what she needed to do.

Gwen studied the set of Andi's jaw and was proud of her bravery, her strength, and her unwavering determination to do the right thing. Gwen was happy to see Melissa never let her hand leave Andi's, but she wished with all her being that it could have been her holding Andi, protecting her. Movement at the front of the room caught Gwen's attention, and she fixed her gaze on Kevin James. A sour taste flooded her mouth and her throat tightened with the effort it took to control the sudden surge of anger. This was the man who had hurt Andi. Before this moment, Gwen hadn't fully understood the magnitude of her hate for this man.

She could never know the price Andi had paid by coming here. And once again, she was awed at Andi's strength.

When they reached the podium, the hearing officer acknowledged Andi and Melissa and asked for Andi to stand and state her full name for the record. With Jimmy at her side, they asked questions regarding the effects the crime had on Andi's life, her mental status, and her feelings about Kevin James being considered for parole. Through it all, Andi remained composed and poised. That composure cracked when one of the men on the panel asked why Andi felt Mr. James continued to pose a threat.

Andi's voice shook as she described the letters she had received from Kevin James while he had been incarcerated. She described the threatening letters James had managed to have other inmates slip to their visitors that had been mailed out to her without the prison knowing.

Andi produced one of the letters, and as she read it to the panel, Kevin James chuckled menacingly. In the letter he'd described in detail the things he planned to do to Andi once he was free. Andi's hands shook as she continued to read, and Jimmy slid her hand around Andi's waist to steady her.

Gwen ground her teeth against her rage as she heard the intimate details of what Andi had suffered. She couldn't imagine the strength it had taken Andi to survive such a brutal attack. Andi had spent over three years of her life protecting everyone around her from this demon, and Gwen realized the sacrifice Andi was willing to make to protect her. Her heart ached with the love she felt for Andi. It was painful to hear all that Melissa and Andi had endured. It was unthinkable that this man would ever be free to harm anyone ever again.

At the conclusion of Andi's speech, the panel thanked her for coming to the hearing and for her unique perspective on the case. Then one of the panelists cleared her throat and apologized to Andi and Melissa for the pain the hearing had caused them.

The panel then addressed Kevin James, asking him about his thoughts and feelings about what he had done and the behavior he had displayed while incarcerated.

Gwen leaned forward as Kevin James stood to make his case. He sounded like a well-educated and reasonable man. He argued that his previous behavior was due to a mental instability for which he was currently being treated. He presented a very convincing argument that he had suffered delusions and had acted during a state of psychosis, and he argued that with his medication he no longer harbored thoughts or fantasies of harming anyone.

The more he talked, the more Gwen realized the evil within the man. Nothing in his posture or his expression spoke of empathy or remorse. Gwen saw what he was saying as nothing more than manipulation. She hoped and prayed the parole board would see the same.

When Kevin James was finished speaking, the hearing officer called a fifteen minute recess and said they would return with their decision after the break.

As Kevin James was led from the room, Gwen's eyes were glued to Andi. They had been asked to remain seated during the break, and Gwen wanted to go to Andi. But she knew she had to be patient just a little longer.

❖

"What do you think?" Melissa asked Jimmy once the panel left the room.

"Hard to say. He made a good argument, but the records don't support his claim of mental stability. More than one of the panelists was visibly affected by your testimonies. We've presented a strong case, but I just can't call this one."

Melissa grimaced and looked to Andi. "How are you holding up?"

Andi felt numb, as if she were standing outside herself in a dream. "Okay. He sounded like he used to during court testimony. He has lots of practice saying what he thinks the court wants to hear."

Earlier than expected, the panel returned. A few minutes later, Kevin James was led back into the room. The hearing officer delivered the panel's decision. "In the matter of the parole of Kevin Dewayne James, this panel has determined there is just cause to believe the inmate continues to pose significant risks to the victims and has not completed rehabilitation. The request for parole is denied. The court recommends—"

"What the fuck? You can't do that!" Kevin James screamed across the room. He struggled against his restraints. "I did what was necessary. Look at them, they're all a bunch of fucking dykes. They deserved what they got. You have no right to keep me here."

Andi flinched. The screams of anger echoed through her soul, stripping her to the bone.

"Mr. James," one of the panelists warned, "you can either compose yourself or you'll be escorted back to your cell."

James's eyes blazed with hatred. He had been glaring at Andi as he spoke, but now the panelist caught his attention. He jerked his arms violently against the restraints at his waist. "You're one of them! You're a fucking dyke. That's what this is about. You just wait, you fucking cunt. I'll show you. You can't keep me here forever." Kevin James lunged forward. "I'll hunt all of you down—"

His last words were cut off as the guard behind him pressed the black rod against his back. It wasn't a blow, just a touch, but Kevin James fell to the floor in a fetal position, his body jerking from the current that had brought him to his knees.

The guards grabbed Kevin James by the arms and dragged him from the room. A foul smell permeated the air, and Andi realized Kevin James had soiled himself.

The outburst had been controlled, but Andi still felt the adrenaline rushing though her body, making her want to lash out at someone or run, run and get away. Melissa's strong arms had pushed against her the instant Kevin James had started his resistance, and Melissa still stood in front of her in a defensive stance. Andi fell back against the bench, her back crushed against the cold wood. She felt as if she were floating away. They had won. James wouldn't be coming for her. But why couldn't she shake the fear? She closed her eyes to shut out the memories, the hate, and the months of dread.

A gentle hand brushed against her cheek as a strong arm slid around her. Andi heard Gwen's sweet voice whispering to her. But that wasn't possible. Gwen wasn't here. She must have passed out. Or maybe this was all a dream. When Gwen's lips pressed against hers, the sensation was so real that Andi couldn't help but reach back. She opened her eyes and was shocked to find Gwen gazing back at her. Shock and relief flooded her. She threw her arms around Gwen, buried her face in Gwen's neck, and held on with all her strength.

"Are you really here?"

Gwen's arms tightened around her. "I'm right here, baby. I'm right here," Gwen soothed. "Its okay, Andi. It's over now."

Andi sighed and lifted her face to Gwen, and placed her hand against her cheek. "What are you doing here?"

"This is where you are. I had to come."

Andi hugged Gwen close again. "I am so glad you did."

When they separated, Andi felt grounded again. She looked around Gwen to Melissa, who stood wrapped in Jimmy's arms.

"Thank you. Thank you for everything." She reached out and took Jimmy's hand. "I can't believe we did it."

Jimmy smiled. "Yes, we did. And with that little show James put on, I don't think we'll have to worry about him for a long time."

Melissa smiled at Andi, and Andi felt a part of her soul slide back into place. They'd had one small triumph that day. Kevin James would not be stalking their lives for now. It was as if the day Kevin James had gone to prison, they had had their lives arrested in prisons of their own making. Like James, they'd gone about their daily routines, spending time in slow motion, waiting for the unavoidable moment when their lives would collide again.

Jimmy's voice was hoarse when she spoke, her own pain and fear thick on her tongue. "Come on, you guys, what do you say we get out of here?"

Chapter Twenty-five

G wen pulled the SUV into the drive and killed the engine. Andi had slept most of the drive home. She studied the faint lines creasing Andi's forehead, the weight of the day's events still evident on her face. Gwen knew it would take a long time to quiet the fear and unrest seeing Kevin James again had created. She swore to herself she would do whatever it would take to see Andi smile and be happy again.

Gwen brushed her fingers lightly along the curve of Andi's jaw and spoke softly. "Andi."

Andi's eyes fluttered open.

"We're here."

Andi smiled sleepily and pushed her cheek into Gwen's touch. "Is this real?"

"What?"

"I started out this day feeling like my life was over. Everything that happened in that hearing made me relive the most horrific moments of my life. My emotions were put in a blender. Then it was over and you were there. And you're here now. So much has happened that I don't know what's real."

Gwen stroked Andi's hair, leaned across the seat, and kissed her lightly on the lips. After a moment she stroked her tongue along Andi's lower lip and pressed more firmly into the kiss. When Andi moaned, Gwen pulled away.

"Feel real yet?"

"Oh yeah. That feels very real."

"Come on, let's get you inside. You must be exhausted."

Andi closed and locked the door behind her after they entered the house. Although the immediate threat had passed, the fear and unease still made her feel edgy and guarded.

"Would you like to lie down and rest for a while? I can go if you need some time."

Andi shook her head. The last thing she wanted was for Gwen to leave. "No, I just want to sit for a while. Some wine would be nice, though. Would you like some?"

"Sure."

"Do you need to go check on Zeek?"

Gwen smiled. "No. She's staying with Morgan for the night. I didn't know what to expect today, and I wanted to make sure I could be here for whatever you needed."

"Thank you," Andi said, then popped the cork on a bottle of Shiraz. She handed Gwen a glass. She settled down onto the couch in her familiar defensive pose, with her back to the corner and her knees pulled up. She sipped the wine and allowed the rich woody palate to bathe her tongue with a soothing blend of flavor and warmth.

Gwen sat down next to Andi. She sipped her wine and brushed her fingers along the smooth skin along Andi's ankle. Andi took Gwen's hand and drew it into her lap. She craved the slightest contact after the long weeks when she had struggled to understand how she would ever be able to have a normal life with Gwen, wanting more than anything to give her all her heart. The fear that had consumed her had threatened to destroy them both.

Gwen was quiet and the look in her eyes was pensive. When she had suggested she leave, Andi had felt the insecurity vibrating from Gwen like a current through the air.

"I'm sorry, Gwen," Andi said. "I know this has been hard for you."

Gwen's clouded gaze met Andi's, and Andi ached with the knowledge that Gwen's doubt was her fault. Gwen placed her wine glass on the table and moved closer to Andi, pulling her into her arms. Andi slipped easily into her arms, curling against her, reveling in the way their bodies molded together as if they were meant to be together. But she needed to be totally honest.

"What happened today doesn't really change my situation, not forever. It just prolongs the waiting. I didn't mean to hurt you, Gwen. I wanted to protect you."

"I know. I know you were trying to do the right thing, Andi, but being without you was killing me. I had to be there."

Andi lowered her head. "I am so glad you were. I felt like I was losing my mind. I wasn't sure I could hold on to reality any longer. But when I felt you, heard your voice…When I looked into your eyes, I knew I would be okay. I knew you would make it all okay."

Gwen tightened her hold around Andi.

Andi shivered. "There was a moment in that room, when I read that letter and I could hear his cold laughter as he enjoyed imagining the terrible things he had threatened to do to me—it was a moment when I wished I had pulled the trigger that night. If I would have killed him then, he wouldn't be able to hurt us anymore."

"I know, baby."

Andi brushed a strand of hair off her cheek with a trembling hand. "Seeing you in that room was the most wonderful feeling I could have imagined. I felt as if I had been sent an angel. As much as I wanted you far away from that evil place, I was so happy when I saw you. Part of me always wanted you there, even if it was wrong."

Gwen was relieved by Andi's admission. She had been desperate to be with her at the hearing. She knew Andi was trying to protect her but it had hurt to have Andi ask her not to come. "Please don't send me away again, Andi. I can't bear it," Gwen whispered.

Andi lifted her face to meet Gwen's eyes. "No. I couldn't. I don't have the strength." She pressed her lips over Gwen's mouth and pulled her into her. She flooded Gwen's mouth with her tongue, and in each stroke Gwen knew the desire, longing, and love that Andi had tried so hard to deny, to keep her safe.

Andi's lips were heaven against her skin. Gwen felt the barriers that had always stood between them crumble. Andi now opened herself to Gwen without reservation, no longer resisting or running from what they both wanted.

"Oh God, Andi, I love you so much. You are everything to me." Gwen's voice trembled as the words spilled out. "I can't lose you again."

"No, I'm not going anywhere. I'm right here, baby." Andi pulled Gwen's head against her chest and stroked her hair. "I love you, Gwen. I love you and I'm so sorry I didn't trust that. God, I need you so much. I love you."

Gwen surged with relief as all the pain of her past melted away to be replaced with a lightness that made her dizzy. Andi loved her. She had waited forever to hear those words. She had felt love in Andi's touch, seen it glowing in Andi's eyes when she looked at her. But hearing the words was euphoric.

Andi lifted her face to hers and kissed her again. This time desire flared like a burst of flame deep in Gwen's belly as Andi pushed her back against the cushions and climbed on top of her, straddling her thighs.

Gwen snaked her hands around Andi's waist, tightening against her hips, pulling her snug against her body. The air melted between them and Gwen gasped at the heat pouring from Andi. She desperately wanted to feel her, skin to skin. She wanted to feel that love as Andi filled her.

Andi played her lips along Gwen's neck and took an earlobe between her teeth with gentle teasing nips. "Take me to bed. I need you against me. I need to taste you. I need you inside me. I need… you."

Gwen groaned. "Oh yes."

Andi took both Gwen's hands as she slid from her lap. "Oh, Gwen, Gwen." Andi pulled her closer, as if her body was drawn by the current of energy flowing between them.

Once they reached the bed, Gwen undressed Andi with slow, tender touches, her fingers barely brushing Andi's skin. Each opened button of her shirt symbolically released Andi from the emotional bonds that had held her prisoner for so long. The smooth silk slid down Andi's arms to pool at the floor. Gwen's hands moved over her skin reverently as if she were a fragile piece of porcelain.

"You are my world. I want this, I want you for the rest of my life."

Andi whimpered. "Mmm. That sounds like a good start."

Gwen studied every inch of Andi's body as if seeing it for the first time. She drew light kisses across Andi's shoulders as her hands played along the smooth planes of her stomach and up her back to release the clasp of her bra. The muscles of Andi's stomach quivered beneath her touch, and it made her ache to have all of Andi against her, inside her.

She undid the slim belt at Andi's waist and opened her slacks. With the slightest dip of her head she brushed a kiss against Andi's breast and felt the nipple harden against her lips. With a flick of her tongue she pulled the erect nipple into her mouth, tracing circles around the tight flesh.

Andi moaned. Gwen feathered her fingers against Andi's hip, pulling her free of her slacks and panties.

Andi's hands raked through Gwen's hair, then fisted her shirt, pulling at the fabric until Gwen stood and pulled the shirt over her head. Her bra quickly followed.

"Sit down," Gwen said. She wanted to go slow. She wanted to explore every inch of Andi's body, to show Andi her love. "You are so beautiful."

Andi wrapped her arms around Gwen and pulled their bodies together. Gwen could feel Andi melting into her as their bodies and hearts joined. When Gwen's leg slid between Andi's thighs she felt her wetness, slick and hot against her skin. Gwen reveled in the feel of Andi. Her softness was heartbreaking, and Gwen's heart swelled with love.

Andi arched her back and pushed against Gwen's thigh increasing the pressure with a thrust of her hips and drew her nails down Gwen's back. Gwen arched her back as searing lines of fire erupted beneath the path of Andi's fingertips. Another eruption of pleasure surprised her when Andi took her nipple into her mouth, sucking hard against the already rock-hard point of flesh. Gwen was quickly losing control and she wanted to slow things down.

"Oh God, Andi. You feel amazing."

Andi released Gwen's breast and shifted. She loosened her grip on Gwen's thigh, gasping when Gwen's hand cupped her sex, parting her with two fingers and sliding along the slick folds to stroke her engorged clitoris. Andi lost herself in the pleasure of Gwen's hand stroking her, her hot lips pressing kisses along her neck to her breasts. Andi claimed Gwen's mouth, stroking her tongue deep inside until she felt pressure building somewhere within, growing outward until it flowed through her arms, down her legs, and through her fingers. Gwen was everywhere. Her breasts brushed against Andi's stomach with each stroke of her hand. Her mouth was hot on her nipple, her teeth scraping lightly across her flesh. It was wonderful, and Andi knew she wanted to have Gwen beside her always. Gwen was all that mattered now.

Andi opened herself to Gwen, wanting to feel more. "I need you inside me. I want to feel you deep inside—" She was silenced as Gwen entered her. Andi wrapped her legs around Gwen's thighs and bore down on each thrust of Gwen's hand. She clutched at Gwen's back, feeling the slick sheen of sweat coating her skin.

"Oh God, Gwen. Oh yes."

Gwen shifted her hand and pressed her thumb against the swollen shaft of Andi's clitoris, and tremors pulsed through Andi's body in rhythmic waves. She slowed, as if wanting to draw out Andi's pleasure.

"Please," Andi whispered.

Gwen obeyed, increasing the pressure to Andi's clit, filling her with each stroke of her hand. She opened her eyes and watched Andi's face as the orgasm claimed her. In that moment they were one. Andi's heart filled and her body surged. Gwen was everything she needed. She was consumed with peace, joy, pleasure. Her body was completely open to Gwen, and she gave herself over to her in a shattering of emotions, culminating in ecstasy. Her body went rigid as her muscles clamped down on Gwen's fingers. "Oh God, yes…"

Every cell in Andi's body was singing. She thought she could hear the hum of the blood in her veins. Her body was acutely aware of each point where her body connected to Gwen's. She pulled Gwen to her, Gwen's head resting against her chest. Andi's breath came in heavy gasps as she tried to recover, and her heart pounded so hard she was sure Gwen could feel the vibration against her cheek. After some moments, Andi finally released her grip on Gwen's fingers.

Gwen trailed her hand up Andi's thigh along her stomach until she cupped Andi's breast. Andi pushed up onto her elbow, rolling to her side to gaze down at Gwen. Andi's eyes were wet. Gwen leaned forward and kissed the tears from Andi's face.

"I'm not crying. Not really. I've just never felt anything like this before."

Gwen continued to kiss along Andi's cheeks, then her eyelids, down her nose, and finally her lips. She could taste the salt of Andi's tears as she swept her tongue into her mouth. She stroked Andi's hair and peered into her eyes. "You are the most amazing, most beautiful woman in the world. I love you."

Andi took Gwen's face in her hands and kissed her again. "You are going to love me even more in a minute," she purred, sliding down, pressing kisses along Gwen's body.

CHAPTER TWENTY-SIX

Gwen woke with both arms wrapped around Andi and Andi's head cradled against her breast. Their bodies were molded together so that every possible inch of flesh was joined. Gwen smiled and gave silent thanks for the woman in her arms. Warm breath kissed her skin as she watched the rise and fall of Andi's breathing, and Gwen reveled in the perfectness of the moment. This was the most peaceful feeling she could have imagined, and having Andi in her arms was like touching heaven.

At the shrill sound of the telephone, Andi's head jerked up. Gwen moaned in protest and Andi pressed a kiss against Gwen's chest before reaching over her to retrieve the phone. An instant later Andi's body tensed, and she bolted upright and sat naked in the middle of the bed, gripping the phone so hard her knuckles were white.

Gwen sat up, reaching for Andi. She could tell by Andi's reaction that something was terribly wrong. The tiny hairs along her arms and at the back of her neck rose in anticipation of a threat. Gwen wrapped an arm protectively around Andi's waist. Andi's words were clipped and it was impossible to decipher her side of the conversation.

"What? Oh God, no. When?…How could this happen?…I know, I will…No…She's here…Okay."

Andi hung up the phone and let it fall from her hands. Her body was shaking and she looked like she was about to run.

Gwen was on her knees in front of Andi on the bed, clasping tightly to her hips. "What's wrong?"

Andi's face had gone so white her lips looked blue and her eyes were unfocused.

"Andi, tell me what the hell is going on!"

This seemed to get Andi's attention, and she looked down at Gwen with sorrow-filled eyes. "I'm so sorry."

"What? What are you talking about?"

"Kevin James has escaped."

Gwen stiffened. Too many thoughts raced through her mind at once, making it difficult for her to focus. After a moment of shock she managed to speak. "How the hell did that happen?"

Andi stepped off the bed and pulled on a pair of jeans. She dressed quickly and moved methodically around the room, betraying no emotion.

Gwen was still trying to figure out what was happening when Andi pulled the 9 mm handgun out of the closet and chambered a round.

"Whoa!" The sight of Andi holding a gun was incongruent with everything Gwen knew about her. "Who was that on the phone? What did they say?" Gwen was up and pulling on her own clothes now as she followed Andi's every move with her eyes.

"That was Mel. She and Jimmy are on their way here now. They've already notified the Norris police. I don't know how he did it, but he's loose and we have to be ready."

Gwen was shocked by the calm in Andi's voice. It was as if she had been preparing for this moment for years, and now that the time had come she knew exactly what needed to be done.

"You should go somewhere safe, Gwen. James doesn't know about you, and you'll be safe if you're not with me. I don't think he saw you in the courtroom, and if he did he won't realize who you are to me. He won't know your name, he won't be after you."

Gwen froze at the words. "No. That's not what we agreed to last night. I'm not leaving you. Not now, not ever."

Gwen saw Andi's resolve break, and tears flooded her lover's eyes.

Andi nodded. "I can't ask you to stay, but I promise I won't ask you to leave."

Gwen crossed the room and took Andi in her arms. "We're going to get through this, Andi. We're going to get through this together."

❖

"It's been three days. Why haven't we heard anything?" Gwen asked, directing her question to no one in particular as she paced the floor.

They had been at Andi's house since the call about the escape, and there had been no news despite Mel's law-enforcement contacts. There had been no sign of Kevin James since he had escaped a medical transport to the psychiatric facility where he was to undergo more extensive treatment after reportedly attempting suicide following the hearing, and experiencing apparent hallucinations. The only information they had was that there had been some sort of accident. An officer involved in the transport said they'd crashed when a truck had crossed in front of the transport van, pushing them off the road, causing the van to flip. Someone had pulled everyone from the vehicle and put James in the truck and called an ambulance for the officers before leaving with James. The truck the officer identified had been ditched a few miles farther down the road, and there had been no sightings since.

Melissa's hands were clenched into fists and a muscle jumped in her jaw. Her anger was almost palpable and the tension was beginning to wear on everyone. "I don't know. This is driving me crazy. We don't even know what to expect. I mean, if James has someone working with him, why did they wait so long? They could have come after us anytime they wanted and we wouldn't have seen it coming."

Andi sat staring out the window at a cardinal that had perched on the telephone wire outside and was trilling its song with confident pride. The contrast of the peaceful melody and the conversation in the room was like mixing oil and water. She turned to Jimmy. "Something doesn't fit," Andi said quietly.

Everyone's attention was instantly fixed on her.

Jimmy lowered the paper she had been reading. "What do you mean?"

"I don't think this person was working with James."

"What? Of course they are. How else do you explain it? Even the staged car accident was the same as last time," Melissa said harshly.

"Think about it, Mel. There is no way James would alert authorities to his escape by calling an ambulance. He would want to get as far away as possible as fast as possible. It doesn't fit. James wouldn't care what happened to those officers. He would only be looking out for himself."

Melissa rubbed her face with both hands. "We didn't think Curtis Boyd had help either. Come on, Andi, we knew there had to be more people involved in the child porn ring. We didn't know about James back then, and we don't know who his contacts are now. This is just one more sick bastard who's been hiding in the wind, waiting for his chance to get James out."

"Maybe," Andi sighed and went back to staring out the window. The cardinal was gone now and she was saddened by its absence. She returned her focus to the room.

Jimmy leaned forward in her chair. "According to the prison records, James hasn't had a single phone call or visitor since his imprisonment, aside from his attorney of course. We know he smuggled out letters to Andi since being there, so maybe he was communicating with someone else the same way."

Something seemed to click in Melissa's thoughts and her expression grew pensive. "But James didn't know he would be transferred to a psych unit, and even if he did, there wasn't enough time for him to set this up by sneaking letters out." She turned to the group, her eyes wide with understanding. "James was a cop. He might have someone on the inside. Someone working for the prison must be involved."

"Or," Jimmy added calmly, "James orchestrated the suicide attempt and the hallucinations to make sure he was transferred."

Andi didn't respond to the new theories.

Gwen crossed the room and placed her hand on Andi's shoulder. "Andi, you okay?"

Andi covered Gwen's hand with her own. Pain settled deeper in her heart. How had she allowed this evil to come into Gwen's world? She had promised not to send Gwen away, but now she didn't see any other way.

As if reading Andi's mind, Gwen leaned down and kissed her cheek. Gwen brushed her lips against Andi's ear and whispered so low no one else could hear, "I'm not leaving, so you can just get that thought right out of your head."

Andi shifted so she could look into Gwen's eyes, preparing her argument, but her words fell short when she saw the set of Gwen's jaw and her determined gaze. The corners of her mouth lifted in a faint grin. She knew it wouldn't do her any good to try to send Gwen away. They were a part of each other now. She would just have to make sure nothing went wrong this time. She knew that this time, she wouldn't hold back when faced with the choice to pull the trigger. She would do whatever it took to keep Gwen safe.

❖

Gwen bustled through the door, her arms full of groceries and a stack of mail. One of the Norris deputies had escorted her around town so she could check on Andi's store, do some shopping, check the mail, and make a quick stop by her house for her laptop, so she could work while at Andi's.

She found the rest of the group in the kitchen, helping Andi bake dog treats. The house smelled like peanut-butter cookies. In that moment no one would have guessed they were basically prisoners in the house, waiting for a storm to hit.

"Mission accomplished," she said, piling the bags on the kitchen counter.

She saw Andi sigh as she stepped into the room. Her eyes looked strained with worry. She knew it had been hard for Andi to let her go out, not knowing if Kevin James was just waiting for an opportunity to strike. She brushed a kiss across Andi's lips.

"I see you three have been busy while I was out." Andi had flour on her cheek and Melissa was up to her elbows in dough. Jimmy's job seemed to be decorator, since she was methodically using a small stamp to press hearts into each cookie before Andi placed them into the oven.

Gwen quirked a smile at Jimmy. "Nice."

"Shut up."

Gwen laughed. "I don't know, Jimmy, maybe you should think of giving up the courtroom for a kitchen. You look good in that apron." She ducked as Jimmy chucked a misshapen ball of excess dough at her.

"All right you two, cut it out. Gwen, you can take over with the cookie cutter." Andi pointed to a sheet of freshly pressed dough.

"Uh...I have some work to catch up on. I think I'll leave the baking to the pros. Keep up the good work there, Jimmy."

Over the last few days, she and Jimmy had developed a unique bond and had turned to playful jokes and pranks to ease some of the tension. They understood each other. They were both trying to protect the women they loved and were trying to keep their own fear and worry from showing.

"How were things at the shop? Was Morgan doing okay?" Andi asked.

Gwen shuffled through the stack of mail that had accumulated over the week. "No problem. I got to see Zeek while I was there too. Morgan has been bringing her to work, and she seemed to be settled into her new job as shop dog." Gwen slid a pile of mail to Andi. "I already tossed the sales ads and other junk. This is your pile."

Andi groaned, digging into the stack of bills, notices, and pet-supply catalogs. A small white envelope caught her eye, and she decided to open it first. She didn't usually receive personal cards or letters, and this was obviously not a bill or business correspondence. The address had been typed and there was no return address. The postmark indicated the letter had been mailed here in town, and Andi thought it was probably from one of her clients.

She slid a finger beneath the flap, tearing the envelope along its edge. Inside she found a small folded piece of paper. Her skin tingled as the faint scent of sandalwood brushed across her memory. Perplexed, Andi drew the paper to her face and sniffed. The scent was unmistakable, but what did it mean? She opened the paper and read the words printed inside, and her breath caught.

"What is it?"

"Nothing," Andi said stuffing the note back into the envelope. "Just a paper cut."

When everyone returned to what they were doing, Andi went back to the note. In small, typed letters it said, *I made it right. Forgive me.* There was no signature. Andi swallowed the lump that had formed in her throat. What could this mean? There was only one person that she associated with that scent, and she couldn't think of any reason she would be in touch now, or what the words could possibly mean.

Andi felt the blood drain from her face, but a small thrill of hope blossomed in her stomach and she flinched, shocked by her callousness. If her theory was right, Kevin James wouldn't be coming for her. But how was this possible? Why now?

Andi folded the piece of paper and stuffed it back into the envelope and put it into her back pocket. She went through the remaining mail as if nothing was bothering her and hoped no one had noticed her sudden change in mood. She couldn't stop thinking about the note and what it might mean. She thought she knew who had sent it, and if she was right, everything she thought she knew about her past was wrong.

Chapter Twenty-seven

A ndi sat in the darkness of her bedroom, listening to the sounds of the night through her window. She longed to be outside so she could watch the starlight glisten off the water of the pool and listen to the unobstructed call of crickets and other nocturnal critters. Being cooped up inside was beginning to wear on her. She felt as if the air was growing stale and the walls were closing in around her.

She thought back on the sound of the heavy metal doors slamming shut behind her as she entered the prison. She knew what it must have been like for Kevin James to spend years in a cell locked behind prison walls. She pulled the small envelope from her pocket and held it to her face. There it was. Sandalwood. She had thought she had been mistaken, but now she had very little doubt who had sent the note. *Oh God, J.C. What have you done?*

Gwen cleared her throat as she came into the room. "I left Melissa and Jimmy watching a movie. I hoped we could have some time to talk." Gwen sat on the edge of the bed and rubbed her hands against her thighs. "Do you want to tell me what's going on? You've been quiet all evening and I can tell something's bothering you."

Andi stuffed the envelope back into her pocket and watched Gwen. Andi pressed her head against the back of the chair and sighed. "I'm just going a little stir crazy. I can't stand being shut up like this."

Gwen nodded. "I know. I thought maybe there was something I could do to take your mind off things for a little while." Gwen grinned mischievously at Andi and patted her hand on the bed.

Andi laughed. "That might work," she said, letting her worry slip aside for a moment to breathe in the simple joy of having Gwen close. She stood and went to Gwen, pushing her down onto the bed. She stretched her body out along Gwen's and wrapped her arms around her, nestling her face against Gwen's neck.

Gwen wrapped her arms around Andi and pulled her tight against her. She stroked Andi's face with the tips of her fingers. "The thought of someone out there wanting to hurt you is driving me crazy. I just want to do whatever it takes to keep you safe."

Andi could hear the worry and strain in Gwen's voice, and she wanted to reassure her. She wanted to believe the nightmare was over, but she couldn't dare share that with Gwen until she knew more. Andi brushed her fingers through Gwen's hair and closed her eyes. "I know, baby. Me too."

Andi saw Melissa jump when the phone attached to her hip began to vibrate. She grabbed the device, glancing at the screen before answering.

"Officer Stuart speaking."

Jimmy muted the television and watched and listened, leaning on the edge of her seat.

"Yes, sir." Melissa's back was stiff as she listened intently to the voice on the other end of the line. "Has that been confirmed, sir?" Melissa began to pace the floor. "I understand, sir. We'll be waiting."

Melissa's shoulders seemed to collapse in on her chest as she ended the call. She looked at Jimmy and then Andi in disbelief.

"What? Did they get James?" Andi asked. The anticipation and dread had been driving her crazy and she was desperate for news.

"Maybe." Melissa looked up, her eyes wide. "You need to get Gwen."

"I'm here—I heard the phone," Gwen said, and she huddled with Andi in an oversized chair.

Melissa paced the floor and held on to her phone as if it were a lifeline. "The chief of police just called. They think they have James."

"What do you mean they think they have him?" Jimmy said, standing and going to Melissa.

Andi sat unmoving. Her heart beat rapidly in her chest, and her palms were sweating. Dear God, let him be dead.

Gwen's gaze was riveted on Melissa, the desperate gleam of hope making her brilliant blue eyes sparkle.

"They received an anonymous tip this afternoon. The caller claimed to know the location where Kevin James was supposed to be hiding. Evidently this place is deep in the backwoods and was difficult to locate. When they got there, they found a body. They think it's James, but that isn't clear. The chief didn't go into detail, but he said he'd let us know as soon as something was confirmed."

Jimmy slipped her arms around Melissa's shoulders, drew her to her chest, and brushed a kiss to the top of her head. "Come on, sweetheart, you need to sit down, you're shaking."

Melissa met Andi's eyes across the room. Andi held her gaze with understanding. They had come so far from where this had all started. She watched Jimmy stroke Mel's hair, her arm wrapped protectively around her shoulder. She was happy to see her friend allowing herself to be comforted. Andi let her gaze shift from Melissa to Jimmy, and then to Gwen. Despite the fear, heartache, and pain, she was forever grateful for the women in this room. This was her family now, and no matter how things turned out, she knew they would be okay.

Andi closed her eyes to the gentle touch of Gwen's fingers in her hair. She could hardly bear the waiting. It seemed her life had been filled with waiting. Her memory flashed to her childhood, to a time when she was a little girl standing outside the school watching the cars moving forward, picking up the other kids and whisking them away, until finally she was the only one left. No one had come for her. Her parents were gone. She thought of all the times she had packed her things into trash bags and waited to be escorted to yet another home, another place where no one understood her silence. Then she thought of the endless days she had spent in her apartment waiting for Curtis Boyd to come after her, the hours waiting for him and Kevin James to kill her, the endless days of the trial, and the timeless years waiting for James to get out of prison and come for her again.

All this time, and she was still waiting. But this time she was waiting for the news that would tell her she was free. It seemed that was what her life had added up to, waiting to be free to live her life, waiting to be happy.

In a hoarse whisper, Andi spoke, her words directed to Melissa. "Do you think it's him?"

Melissa met her eyes and shrugged. "I don't know. The chief wouldn't give any details over the phone, but his voice sounded like he thought it was James."

Andi nodded. She hiked her leg over Gwen's lap and curled her body around Gwen's. The rhythmic thud of Gwen's heart was like a beacon keeping her on course, reassuring her that she was safe and loved. The faint memory of sandalwood tickled her thoughts, and she closed her eyes against what she thought she already knew. If she was right, Kevin James was dead, and she knew who was responsible. The question needling her now was what would she do about it.

It was the middle of the night before they received the news they were waiting for. Andi gripped Gwen's hand waiting for the final word that it was over as she watched Melissa answer the phone.

Melissa put her phone on the table and faced Andi. Her expression was unreadable, as if she didn't know how to feel. "They found him. The place had been torched and they found the body in the debris. It isn't clear right now if the fire was intentionally set or accidental. There were items found at the location to suggest the cabin was used for the manufacture of methamphetamine. It's possible James accidently set off some of the highly combustible chemicals. The important thing is that they confirmed it's him."

Jimmy grabbed Melissa in a hug. "Oh, thank God."

Gwen was silent and Andi could feel her watching her.

Everything she learned just solidified her belief that someone had done her a grave favor. As much as she had wanted Kevin James dead, she always thought it would come down to a battle between James and herself. Killing Curtis Boyd had been an accident, a fluke, a one in a million shot, and she was still uncertain how she should feel about what she had done. She knew what it would cost her to take a life intentionally, and she couldn't imagine anyone paying that price for her.

Jimmy was the one to ask the one lingering question. "Any leads on the person who helped him escape?"

"Nothing much. We're lucky to have anything at all. The two officers that were injured in the crash can't remember anything about the person who pulled them out of the van. Hell, they barely even remember being on the transport. They were given tox screens at the hospital and both tested positive to Rohypnol. It appears they were injected with the drug on the scene. If they saw anything, they don't remember it."

Andi's body began to shake uncontrollably, tears fell from her eyes in streams, and the air seemed too thin to breathe. She thought she was going to be sick. "I need a break." Andi stood, then turned to Gwen and held out her hand. She didn't have to say anything. Gwen simply took her hand and followed her.

Andi heard the door to her room click shut as she climbed onto her bed. A moment later, she felt Gwen climb in bed next to her and wrap her arms around her. She sank into Gwen's embrace. She turned to face Gwen, thankful for her patience. "I think I know who did this."

Gwen studied her, confusion clouding her gaze. "What do you mean?"

"The other day when you brought in the mail, there was a note. I recognized a familiar scent on the paper." Andi pulled the envelope from her pocket and handed it to Gwen.

Gwen frowned as she read the brief message. "So you think someone you know killed him?"

Andi stilled. "Yes," she whispered. "I think it was J.C. I think she orchestrated the escape, kidnapped James, and then killed him."

"I don't understand. Why would she do something like this?"

"I think it was her way of making up for what she did and what she didn't do in the beginning."

"What are you going to do?"

"I don't know. I don't really have any evidence of any of this. It's really just my theory. But I believe she's the one. And if I'm right, this whole nightmare really is over."

Gwen brushed her fingers through Andi's hair. "I don't know who did this, or why, but I'm just happy you're safe."

Andi felt the weight of the world lift from her heart. Kevin James was gone. There would be no more hiding, no more fear, and most of all she had the most wonderful, beautiful woman in the world in her arms.

"I don't know how to feel right now. I think part of me still doesn't believe it's real. Part of me is relieved. But mostly I feel hopeful." Andi traced her finger along Gwen's jaw. "For the first time I believe in the future. It feels amazing." She smiled. "I don't think I could have gotten through any of this without you. I never could have dreamed I could be this happy. Now that I know I can have a life, I can't imagine a single day of it without you. I love you, Gwen."

Gwen smiled and leaned close until their lips touched. Relief washed over her. She felt like she had been holding her breath for weeks, afraid she could lose Andi at any moment. To hear Andi say she wanted to be with her was like having her prayers answered.

"I feel like I've been waiting all my life to hear you say that." She kissed Andi. After everything they had been through, she had no doubt that Andi loved her. And more than anything, she loved Andi. They had been through so much together in such a short amount of time. She knew there was nothing that could come between them now. And she couldn't wait to spend the rest of her life showing Andi just how much she was loved.

"I love you, Andi."

❖

"What do you think they're up to?" Gwen asked, handing a cup of coffee to Jimmy.

"I don't know. I'm sure they'll let us know something soon." Jimmy leaned back in the deck chair, stretched out her legs, and crossed her feet at the ankles. She laced her fingers together and wrapped her hands behind her head, giving the appearance of complete calm. She took a deep steadying breath and regarded Gwen quizzically.

"You know this isn't over, even with James gone. I've seen what this has done to Melissa, and I know scars like that won't heal just because that bastard is gone. Andi's going to go through a lot. Think you can handle that?"

Gwen sat down opposite Jimmy and watched Andi through the glass door. "I can't imagine what the three of you have been through. Just these last few weeks have been enough to drive me crazy. But I love her. No matter what it takes, I'm going to see to it that she gets through this."

"Good. She's tough, and it isn't easy for her to accept help, but she loves you. Don't let her run away from this."

Gwen regarded Jimmy for a few moments before asking, "How do you do it? How have you gotten through all this?"

Jimmy smiled. "I didn't really have a choice. I fell in love. Melissa is my life. There isn't anything I wouldn't do to protect her."

There was something in Jimmy's voice, or perhaps in her demeanor, that made the hairs stand up on the back of Gwen's neck. She thought of the wild look of panic and pain she had seen in Andi's eyes the day Kevin James had escaped. She remembered her own desperate desire to kill Kevin James herself if that was what it took to keep Andi safe. "Yeah, I know what you mean."

Jimmy broke eye contact, leaning her head back and closing her eyes.

Gwen thought about what she had said and wondered if it was true. It was one thing to believe you were capable of the unthinkable, but it was another thing to go through with it. She hoped they would never have to find out.

Both Jimmy and Gwen looked up at the sound of the door opening. Gwen rubbed her hands nervously against her jeans as her eyes roamed every inch of Andi's face and she tried to read what was happening through the lines around her eyes, in the curve of her lips, and from the easy gait in her step.

Laughter rang out as Andi and Melissa came through the door. Gwen reached for Andi, gently lacing their fingers together.

Melissa's eyes were fixed on Jimmy as a faint smile began to lift the corners of her lips. "It's all settled. New Year's is at our house this year."

Gwen brushed the hair back from Andi's forehead and peered into her eyes. "You guys were in there for a long time. What kind of surprises did you two cook up?"

Andi looked at her with a playful smile on her lips. "We may have one or two things in the works." Andi sat down across Gwen's lap, sliding her arm around Gwen's shoulders. She was still amazed by how right Gwen always felt when they touched. Her skin tingled as the flood of happiness cascaded through her body and nuzzled into her soul.

Gwen reached up and placed her hand to Andi's cheek. "You okay?"

Andi felt her entire body respond to Gwen's touch. She slipped her hand over Gwen's and pressed it to her cheek, relishing the warmth against her skin. Her wait was over. She hugged Gwen close. With each breath, she felt the weight of her past lift. From now on she was only looking forward into tomorrow. "I will be." She sighed into Gwen's chest. "I have you."

Epilogue

Four months later, Andi sat in a secluded corner of the bookstore, sipping her coffee as she looked through a magazine someone had left on the table. She hadn't been there long when another woman came up to her and asked to sit in the plush reading chair next to her. She looked up and studied the woman curiously. She had long blond hair, honey-brown eyes, and long lean arms and legs that showed defined muscles beneath her snug-fitting faded jeans and black T-shirt. J.C. was thinner than Andi remembered and her hair was longer, but she looked good, just a little too thin.

"Please," Andi said gesturing to the empty chair.

"Thanks."

Andi waited for her to get settled, watching how J.C.'s frame draped into the soft leather chair. "How have you been, J.C.?"

"Things are okay. I heard about the mess with James a few months back. I'm glad that all worked out."

Andi murmured in agreement. "I never thought I would be free of all that again. I sometimes have to remind myself that it's over when I find myself looking over my shoulder or jumping at the slightest noise in the dark."

J.C. gazed at Andi as if appraising her. Her look was neither seductive nor malicious, but it made Andi self-conscious.

"Tell me what's been going on with you, the past four years, J.C."

The corner of J.C.'s mouth twitched and drew down into a slight frown. "Nothing much, work mostly." She paused for a moment, still studying Andi. This was the first time they had seen each other in the years since they'd parted.

"Why did you ask me here, Andi? It isn't like we've kept in touch over the years."

It was Andi's turn to assess J.C. and determine just how far she wanted this conversation to go. She pursed her lips into a thin line of determination, took a deep breath, and decided to go for it. "I know you sent the note."

J.C. didn't give away any sign of understanding what Andi was talking about, but Andi knew this woman, and she saw the faint flicker in her eyes that confirmed everything.

"What are you talking about, Andi?"

"I know it was you. It smelled like you. You can't convince me you don't know what I'm talking about. But I need to know what you meant. What did you want to be forgiven for?"

J.C. shifted in her chair. She cleared her throat as if the words were stuck. "I know you must hate me for what I did. I didn't want to leave you back then, Andi. But there were things happening that I couldn't tell you about. The short of it was I decided you were safer without me in the picture. I didn't know Kevin James was part of the whole mess until it was too late. He made waves for me at work, and I wasn't strong enough to stand up to all the guys and my dad. I wasn't there when you needed me, and that's something I've regretted every day since."

Andi was surprised. She had always believed it had been easy for J.C. to leave. She had believed she wasn't worth saving.

"In the note, you said you made it right. What did that mean?"

There was a long silence, and when J.C. didn't answer, Andi began to grow more certain that her suspicions were right.

"Did you kill him?" Andi whispered.

J.C.'s eyes flashed up at her, the embers of hatred still glowing in her gaze.

"What I meant was that I had gathered evidence that James was involved in the child porn stuff with Curtis Boyd. I had enough to send him away for the rest of his miserable life. I thought if he was sent away for good, you could finally go on with your life. I wanted to give you that."

Andi was shocked by the news that J.C. had been working all this time to help her. "Why didn't you say something to me? It's been years, J.C."

"Come on, Andi. We both know I'm the last person you wanted to see. I screwed things up, and I could never take that back."

Andi thought about it for a while as she stared at a scar that ran across the back of J.C.'s hand. It was new and she wondered what had happened to cause such an angry wound. She noted that although J.C. had an answer for the message she had sent, she hadn't denied killing James. J.C. had hurt her, but maybe there were things that she just couldn't understand. After all, hadn't she done the same thing to Melissa? She had left when Melissa needed her after the attacks, and she had left without explanation too.

"I guess we all did the best we could back then. I'm not very proud of some of my choices either."

J.C. looked down at her hands. "I'm really sorry, Andi. You always deserved more than I could give you. I wish things had been different."

"Yeah." Andi smiled faintly and dropped her gaze to study the pattern on the carpet at her feet.

J.C. rubbed her hands along the arms of the chair nervously. "Despite everything, you seem happy."

Andi smiled a real smile this time. "I am happy. I've met someone. She makes all the difference."

J.C. nodded. "I'm glad."

"What about you, J.C.? Is there anyone special in your life?"

"No. Not since you."

Andi flinched.

"I know I didn't do a very good job of letting you know, but you were important to me. I guess I just didn't have anything to offer you in return."

Andi softened at the pain she heard in J.C.'s voice. It was time to let go of the anger and resentments. "I think you have plenty to offer, J.C. I hope you'll believe that when the right person comes along."

"Yeah, well…" J.C. drew in a deep breath. "I better get going. It was good to see you, Andi. Good luck with your new life."

Andi stood when J.C. gathered her long body out of the chair and turned to say good-bye. Andi hesitated for a moment and then wrapped her arms around J.C's shoulders, pulling her into a hug. "Thank you, J.C."

J.C.'s hands slid tentatively around Andi's back and returned the embrace. Andi felt her release a long mournful breath as if she was letting go of a heavy weight. When J.C. withdrew, her eyes glistened with unshed tears. "Take care of yourself, Andi."

Andi nodded and backed away from J.C. She watched the woman who had once been the center of her world walk out of her life for the second time. But this time their parting seemed to seal a door to the past, closing old wounds and leaving a feeling of peace.

Andi might never know the truth about what happened to Kevin James, but she knew she would be forever grateful that he was gone from her life.

A cool hand brushed her arm, pulling Andi from her thoughts. She turned to see Gwen standing next to her, eyes sparkling, her smile warm. "How'd it go?"

"Good. It was good." Andi slid her hand into Gwen's. "I'm glad she came."

"Did you find what you were looking for?"

"Yes. I think I did." Andi leaned her head against Gwen's shoulder and breathed in the crisp clean scent of her. Everything seemed to fall into place and she felt her heart warm. "I found you."

Gwen brushed her fingers along the line of Andi's jaw, lifted her head with two fingers, and leaned down and kissed her lightly on the lips. "What do you say I take you home now? I want to be close to you. I want to make love to you. I don't want you to have any doubts about where you belong."

Andi smiled and leaned into Gwen. "I'd like that. And just so you know, I have no doubts where I belong. You have me. All of me. Always. With no boundaries."

About the Author

Donna K. Ford is a licensed professional counselor who spends her professional time assisting people in their recovery from substance addictions. She holds an associate degree in criminal justice, a BS in psychology and an MS in community agency counseling. When not trying to save the world, she spends her time in the mountains of East Tennessee enjoying the lakes, rivers, and hiking trails near her home. Reading, writing, and enjoying conversation with good friends are the gifts that keep her grounded. She is grateful to share her life with her loving partner, two adoring cats, and one crazy beagle that keep life interesting.

Books Available from Bold Strokes Books

Switchblade by Carsen Taite. Lines were meant to be crossed. Third in the Luca Bennett Bounty Hunter Series. (978-1-62639-058-4)

Nightingale by Andrea Bramhall. Culture, faith, and duty conspire to tear two young lovers apart, yet fate seems to have different plans for them both. (978-1-62639-059-1)

No Boundaries by Donna K. Ford. A chance meeting and a nightmare from the past threaten more than Andi Massey's solitude as she and Gwen Palmer struggle to understand the complexity of love without boundaries. (978-1-62639-060-7)

Sacred Fire by Tanai Walker. Tinsley Swann is cursed to change into a beast for seven days, every seven years. When she meets Leda, she comes face-to-face with her past. (978-1-62639-061-4)

Queerly Beloved: A Love Story Across Gender by Diane and Jacob Anderson-Minshall. How We Survived Four Weddings, One Gender Transition, and Twenty-Two Years of Marriage. (978-1-62639-062-1)

Frenemy of the People by Nora Olsen. Clarissa and Lexie have despised each other as long as they can remember, but when they both find themselves helping an unlikely contender for homecoming queen, they are catapulted into an unexpected romance. (978-1-62639-063-8)

Timeless by Rachel Spangler. When Stevie Geller returns to her hometown, will she do things differently the second time around or will she be in such a hurry to leave her past that she misses out on a better future? (978-1-62639-050-8)

Second to None by L.T. Marie. Can a physical therapist and a custom motorcycle designer conquer their pasts and build a future with one another? (978-1-62639-051-5)

Seneca Falls by Jesse Thoma. Together, two women discover love truly can conquer all evil. (978-1-62639-052-2)

A Kingdom Lost by Barbara Ann Wright. Without knowing each other's fate, Princess Katya and her consort Starbride seek to reclaim their kingdom from the magic-wielding madman who seized the throne and is murdering their people. (978-1-62639-053-9)

Uncommon Romance by Jove Belle. Sometimes sex is just sex, and sometimes it's the only way to say "I love you." (978-1-62639-057-7)

The Heat of Angels by Lisa Girolami. Fires burn in more than one place in Los Angeles. (978-1-62639-042-3)

Season of the Wolf by Robin Summers. Two women running from their pasts are thrust together by an unimaginable evil. Can they overcome the horrors that haunt them in time to save each other? (978-1-62639-043-0)

Desperate Measures by P. J. Trebelhorn. Homicide detective Kay Griffith and contractor Brenda Jansen meet amidst turmoil neither of them is aware of until murder suspect Tommy Rayne makes his move to exact revenge on Kay. (978-1-62639-044-7)

The Magic Hunt by L.L. Raand. With her Pack being hunted by human extremists and beset by enemies masquerading as friends, can Sylvan protect them and her mate, or will she succumb to the feral rage that threatens to turn her rogue, destroying them all? A Midnight Hunters novel. (978-1-62639-045-4)

Waiting for the Violins by Justine Saracen. After surviving Dunkirk, a scarred and embittered British nurse returns to Nazi-occupied Brussels to join the Resistance, and finds that nothing is fair in love and war. (978-1-62639-046-1)

Because of Her by KE Payne. When Tabby Morton is forced to move to London, she's convinced her life will never be the same again. But the beautiful and intriguing Eden Palmer is about to show her that this time, change is most definitely for the better. (978-1-62639-049-2)

Wingspan by Karis Walsh. Wildlife biologist Bailey Chase is content to live at the wild bird sanctuary she has created on Washington's Olympic Peninsula until she is lured beyond the safety of isolation by architect Kendall Pearson. (978-1-60282-983-1)

Tumbledown by Cari Hunter. After surviving their ordeal in the North Cascades, Alex and Sarah have new identities and a new home, but a chance occurrence threatens everything: their freedom and their lives. (978-1-62639-085-0)

Night Bound by Winter Pennington. Kass struggles to keep her head, her heart, and her relationships in order. She's still having a difficult time accepting being an Alpha female. But her wolf is certain of what she wants and she's intent on securing her power. (978-1-60282-984-8)

Slash and Burn by Valerie Bronwen. The murder of a roundly despised author at an LGBT writer's conference in New Orleans turns Winter Lovelace's relaxing weekend hobnobbing with her peers into a nightmare of suspense—especially when her ex turns up. (978-1-60282-986-2)

The Blush Factor by Gun Brooke. Ice-cold business tycoon Eleanor Ashcroft only cares about the three P's—Power, Profit, and Prosperity—until young Addison Garr makes her doubt both that and the state of her frostbitten heart. (978-1-60282-985-5)

The Quickening: A Sisters of Spirits Novel by Yvonne Heidt. Ghosts, visions, and demons are all in a day's work for Tiffany. But when Kat asks for help on a serial killer case, life takes on another dimension altogether. (978-1-60282-975-6)

Windigo Thrall by Cate Culpepper. Six women trapped in a mountain cabin by a blizzard, stalked by an ancient cannibal demon bent on stealing their sanity—and their lives. (978-1-60282-950-3)

Smoke and Fire by Julie Cannon. Oil and water, passion and desire, a combustible combination. Can two women fight the fire that draws them together and threatens to keep them apart? (978-1-60282-977-0)

Asher's Fault by Elizabeth Wheeler. Fourteen-year-old Asher Price sees the world in black and white, much like the photos he takes, but when his little brother drowns at the same moment Asher experiences his first same-sex kiss, he can no longer hide behind the lens of his camera and eventually discovers he isn't the only one with a secret. (978-1-60282-982-4)

Love and Devotion by Jove Belle. KC Hall trips her way through life, stumbling into an affair with a married bombshell twice her age. Thankfully, her best friend, Emma Reynolds, is there to show her the true meaning of Love and Devotion. (978-1-60282-965-7)

Rush by Carsen Taite. Murder, secrets, and romance combine to create the ultimate rush. (978-1-60282-966-4)

The Shoal of Time by J.M. Redmann. It sounded too easy. Micky Knight is reluctant to take the case because the easy ones often turn into the hard ones, and the hard ones turn into the dangerous ones. In this one, easy turns hard without warning. (978-1-60282-967-1)

In Between by Jane Hoppen. At the age of 14, Sophie Schmidt discovers that she was born an intersexual baby and sets off on a journey to find her place in a world that denies her true existence. (978-1-60282-968-8)

Secret Lies by Amy Dunne. While fleeing from her abuser, Nicola Jackson bumps into Jenny O'Connor, and their unlikely friendship quickly develops into a blossoming romance—but when it comes down to a matter of life or death, are they both willing to face their fears? (978-1-60282-970-1)

Under Her Spell by Maggie Morton. The magic of love brought Terra and Athene together, but now a magical quest stands between them—a quest for Athene's hand in marriage. Will their passion keep them together, or will stronger magic tear them apart? (978-1-60282-973-2)

Homestead by Radclyffe. R. Clayton Sutter figures getting NorthAm Fuel's newest refinery operational on a rolling tract of land in Upstate New York should take a month or two, but then, she hadn't counted on local resistance in the form of vandalism, petitions, and one furious farmer named Tess Rogers. (978-1-60282-956-5)

Battle of Forces: Sera Toujours by Ali Vali. Kendal and Piper return to New Orleans to start the rest of eternity together, but the return of an old enemy makes their peaceful reunion short-lived, especially when they join forces with the new queen of the vampires. (978-1-60282-957-2)

How Sweet It Is by Melissa Brayden. Some things are better than chocolate. Molly O'Brien enjoys her quiet life running the bakeshop in a small town. When the beautiful Jordan Tuscana returns home, Molly can't deny the attraction—or the stirrings of something more. (978-1-60282-958-9)

The Missing Juliet: A Fisher Key Adventure by Sam Cameron. A teenage detective and her friends search for a kidnapped Hollywood star in the Florida Keys. (978-1-60282-959-6)

Amor and More: Love Everafter edited by Radclyffe and Stacia Seaman. Rediscover favorite couples as Bold Strokes Books authors reveal glimpses of life and love beyond the honeymoon in short stories featuring main characters from favorite BSB novels. (978-1-60282-963-3)

First Love by CJ Harte. Finding true love is hard enough, but for Jordan Thompson, daughter of a conservative president, it's challenging, especially when that love is a female rodeo cowgirl. (978-1-60282-949-7)

Pale Wings Protecting by Lesley Davis. Posing as a couple to investigate the abduction of infants, Special Agent Blythe Kent and Detective Daryl Chandler find themselves drawn into a battle over the innocents, with demons on one side and the unlikeliest of protectors on the other. (978-1-60282-964-0)

Mounting Danger by Karis Walsh. Sergeant Rachel Bryce, an outcast on the police force, is put in charge of the department's newly formed mounted division. Can she and polo champion Callan Lanford resist their growing attraction as they struggle to safeguard the disaster-prone unit? (978-1-60282-951-0)

Meeting Chance by Jennifer Lavoie. When man's best friend turns on Aaron Cassidy, the teen keeps his distance until fate puts Chance in his hands. (978-1-60282-952-7)

At Her Feet by Rebekah Weatherspoon. Digital marketing producer Suzanne Kim knows she has found the perfect love in her new mistress Pilar, but before they can make the ultimate commitment, Suzanne's professional life threatens to disrupt their perfectly balanced bliss. (978-1-60282-948-0)

Show of Force by AJ Quinn. A chance meeting between navy pilot Evan Kane and correspondent Tate McKenna takes them on a roller-coaster ride where the stakes are high, but the reward is higher: a chance at love. (978-1-60282-942-8)

Clean Slate by Andrea Bramhall. Can Erin and Morgan work through their individual demons to rediscover their love for each other, or are the unexplainable wounds too deep to heal? (978-1-60282-943-5)